COV

Sandy Sullivan

EROTIC ROMANCE

Siren Publishing, Inc.
www.SirenPublishing.com

A SIREN PUBLISHING BOOK
IMPRINT: Erotic Romance

COWBOY LOVE
Copyright © 2010 by Sandy Sullivan

ISBN-10: 1-60601-558-3
ISBN-13: 978-1-60601-558-2

First Printing: February 2010

Cover design by Jinger Heaston
All cover art and logo copyright © 2010 by Siren Publishing, Inc.

Printed in the U.S.A.

PUBLISHER
Siren Publishing, Inc.
www.SirenPublishing.com

DEDICATION

To my husband Shaun - Your support has been invaluable. You are my own Cowboy Love.

To Cathy Gehret – We did it girl! Thank you for everything.

COWBOY LOVE

SANDY SULLIVAN
Copyright © 2010

Chapter 1

The orange glow of the morning sun streamed over the hillside, infusing color over the pale blue above her head. The cool air lifted the tendrils of her hair, brushing the ends across her cheek in a caress, while the heat of the sun warmed her skin.

The heady scent of the roses budding along the fence filled her nose with their sweet perfume. Her muscles began to relax in the familiar surroundings of a working ranch. Growing up riding, roping, handling horses and cattle alike made this feel like home, but the noises coming from nearby drew her to find out what was happening on the other side of the bushes.

"Damn it!"

Amy cocked her head to listen, but only the jingle of spurs met her ears. The familiarity of the sound made her heart skip a beat. Frown lines settled between her eyes as she tried to figure out where the noise came from. When curiosity got the better of her, she pushed open the small gate, letting it click behind her.

Coffee cup in hand, Amy moved through a small walkway obviously used many times over the years until she could clearly see a round pen a short distance away. The structure caught her attention the night before as they had driven by the neighbors' house on their way to Chris' parents' ranch, only now it had an occupant.

As she moved closer, she saw a noticeably angry cowboy lying in the dirt as the brown and white mare stood over him, shifting uncertainly. The young man's black Stetson lay a good distance, where it apparently landed when he got unceremoniously dumped in the center of the corral.

While she watched, the cowboy jumped to his feet, a stream of expletives coming from his mouth as he stomped to the railing at the side of the pen, oblivious to his audience.

Amy smiled into her cup, amused at the cowboy's predicament. Able to sympathize, she had the insane urge to rub her hip, remembering her own butt in the dirt more times than she cared to admit. She took a sip from the cup of hot liquid warming her hands and the heat spread through her as it slid down, settling in her belly.

When she raised her eyes, her gaze found the cowboy again across the expanse of the pen and her breath caught as goose bumps rose along her arms. The upper body revealed to her stare as he stripped off his t-shirt was perfect, with the right amount of dark curls spattered along the sculpted lines. His well-muscled body, tanned from many hours in the hot Texas sun, greeted her as she stared, tracing the line of hair to the waistband of his jeans. His washboard abs rippled when he moved and she licked her parched lips as he tossed his shirt over the railing. A single droplet of sweat cut a path from near his ear, along his torso, stopping to rest on the end of his male nipple for a moment, before dropping off into the dust at his feet. The insane urge to follow the line of salty liquid down his body with her tongue zinged through her, wetting the piece of silk between her thighs. She shivered at the thought. His almost black locks curled a little at the ends where it touched the back of his neck and a two days' growth of whiskers gave him a scruffy appearance. *Whisker burn? Interesting.*

Completely unaware of being observed, the cowboy stomped toward the horse, his frustration evident by his stride. He grabbed the reins of the reluctant animal, swung back into the saddle and jammed his boots into the stirrups, just as the mare started to sidestep.

And the ride was on.

Unconsciously, her feet carried her closer to the pen until she stood at the rail and watched in silence. The reins gripped tight in his fist, he hung on as the horse whirled and kicked, trying desperately to dislodge the rider on her back. A few short minutes later—*thump*, in the dirt he went again as his curse ripped through the air.

"Son of a—"

Once he realized he had an audience, dark brown eyes fixed on her as he pulled himself up from the ground and the air snapped and crackled like an approaching thunderstorm. He stared for a moment before picking up the rawhide and leading the horse toward her, a questioning raise of his eyebrow and a slight smile gracing his lips.

She met his stare, her heart pounding in her chest like a jackhammer on overdrive, as his long stride brought him closer, until he stood at the railing.

Taking a deep breath, she stepped between the split rail fence and greeted him as he reached her side.

"Mind if I try?"

Without waiting for an answer, she handed him her coffee cup, ignoring his glance as she took the rawhide from his hand. The brush of her fingertips against his sent ripples of heat shooting up her arm and their eyes met for a split second before she turned away. She gathered up the piece of leather and walked the skittish mare several feet even as his gaze rested on her. The unspoken challenge hung in the air. She 'had a gift' as her dad called it, and helping this handsome cowboy just felt right.

While Amy stroked the mare's nose, rubbing along her neck, talking quietly, and whispering sweet words of encouragement, the horse began to calm under her hands. The animal stood utterly still as Amy talked and touched, flicking her ears with each word she spoke.

The world stopped spinning as Amy worked, calming the mare, encouraging her and touching her. The soft hair across her palm soothed her own soul and calmed the skittish mare.

When Amy reached for the reins and moved them over the horse's neck, the cowboy took a step in her direction, but her raised palm stopped him, not wanting him near as she stepped into the stirrups. A very real possibility existed the animal would buck, throwing her in the dirt, too.

The reins in her hand, Amy slid her foot into the stirrup, pulled herself up and swung her leg over the saddle, settling firmly on the seat. She let the mare get used to her weight before she attempted any movement. Amy started from the beginning, only wanting the animal to allow to her sit and possible walk without getting thrown.

The mare turned to peer at the rider on her back. Her big doe eyes shone bright with trust, but looked at Amy like she was trying to figure out how the rider got up there. Amy whispered to her, stroked her neck and shifted in the saddle.

The cowboy's shirt back in place helped her remain focused, but she found the penetrating hot stare of the brown eyes across the corral intoxicating. She did her best to ignore him even as her nipples hardened into little nubs and her pussy throbbed. The sight of those finely sculpted muscles and plains of his chest, forced the ache between her legs to intensify with a need for something that hadn't been satisfied in a while.

I wonder what licking would do.

Shaking her head, she pulled her thoughts back to the mare. She squeezed with her knees and clicked her tongue, urging the skittish animal forward. The mare took several uncertain steps as Amy encouraged her with soft words and a stroke to her neck.

She walked the horse around the corral, surprised when the animal appeared to be amazingly attentive and cooperative, making it much easier. Deciding to test her abilities a little, Amy nudged her with her knees and clicked her tongue, hoping the mare would canter. Breaking into a slow gallop around the pen, Amy could see the astonished impression from the side of the arena out of the corner of her eye.

After riding the span of the pen several times, she pulled her back to a slow walk and rode in the direction of the young man. Dismounting, she tugged the reins loose from the mare's neck, walked the few feet to his side, and handed him the reins.

"A gentle hand and soft words win the woman's heart."

She smiled at the cowboy's stunned expression as she made her way between the railings and headed back the way she had come.

Just as she reached the fence connecting the two houses, the low timbre of his voice met her ears. "Wait! What's your name?"

Looking over her shoulder, she gave him a secretive smile, a small shake of her head and a sexy wink, before moving through the gate and disappearing.

She reached the back door of her friend's parents' house with a smile on her lips. *That was fun.*

Stepping through the doorway, she saw Chris sipping her coffee at the kitchen table.

"Where have you been?"

"Just checking out your parents' property." She poured herself another cup before she sat down, stirring the contents before bringing it to her lips.

"Find anything interesting?"

"Um…you might say that." She allowed a small smile to flitter across her mouth prior to changing the subject. "So what are we going to do today?"

"Well, I thought we could go shopping at the mall in town this afternoon, get dinner at The Grill and then hit Pete's tonight."

"Pete's?"

"Yeah, it's one of the local cowboy bars. Nice place, good dance floor and most important, strong drinks."

"Sounds fun."

Chris gave her a curious glance as she said, "You aren't one for bars, Am."

"We're here to unwind and relax, right? It sounds a perfect place to start." She shrugged, dismissing Chris' observation. "I want to drink, dance and have a good time. If there are plenty of men and a dance floor, I'm happy."

"Well then, we're set, I guess. Let me get dressed and we'll hit the mall. Buying new clothes always puts me in a better mood, anyway." Chris stood and moved to the sink, setting her cup inside before she went down the hall toward her room.

"Would you like something to eat?"

"Oh, no thank you. Coffee will be fine. I'm not much of a breakfast eater, anyway."

"You were gone quite a while. Did you enjoy your jaunt around the ranch? It is nice and relaxing here. I'm sure you'll forget all about the sleezeball." Catherine's a-matter-of fact tone made Amy smile.

With Catherine's statement, Amy's thoughts drifted back to their arrival at the house the night before, and the words of wisdom concerning her relationship in the company of Jack Miller.

* * * *

The porch light flipped on as the two women walked toward the front entrance. Amy smiled, as they stepped up and Chris' mom peered out at them.

"Hello." Amy reached for the screen.

"You must be Amy." The gray-haired woman on the other side flipped the latch.

"Yes, ma'am."

"I'm glad you're here." Chris' mom wrapped her in a warm hug.

"Me, too." Amy hugged the woman in return.

Chris did the introductions as the two women pulled apart. "Mom, this is Amy. Amy, this is my mom, Catherine."

"It's so nice to meet you. I've heard a lot about you."

"It is nice to meet you, too. Chris has told me so much about you over the years. I feel I already know you." Amy groaned. "It's all right. She hasn't told me anything bad, but she did tell me about these men you keep hanging around. I must say, you need to find you a decent man."

"Lord, Chris, did you have to tell her my mistakes concerning my love life?" Amy rolled her eyes, folding her arms under her breasts.

"Of course! She's been giving me advice to give to you!"

"Did you tell that no-good bull-rider to buzz off?" The three women walked into the living room and sat down on the couch.

Amy sighed. "Yes ma'am."

"Trust me, sweetheart, you did the right thing then." Catherine patted her hand in comfort.

"I know."

"A pleasant weekend here in the promised land will do you good, girl. Kick back, relax and enjoy your days. Who knows, you might meet some polite, home-grown cowboy and want to settle down right here."

Amy laughed. "The last thing I need is another cowboy."

As the conversation from the night before faded from her mind, she noticed Catherine's sly look across the table.

"Um, yes. It was…interesting." Amy tried to hide her smile by taking a sip out of her cup.

"I'm glad. Handsome young man, isn't he?" Catherine said as she stood and headed for the doorway. Giving Amy a quick wink, she disappeared down the hall as Amy sat in stunned silence, the words flittering across her mind. How had Catherine known? Had she seen her next door? Amy wasn't sure, but she loved Chris' mom already. Catherine had to think highly of the gorgeous cowboy otherwise, she assumed Chris' mom would have warned her to stay away from him.

"Ready?" Chris walked into the kitchen a few minutes later, dressed and all set to start their adventure.

"Yep, let's go." Amy returned her cup to the counter and grabbed her purse sitting on the couch as they headed for the door.

Disappointment clouded her mind for a moment when they drove past the round pen, now sitting empty and still. Another glimpse and or an introduction would have completed her morning. She shrugged as she thought, *oh well.*

For the rest of the day, the two women shopped, hitting several different stores. Amy found a number of things at one of the local western places, while Chris bought a few things elsewhere. Chris liked to shop at more of the modern locations, preferring the classy style to Amy's comfortable jeans, tank tops and boots.

Numerous times during their shopping spree, the temptation to ask Chris about the cowboy flittered over her mind, but she resisted. Asking would only give Chris the idea she had an interest beyond mere curiosity and she didn't, did she?

Standing in a dressing room in front of a long mirror, turning this way and that as she scoped out the little black dress hugging her curves, her thoughts persisted. *I have to admit, he is down right gorgeous.* The expression on his face when she returned the reins to him, made a wistful smile cross her lips, getting bigger as she pictured their encounter again. She almost laughed at the surprise written on his face. That was the normal reaction from anyone who had never seen her work a horse before.

Her teenage years were spent learning the trade from her dad, and he taught her everything he knew. The ability to break a mare or gelding to rider with little more than a soft voice and a kind hand came naturally.

"Well, what does it look like, Am?"

She came back to the present as she heard Chris call from outside the dressing room. Sighing in resignation, she opened the door and stepped out.

"Wow. That hugs every curve perfectly. You would definitely catch some attention wearing that little outfit."

"I do like the way it fits." Amy twisted and turned, studying her reflection in the mirror. "And I really don't have a nice dress to wear out."

"Then splurge. It's not that expensive, anyway." Chris walked toward her, checking the tag under her arm. "Look, it's on sale."

"A hundred dollars, Chris? I never spend that much on myself." Amy frowned, smoothing the fabric over her hips.

"Well, maybe you should start. You earn it—spend some, for crying out loud."

"I know, but I'm always afraid I will need it for something like tires for my car or a rainy day emergency." Amy looked wistfully at the dress. *I really do love this dress.*

Chris took Amy's hand in hers, "Amy, this is your weekend. Take advantage and live a little."

"Are you sure it looks okay?"

"You are a knockout in that dress. It's perfect."

"Okay, you've convinced me. I'll buy it."

"And the cute shoes?"

"Yes, and the cute shoes."

"Good. Now, I'm starving!"

Shaking her head, Amy retreated into the dressing room with a smile.

Once they went through the checkout with their purchases, they headed for the exit near the car to find something to eat. Chris mentioned a steak place, and it sounded wonderful. Amy was pretty hungry herself and she planned on drinking tonight, even possibly getting drunk. A heavy dinner could stave off the hangover come tomorrow morning.

"Hey, when we're done eating, how about we run back to your parents' house and shower. I don't want to go to the bar all sweaty from running around all day." She stuffed her packages behind her before slipping into the driver's seat.

"Yeah, we can do that. You never know who might be bar hopping tonight."

She gave Chris a sideways glance, she remembered the guy her friend had been trying to set her up with for the last six months.

"You aren't trying to hook me up with that guy, are you? You promised you wouldn't even mention his name this weekend."

"No, I'm thinking for myself."

"Good. You don't need to be playing matchmaker while I'm here. I really don't want another guy in my life right now." Her tone did not sound convincing even to her own ears as her thoughts drifted back to early that morning for a moment.

"Of course you don't. Men are bastards, right?" A sly glance from Chris and wariness tingled down her spine.

"Yes, they are."

Chapter 2

Chris and Amy pulled up to the bar about eight, finding a spot to park. Tons of cars already lined the parking lot so they took a slot a little farther from the entrance.

"This must be the happenin' place." Several people milled about as Amy and Chris moved inside.

"Yep. Everyone comes here on Friday nights."

George Strait's voice crooned, "Amarillo By Morning" as the cool air of the bar caressed her face. Once inside, the two found a table to the left of the stage against the wall and she sat down facing the door as Chris took the chair opposite her. A long mahogany bar covered one whole wall and several customers inhabited the barstools as they talked and laughed with others nearby. Bright gilded mirrors hung behind the bartenders, reflecting faces of the people standing close. Bud Light, Michelob, Corona and every other type of beer a person could think of, neon signs flashed brightly with colors of red, gold, blue and white. The large mechanical bull in the corner drew her attention. A small grin lifted the corners of her mouth. *Something new to try.*

"I thought you said they had a band," raising her voice to be heard over the music blaring from the speakers on the stage, standing to their left.

"They do. Doesn't start until nine."

A blue-eyed blonde cowboy stopped at the table and took their drink order. Amy admired the tight fit of his Wranglers as he walked away, before her attention returned to her friend. "So how many of these people do you know?"

Chris scanned the mass before she answered, "Almost everyone. I went to school with most of these people. I do see a few new faces."

Amy's gaze moved over the throng, hopeful of catching a glimpse of the cowboy from this morning, but no one appeared familiar. *There are lots of good-looking men here, though.* The crowd was divided a little unevenly, with the men out-numbering the women close to three-to-one.

Chris waved at someone she knew, and as the cute guy reached the table, she stood and made the introductions.

"Amy, this is Rob."

She stuck out her hand and said, "Nice to meet you."

"You, too." His blue eyes twinkled as they met hers and he snaked an arm around Chris' waist.

"Rob and I have known each other for years."

Her eyebrow arched in question, and she smiled at the man next to her.

"Really? I'm sure you can tell me some awesome stories to blackmail my best friend with."

Giving her a wide smile and a wink, he replied, "I bet I can. We'll talk soon."

"You will not!" Chris exclaimed, pushing him from her side with a giggle. "I'll catch you later."

"Sure, Chris. Behave yourself, young lady." He winked before he headed toward the bar.

Amy shook her head. Chris complained she never had a serious connection. Her serious relationship just walked away from her side.

Her eyes moved over the group again, watching as they shifted and mingled, reacquainting themselves amid the others in the room. As more people came in the doors of the bar, she skimmed each face, almost hoping.

A moment later, she caught the sight of someone in a white long sleeved shirt and black cowboy hat, weeding through the crowd carrying a guitar case. Unable to make out his features, she watched as he worked his way toward the stage. *He has to be with the band.* Her interest piqued, she continued to be fascinated by the way he moved as the word graceful came to mind.

Right before he reached the edge of the dance floor, he turned and Amy could make out his features. Her breath caught in her throat. *My cowboy. No, not mine, hell, I don't even know his name but the guy from the corral.* This time he was dressed to impress, with a pressed western style shirt and tight Wranglers emphasizing his nice ass and polished boots. *Damn! He's just as nice all cleaned up.* Her appreciative glance raked over him from head to toe.

When he finally turned in her way and his gaze met hers across the room, surprise registered on his face, and he took a step in her direction. One of the band members approached behind him, grabbing his arm and ushering him toward the stage before he could go any farther.

Once he reached the stage, he stepped onto the platform prior to swinging his glance back to her. Her heart hammered in her chest and her mouth went as dry as the Sahara desert. She wasn't able to drag her eyes from his, even if she wanted to. He tipped his hat and gave her one of the sexiest grins she had ever received before turning to remove the guitar out of his case.

When he broke their eye contact, a voice finally permeated the fog encompassing her mind.

"Hello? Amy?" Chris waved her hand in front of her face.

"Uh…what?"

"Who are you flirting with?"

"I'm not flirting with anyone, why?"

"You did, too. You weren't paying attention to a word I said."

Chris looked in the direction of Amy's stare and saw the handsome man up front as she gave him a hearty wave. She flashed Amy a secretive little smile before she changed the subject as the band started to warm up.

For the next hour, his rapt attention from across the room sent shivers across her arms. The air seemed to be sucked from her lungs as several different men twirled her around the dance floor. Unsure of the culprit, the dancing or his heated gaze, she struggled to calm her breathing as the band took a break.

"We'll be back in fifteen, folks."

The song ended and she headed back to her table. She watched as he set his guitar down and hopped down in front. He was quickly engulfed in a party of four women sitting at his feet.

Amy continued to study him from a distance as he stopped to talk, but his eyes met hers over their heads. Finally, able to pull away from them, he walked in her direction, keeping her pinned to her chair in nervous anticipation.

As he approached, Chris stood up and enveloped the handsome cowboy in a warm hug.

"Tanner, you devil. What have you been up to?"

"Same old stuff." He wrapped his arms around Chris, hugging her tight.

"Sit down, sit down. I haven't talked to you in forever. How are things with the band?" They both slid into the empty seats while Amy watched the exchange.

"Good. We are doin' shows all over."

His eyes moved over her face as a small smile lifted the corners of his mouth, before returning to Chris. The little grin made her breath hitch in her throat even as her body grew warm from his gaze, and made her incredibly aware of how the room seemed smaller. His very essence filled the space between them and the air crackled as Amy shifted nervously in the chair.

"I haven't heard you play in Dallas."

"No, we haven't done anythin' up there in a while. Is that where you're livin' these days?"

"Yeah, working at a hospital on the outskirts of town."

"Really? You must be keepin' busy, then."

"We work all the time, more than we want to." Amy's pulse went into overdrive as their eyes met and one corner of his mouth lifted in a flirty smile. "I'm sorry. I guess I didn't introduce you two. Tanner, this is Amy. We work together in Dallas. Amy, this is Tanner. He lives next door to my parents."

"Well, hello again." Tanner smiled, his eyes crinkling at the corners.

"Nice to meet you."

"Again?" Chris questioned with a quizzical expression. "You two know each other?"

"Sort of," Tanner replied, his eyes never leaving her face.

"Care to explain?"

"She caught me in the dirt this mornin' tryin' to break a mare," Tanner explained as his glance finally swung back to Chris.

"Ah...I see." A mysterious smile rippled across Chris' lips.

"It was kind of hard not to notice when I heard some pretty descriptive cuss words coming from over there," Amy responded, as Tanner blushed under his tan.

"Sorry," he murmured, his caressing glance returning to Amy.

"No problem. It's not like I haven't heard them before, and probably said a few myself. I've had my butt in the dirt more times than I care to remember."

A small smile crept across his lips and she could almost read his thoughts as heat crept up her cheeks.

"Where'd you learn to tame a horse?" he asked curiosity bright in his eyes.

"My dad. He's been doing it for years. A gift or a curse, however you want to think of it."

"I've never seen anyone do that before." His eyes slid over her face, making the heat rise on her cheeks. "Incredible."

"Yeah, well, I try not to advertise."

"Why not? You could make a fortune."

"I'm not interested in doing it all the time. Nursing is where my heart is."

"Ah…well, I need to get up on stage. I'll come back on my next break. I would really like to hear more." The heat he projected with one glance made her inhale sharply. He smiled and winked, before turning and heading back toward the platform.

Chris cocked an eyebrow and Amy could almost see the questionings swimming through her mind. "What?"

"How come you didn't tell me you met Tanner this morning?"

She shrugged nonchalantly. "No big deal."

The gears turned bright behind Chris' face and Amy groaned silently.

"Not a big deal? The looks you two exchanged say something else entirely different."

"Really, Chris, it's nothing."

"Um…sure, Amy. Okay."

The next several songs brought a barrage of good-looking cowboys, asking for a dance from both the beautiful women. Amy accepted each one who asked; sure her fascination with the guy on the stage was a passing fancy.

One his second break, Tanner returned to their table, sliding into the seat next to her.

"You're pretty good. Do you write your own songs?" She nervously pushed a piece of hair behind her ear and fidgeted in the seat.

"Thanks, and I do write some."

She shifted her chair, putting a little more distance between them. His nearness made her tremble, and she wasn't sure she liked the reaction.

"Have you been singing long?"

"Yeah, it seems like forever. My dad bought me a guitar for my ninth birthday and I've played ever since. We didn't start gettin' gigs until the last couple of years."

"Do you play outside of Texas?"

"No. We don't do anythin' too far from home yet, but I'm workin' on getting some stuff elsewhere. You live up near Chris and work together, right?"

"Yeah, on the same floor at the hospital."

"Have you known her long?"

"About five years. We met right after I moved to Dallas."

"Where did you grow up?"

"Oregon."

"Oregon? Why'd you move to Texas?"

"I needed to start my own life, I guess. My parents own a small place near the southern Oregon border. I got tired of the rain."

The death glare she was receiving over his shoulder from the dark-haired woman near the front, almost made her laugh.

"Your fan club?" Amy nodded toward the stage.

He looked back and the girl waved at him. Without returning the gesture, he returned his attention to Amy. "Yeah, I guess. They're here every weekend. I've known most of 'em for a long time."

Amy raised her hand and waved at the girl over his shoulder with a bright smile. The woman whipped around as if she had been slapped, presenting Amy with her back.

Tanner flashed a warm grin as he laughed. "That's mean."

"Well, she's been giving me a death glare since you came over here." She shrugged. *I don't have time for petty jealousy.* Her attention returned to the handsome man in front of her.

"She's wanted me to go out with her for quite sometime, but she's not my type. I can't seem to get through to her though."

"So what *is* your type?" Amy asked before she could stop herself, nervously picking up her drink to drag her eyes away from him. *What do I care what kind of woman he dates anyway?*

"I don't know. Someone not so pushy I guess."

"Yeah, I know what you mean," Amy murmured, her eyes still fixed on the glass in her hand.

His question startled her as he asked out of the blue, "Would you dance with me?"

Shifting, she lifted her eyes, gazing over his shoulder to the stage behind him as she grinned. "The band is on a break."

"There's still music. Please?"

He stood and held out his palm. Giving him a small smile, she replied, "All right." She placed her hand in his as the warmth of his grasp curled up her arm. *Why do I think this is a mistake?* She let him lead her onto the dance floor as the song changed. The slow ballad drifted over them as he took the hand he held and place it on his shoulder. He slid his arm around her waist and grasped her other one as he brought their bodies almost close enough to touch. They moved together as if made to, while the melody drifted over them and the room disappeared.

She wasn't sure why she allowed him to pull her closer. She rested her cheek next to his, feeling the soft scrape of his whiskers on her sensitive skin. The scent of his cologne wafted to her nose, and she fought the urge to bury it against his neck. The stares that followed their path around the floor prickled her skin, but she didn't care as she closed her eyes to the sensations rippling through her with a simple dance.

When the song ended, she pulled back in his arms, but he refused to let her go for several seconds.

Lord, he's got pretty eyes. Her lips parted on a sigh that escaped her as his iris' turned dark brown, and his gaze moved to her mouth. For a brief moment, she watched as his mouth drifted toward hers, anticipating the feel of his lips. When his lips whispered over hers softly, she sighed and leaned toward him.

He jerked when a slap landed on his back as his drummer said, "Dude, we need to get up there."

Heat crawled up her neck as embarrassment rushed through her and she pulled completely away from him. Turning on her heel, she headed back toward the table she shared with Chris. *I can't believe I let him kiss me right here in front of everyone! Lord, Amy, what the hell are you thinking?*

"What was that all about?" Chris asked, as Amy slid into the chair across from her.

"I don't know, but I need some air. I'm going outside for a minute."

She stood again and headed toward the door, fully aware of the brown eyes that followed her. When the hot, sticky night air hit her face, beads of perspiration formed under her hair at her neck and she grumbled. She walked down the few stairs of the bar focusing on reaching her car, intending on clearing her head for a moment before going back inside.

"Amy, wait!"

She reached the car and turned to find Tanner a few short feet away. Feeling out of control, she tried to put on her standoffish persona, hoping he might get the hint and leave her alone. His nearness made her feel vulnerable and excited at the same time. Amy suspected if she allowed herself to delve into the feelings he aroused, he would hurt her more than Jack ever could.

"You're leavin'?"

"No. Maybe. I don't know." She propped herself against the car, folding her arms under her breasts.

"Is there somethin' wrong?"

Her insides quivered at the warmth in his eyes.

"No, I needed some air. It was getting hot in there." Her face flushed from the heat of the night or the look in his eyes, she wasn't sure.

"I know what you mean," he murmured, shifting from one foot to the other.

"I thought you had started playing again."

"We did, but when you rushed out, I wanted to make sure you were okay."

"I'm fine. I'll be inside in a minute," she said, almost cringing at the dismissal in her tone.

"All right." He turned and headed back toward the bar, meeting Chris on the steps.

"Everything okay?"

"I guess." Tanner shrugged with a puzzled look over his shoulder at Amy then went back inside the bar.

Chris walked the last few feet to the car.

"What happened?"

"Nothing, why?"

"There seemed to be some tension between you two."

"There is *nothing* between us, Chris. I just met him for crying out loud."

"I know, but it's not like you aren't attracted to him."

"He's just another guy. Good looking one, I'll admit, but he's still a guy, probably wanting nothing more than to get laid," Amy said, pushing away from the car. "I'm going inside. There are plenty of good-looking men in there, and I think that I'll find a few to dance with. Besides, I want to try that mechanical bull in the corner."

Chris' frowning stare rested on her back as she made her way toward the door. She was there to unwind and relax, not find another man to take Jack's place.

When she reached their table, the flood of men came close behind. One cute blond cowboy found his way to her side, asking her for the next dance. As she stepped into his arms, the glare from the stage was almost enough for her to rethink her decision about dancing with others in the room, almost.

She spent the rest of the set in the embrace of whoever asked, aware that Tanner refused to play anything slow. When he took his next break, she made sure to be caught up talking with one cowboy on the other side of the room. Tanner slid into the chair opposite Chris before Amy turned her back to him. His hot gaze rested on her and the hair on the back of her neck prickled in response, while she tried to focus on what the man in front of her said.

Adam? John? Damn! I can't even remember the guy's name. Smiling, she said, "Thanks for the talk. I'm gonna try my hand or rear, on the bull."

"Mind if I watch? There is something totally hot about a woman on a bull."

She shrugged. "Suit yourself."

Her center of attention shifted to the black and white spotted rawhide covered metal bull in the corner. Several patrons already tried to ride the thing while the crowd around them laughed hysterically. Of course, most were already drunk by the time they got on the bucking, twirling contraption. She wasn't drunk yet, but if she kept drinking at the rate she had been, she would be shortly.

She approached the inflated area as the last rider slid off the side, laughing uncontrollably. Amy waved to the operator, making sure the man knew she wanted to be next. He motioned for her to go ahead with an I'm-not-going-to-tell-you-not-to smile.

She stuck her foot in the makeshift stirrup and hoisted her body into the patent leather saddle fixed on the back. The crowd hooted and hollered as she let a saucy smile ripple across her mouth and lifted her arm high above her head. "Let'er rip."

The bull slowly rocked back and forth, gaining speed as the guy with the control moved the ball around in his hand. Her arm swung side to side while she kept her balance, gripping the tanned sides of the contraption with her thighs. She managed to stay on until her time was up and the crowd cheered as she got off. After making a sweeping bow to the delight of the onlookers, she straightened up only to catch the appreciative observation of Tanner. More than a little tipsy at this point, she sauntered to his side, wrapped her hand behind his neck and fastened her lips on his. His arms went around behind her as he tipped his head, fitting her mouth better against his own and her blood roared in her ears. His tongue slipped along the crease of her lips and when she opened her mouth to his seeking tongue, he pushed inside, taking everything she had to offer.

When she finally broke the kiss, they were both panting for breath. "Thanks. I figured I deserved some sort of prize for my ride." She stepped over the inflatable ring, around his side and lost herself in the crowd of people as she tried to still her racing heart.

Why the hell did I do that? Must be the rum—rum does bad things to my brain waves. No more alcohol for me tonight. I'll give the other men in the room my full attention. That should prove my attraction to Tanner to be nothing except a passing fancy, wouldn't it? Unfortunately, it backfired as Tanner began avoiding her as well, spending his breaks with several women in the bar. He played the room like a guitar, stroking and strumming the women around him, leaving each one the impression he would spend a little more time with them, but always walking away in the end.

As the evening wound down, Tanner said from the stage, "That's it, folks. Enjoy the rest of your night, and please don't drive if you've been drinking. We'll see y'all next weekend. Good night." He flipped the switch on the microphone to shut it off and put his guitar away as the four women at his feet moved closer.

Chris walked to Amy's side as she said, "Are you about ready to go?"

"Yeah, let me get my purse," she replied, pulling her gaze from the man on the stage and shifting toward their table. She bent down to pick it up and as she turned around, Tanner stood behind her. She jumped in surprise, placing her hand on her chest to still her racing heart.

"You scared me."

"Sorry. I didn't want you to leave before I could talk to you." He stepped closer, almost blocking her retreat, enveloping her senses with his presence. "I had hoped to dance with you again."

"Yeah, well, it didn't work out that way." She fumbled with her purse, avoiding his searching gaze.

"I guess not," he whispered. Her head came back up when she heard, "Would you like to get a cup of coffee?"

"I appreciate the thought, Tanner, but maybe some other time."

"How about tomorrow?"

"Tomorrow?"

"Yeah. Will you have supper with me?"

"Are you asking me out?"

"Yeah, I guess I am. What do you say?"

The hopeful appearance on his face gave her pause.

"I don't know, Tanner, I mean, we just met." She wanted to be evasive and not encourage him, but on the other hand she wanted…what, she didn't know.

"I thought that's what dates were for."

His pleading eyes met hers and melted her resolve to avoid being alone with him. She had a bad feeling about this, but with a wary smile, she relented. "Okay."

Giving her that smile that turned her insides to mush earlier and made her think of his mouth on hers, he said, "How about I pick you up at Chris' at six? We can have supper, and go dancin' or whatever."

Or whatever. Whatever could mean… Her stomach clenched and liquid seeped onto her panties as she thought of their shared kiss. *Damn, he can get me hot and wet with a kiss.* "I suppose that would be all right."

Snapping his fingers he said, "Wait. Would you like to go for a ride tomorrow? We could take a couple of horses, grab a picnic lunch and go down by the river. There is a really nice spot where I like to go fishin'."

"Fishing?"

"Yeah, fishin'. Do you like to fish?"

"Actually, yes. It's been a long time since I went fishing or riding for pleasure. I usually don't have time to kick back."

"Great! I'll grab a couple of poles and ride over about eleven, if that's okay with you."

"How about I walk over and meet you at your house? I'm kind of picky about my mount."

With an impish grin, he replied, "I bet you are."

Blushing when she realized the double meaning, she stuttered, "I mean, what I meant was—"

He interrupted her with a devilish smile as he said, "I'll see you at eleven or so."

"Eleven it is."

"Sweet dreams," he whispered with a wink.

"Night," Amy whispered as he turned back toward the stage, just as Chris reached them.

"Night, Chris," he said, tipping his hat to her as he passed.

"Night, Tanner."

Amy's gaze fastened on his nicely rounded ass displayed to her view as he walked away and she sighed.

"Did I give him enough time?" *Chris is so setting me up.* Amy frowned at her friend before she turned and headed for the door. "Well, what did you expect me to do when he moved toward you? I got the impression he wanted to talk to you, and I didn't want to get in his way."

Once they reached the car, she opened her door and slid inside, without a word. Chris followed suit by opening the passenger side and climbing in.

She flipped it into drive and pulled out of the parking lot, spraying gravel behind her as silence prevailed inside the car.

"Come on, Am, talk to me."

"No." Her gaze focused on the road in front of her, while her hands gripped the steering wheel until her knuckles turned white.

"Why? I thought I was helping you."

Amy grumbled, "You set me up, Chris. Trying to push me together with Tanner isn't a good idea. I don't want to get involved with someone, no matter how gorgeous they are."

"I only gave him a chance to talk to you. So what happened?"

"He asked me out."

"He asked you out?"

"Yes, he did."

"That's cool! Tanner is a super guy."

Amy looked at her friend, remembering something Chris had said about the guy she had been trying to hook her up with for a long time. *No, it couldn't be. Chris hadn't even tried to introduce them.* She returned her focus to the road without a comment.

"So what are you going to do? Did you say yes?"

"Yes, I did, but I think I'll tell him I can't. I don't think it's such a good idea." Her frown continued to pull her mouth down at the corners. She didn't like this one bit.

"Why?"

"You saw what happened on the dance floor." *Surely that's enough of an explanation. I don't have to spell it out for her, do I?*

"Yeah, so?" Chris sounded confused. "What about when you kissed him after riding the bull? He didn't instigate that, you did."

"I know, and I shouldn't have. I don't want to give him any ideas. The last thing I need is a long distance relationship or to get involved with another cowboy."

"I'm not sure I understand what the problem is. Good grief! You aren't going to fuck him, are you?"

"No!" Amy's gaze swung to her friend in surprise. Not that she hadn't thought about something along those lines, or at least his lips on hers, but for Chris to say it out loud, put her on the defensive.

"Well, it's only one date. Besides, it's not like you are a virgin or anything. You've had lovers before."

"Thanks, Chris."

"I didn't mean it like that. I think you are reading way too much into this."

"Maybe."

"You're attracted to him, right?"

She inhaled sharply before she answered, "Yeah, you could say that."

"Well, what's the big deal? I say go for it. Have a good time and worry about the consequences later. All I'm saying is don't shut the door before the horse is in the barn."

She frowned, knowing her friend meant well, but she was afraid. Never having been this quickly attracted to a man before, the thought of walking away after the weekend came to a close, did not appeal to her.

The two women fell silent for the rest of the ride, but as they pulled into the drive, Chris said, "Amy, listen. There isn't any harm in going out with Tanner one time. I think you two probably have a lot in common. If nothing else, you might end up with a good friend."

"I guess you're right. No big deal." *Yeah right, Amy,* her heart whispered. *His stare curled your toes. If a look could do that, what do you think making love with him would do?*

Once they reached their respected temporary bedroom doors, Chris said, "Tanner is different from the guys you are used to dating. Those stuck-on-themselves guys you've been seeing, only make you doubt yourself. Tanner is a simple cowboy. Be careful. I don't want either of you to get hurt."

Amy shrugged, Chris was right.

"I'm tired of seeing you miserable. You are a beautiful girl, inside and out. It would be great to see you with someone who would appreciate you for yourself and who isn't the type to abuse women. Tanner is too sweet for that. I'm not saying he's Mr. Right. It's only one date. Take advantage of it."

Without waiting for a reply, Chris went into her room and shut the door behind her, leaving Amy standing in the hall.

When Amy stepped into the room, the moon shone brightly through the window, casting silver ribbons on the floor. She pulled off her boots and clothes, slid her t-shirt on and pulled the covers back on the bed, climbing underneath. She focused on the ceiling overhead as shadows danced across and visions of Tanner smiling at her from the stage flashed through her mind.

Damn! Heat infused her body, making her squirm under the sheets. She'd never had anyone look at her with such hunger, like he would devour her, given the chance.

That's it! I need to put him out of my mind; otherwise I'll never get any sleep tonight. She rolled onto her side and closed her eyes.

As sleep finally claimed her, dancing brown eyes and a wicked smile plagued her dreams.

Chapter 3

The next morning, she woke late. She did not remember her dreams from last night specifically, but she awoke very much aware of her body and its needs. The sun shone bright in the sky when she rolled out of the bed, grabbed her robe and wandered into the kitchen for coffee.

"You girls came home rather early. I sure didn't expect to see you two until the wee hours of the morning."

"Why am I not surprised to find you out here and knowing exactly what time we got in? We didn't come in until after two a.m."

"It comes from many years of keeping track of Chris and her siblings. They constantly came in past curfew." Catherine's smile warmed her heart.

Thoughts of Chris getting in trouble on a daily basis made her smile. She could imagine her friend sneaking into the house, only to be caught by her mother who stood guard over the front door.

"Did you girls have a good time?"

"Um, it was fun, I guess."

"Fun? You say one thing, but your face tells me something else." Amy blushed under her scrutiny.

"Well..." she started, before being interrupted as Chris wandered into the kitchen.

"The world must be coming to an end," Catherine remarked, feigning surprise. "She's up before noon."

Chris gave her mother a smirk and a shake of her head as she headed toward the coffee. "How am I supposed to sleep with the noise going on in here?"

"Amy and I were talking about last night."

"Did she tell you she has a date with Tanner today?"

Catherine's surprised gaze returned to her. "No, she left that part out.

That would explain the pretty blush."

Feeling completely out-numbered, Amy rolled her eyes and stood. "I'm going to go take a shower. If you'll excuse me."

"Of course." Catherine winked and laughed as Amy took her coffee with her and walked back down the hall to her room. *Those two obviously think Tanner hung the moon. You had better be careful or they'll have you married off to the guy.*

She grabbed some clean clothes and walked into the bathroom, turning on the water. A hot shower, that's what she needed. *Or maybe I should take a cold one.* Tanner's eyes, hot with desire, swam before her. Shaking her head to displace her erotic thoughts, she stripped her clothes off and stepped into the stream of water. She quickly showered and redressed in clean jeans, a tank top and her boots in preparation for their ride. She was looking forward to this. It had really been too long since she could just enjoy herself and not worry about a competition or whether she looked nice enough for the company she would be keeping.

Once dressed, she glanced at her watch grumbling, "Shoot. I better hurry. It's almost eleven."

When she stepped into the front room, Catherine, Robert and Chris greeted her.

"My, don't you look pretty." Catherine took in Amy's attire.

Amy shrugged. "Nothing special."

"Yes, well, I still think you look nice. Have a nice time with Tanner." Catherine grinned as she reached the front door.

"With Tanner?" Robert questioned.

"Yes, dear. Amy and Tanner are going riding."

She shook her head as she slipped out through the screen, as Catherine continued to explain to her husband why she and Tanner were going somewhere together.

The balmy breeze picked up her hair from her shoulders, spreading it softly against her back, as she walked down the drive toward Tanner's. The smell of hay, animals, sunshine and leather lifted her spirits while they calmed her soul.

It was a bit farther going this way than cutting through the garden, but it put her closer to the barn. She approached the house, noticing Tanner standing near the shelter, brushing a beautiful sorrel gelding.

"Morning," she said, walking up behind him.

He turned as he heard her voice, giving her an appreciative smile. The sunglasses he wore, shielding his eyes from her, but she could tell they ran down her body by the shivers it caused on her skin as his grin widened.

"Mornin'," he replied, setting the brush aside. "You can pick any of the horses in the corral. They are all broke to ride."

"Thanks," she said, eyeing the wonderful group of horses in the pen nearby.

"Mornin', young lady."

She turned to find an older version of Tanner standing at the open door of the barn. Appearing to stand a little shorter than his son's six feet, the same brown eyes twinkled as they met hers, although a few more years of experience wrinkled the corners.

"Good morning," she replied.

"I'm Scott Lewis, Tanner's dad." He held out his hand.

"It's nice to meet you, Mr. Lewis."

"Please, call me Scott. Mr. Lewis makes me feel old."

"All right, Scott," she said with a smile.

"Dad, this is Amy," Tanner said, but paused, pushing his sunglasses on top of his head. "You know, I don't even know your last name."

"It's Russell." Amy grinned.

"Amy Russell," Tanner finished. "She's a friend of Chris' from Dallas."

"It's real nice to meet you, Amy. I watched you work the horse yesterday. Pretty amazin'. I haven't seen anyone do that in twenty years. You happen to be related to John Russell?"

Her gaze returned to Scott, laughing as she said, "Yeah, you could say that. He's my dad."

"Well, hot damn! You're John Russell's little girl?"

"Yes, I am. Do you know him?"

"Hell yeah!" he exclaimed. "We used to ride rodeo together way back when."

"Really? What a small world."

Scott looked hard at her for a moment and said excitedly, "Your dad called you little squirt!"

"Yes, he did, still does at times." Amy laughed, thinking about her dad and how he would kid her.

Scott grabbed her in a hug, pulling her against his large frame in a warm embrace. "I used to tease you when I caught John at a rodeo. I can't believe you are all grown."

* * * *

Tanner's gaze moved back and forth between the two people in amazement. His dad knew Amy's dad? It blew his mind to think their families knew each other, or at least used to.

"Where's your dad now?" Scott asked.

"He and Mom settled on a piece of land in Oregon. He'll be surprised to know I ran into you."

"Wait a minute. You went to rodeos with your dad?" Tanner questioned, getting into the middle of the amazing reunion.

"Yeah, all the time when I was little. I rode after I got into high school. I've started doing the rodeo thing on the weekends now, when I can."

"What do you do now? Barrels?"

"You wouldn't believe me if I told you."

"Yes, I will."

"Trust me, you won't."

"Don't tell me you ride bulls?" He kept his voice teasing. The more he learned about this incredible woman, the more she fascinated him.

"No."

"Then what?"

"You will not believe me so just drop it, okay?"

"Come on, Amy, tell me."

She shifted uneasily. "All right, I team rope," she murmured quietly.

"No way!"

"I told you that you wouldn't believe me."

"I've never heard of a woman team ropin'. What position?"

Rolling her eyes and sighing heavily, she said, "Heeler."

"You have to be kiddin' me." He grunted. "How come I've never heard of you competin'?"

* * * *

She found the need to constantly defend her riding around men aggravating and it pissed her off. Every rodeo she went to someone questioned her abilities, and on many occasions, she had to prove them wrong. People she knew even made bets when they would hear a cowboy say he did not believe she roped.

"I don't go around advertising it, Tanner," she said, exasperated as anger built in her chest. It really bothered her that he didn't believe her.

"I still don't believe it."

"Fine. Is there someone on your place that ropes?"

"Yeah."

"Get him and I'll prove it to you. Where can I find a good roping horse?" She looked toward the corral, shading her eyes from the sun.

"Take your pick. I'll find Larry." Tanner turned his back and headed toward the back of the barn.

He returned a short time later with Larry in tow. He had explained to the man the situation and Larry seemed more than happy to oblige. She still stood near his dad, looking over the horses in the corral.

"Come with me. There are more in the barn." She followed him, anxious to see if there happened to be a different horse that might work for her demonstration.

She walked toward the back where a chestnut gelding poked his head out of the stall. Taking her hand and running it up the animal's nose and across his neck, she looked over the stall door, surveying him.

"I'll take him," she said with confidence, aware of Tanner's surprised look. She knew a good roping horse when she saw one.

"All right. I'll get some tack. There's a lead rope hangin' there by the door."

Grabbing the twisted nylon, she slipped it into the ring under the animals halter, pulled the lock on the stall and led the beautiful horse to a spot where she could tether him.

Tanner returned with a gorgeous saddle, bridle and blanket for her use.

"You don't have a saddle that's a little more worn? I hate to use something so nice." She ran her hands over the tooled leather, still crisp and stiff from non-use.

"It's okay. It's the best tack we've got. I wouldn't want you to have a problem ropin' with defective tack."

"Give it to me," she snapped, pulling the tack from his hands and briskly saddling the horse. His joking tone just set her nerves on edge as she bristled with anger.

Larry sat already astride his horse in the pen, waiting for her. Tanner opened the gate to the pen after she had mounted and pulled it shut behind her as she rode over to the shoot. She nodded to the man already in position with the cow between them, bawling.

She put her sunglasses on to cut the glare, and she readied the rope for their first run. Watching the cow and her partner, she made sure everything was set properly, before she nodded for Tanner to release the cow.

The animal shot out of the holding shoot like a bullet and Larry took off, cleanly roping the horns, as Amy brought up the back. She threw the rope with perfect timing, hooking both back feet, and her horse instinctively stopped on its rear haunches, pulling it tight.

The scenario played out several more times, each ending in the same fashion. Time came for their final run and she could tell by her partner's posture he wasn't happy about a female showing him up. As he roped the horns, he pulled the cow's head enough to throw her timing off, causing her to miss. As she rode over to the cowboy, she said, "It's a good thing you don't do this with me all the time, or I'd kick your ass for pulling that cow's head."

A stunned expression rippled across his face as he replied, "Sorry."

Heat crawled up her neck as her anger built to an explosive level. She had proven she indeed knew what she was doing, but it felt like a hollow victory to her heart. Tanner didn't believe her and that hurt more than she wanted to admit. She pulled the horse back around and rode toward the fence where Tanner and Scott stood watching each run in earnest. The proud raise of Scott's eyebrows and the frown on Tanner's face should have made her anger dissipate, but it didn't. When she pulled the horse up, she hooked her sunglasses with her finger, pulling them down her nose slightly so she could see him over the top rim.

"Satisfied?" Not waiting for an answer, she swung the horse around and headed back for the barn, fuming.

The gate opened to the pressure of her boot, and she rode the gelding inside. *I thought he might be different, but I guess I was wrong.* She dismounted and began stripping the horse of the weight of the saddle. Once free, she slid it over the side of the gate in a jerking motion.

She stiffed as she heard shuffling behind her and his hand came down on her shoulder.

"Listen, Amy, I'm sorry I doubted you. I should have known you wouldn't lie to me."

"I don't give a damn whether you believe me or not," she murmured, shrugging off his touch.

"Let me get the saddle." He moved to take the heavy tack back to the storage room.

"I can get it myself," she grumbled, pulling it from the gate when he tried to reach for it.

"Come on, I said I'm sorry."

She whirled around as she snapped, "You know what? I thought maybe you were different, but I guess not. I thought you might believe me when I told you about the team roping, but you didn't. You're like all the rest. You don't think a woman can do anything, much less do something that is predominantly a man's sport."

"I said I was sorry," he whispered. Pulling the heavy saddle from her arms, he slid it back over the gate before turning to wrap his arms around her, tugging her to his chest.

She pushed against him, but he refused to let her go until she finally quit fighting him.

Giving up, she buried her face next to his shoulder, allowing him to stroke her back for moment before she pulled out of his arms.

"It doesn't matter. I'm sick of proving myself to people. It gets really tiresome," she grumbled as she grabbed the saddle again and headed off to the tack room.

She pushed the saddle onto the stand, making sure it wouldn't fall before she turned around and Tanner stood in the doorway.

"I wish I knew what to say."

"Never mind. I don't care, anyway." She tried to sound convincing, but it didn't work. What he thought meant a lot, unfortunately.

"No. I'm not going to let it go. I upset you, and I'm sorry."

"Listen, Tanner, its fine. Forget it. I'm heading back to Chris' parents place."

He took her shoulders in his hands, but released one to put a finger under her chin, forcing her to raise her eyes to his.

"We're goin' fishin', aren't we?" She could see the teasing glint to his eyes as he tried to make it up to her.

"I don't know if I want to be around you right now."

"Amy, come on. I've already apologized. I promise I'll never doubt you again. I should have known better, anyway. The way you handled that mare yesterday, I wouldn't be shocked to find out you could do everythin' you've put your mind to." Skimming his fingers across her jaw, he continued, "I want to spend the afternoon with you. Don't go."

The warmth of his hands caused heat to seep to her core as she saw the sincerity in his eyes and she finally relented. "All right, I'll go."

"Fantastic! You can pick out a horse out of the corral or you can ride Buster there, if you like. I'll go get the picnic from my mom and the fishin' poles." She watched him turn on his heel and move toward the house, a quickness to his step.

She sighed as she tipped her head back on her shoulders and asked the Lord above for some guidance. *Why did you give in? His doubting cut deep, deeper than any man has before. He's going to hurt you and hurt you bad,* her heart whispered as she grabbed a different saddle and headed back to gelding standing nearby. She quickly saddled him, mounted and rode into the bright sun, heading for the front of the house. Tanner waited with his horse, two saddlebags and two fishing poles

As she approached, her head told her, *you are going to regret this, Amy. He's too cute for your own good, girl, and you are going to get your heart broken if you aren't careful.*

"Ready?"

"Yes. Which way?"

"Follow me," he answered, giving his horse a quick kick, moving into a canter with Amy right on his heels.

Chapter 4

Amy pulled up beside him as they rode out of the yard as she asked, "Did your dad put you on a horse as early as mine did?"

"I've been ridin' since before I can remember so yeah, probably so."

She smiled. "I guess that's the way it is when your dad rides rodeo."

"How often do you get to compete?"

"If we can find one, we go every weekend we're off."

"We?"

"Yeah. A guy at work and I ride together. He works in radiology. His name is Jason Clark. He's a super guy."

"When do you compete next?"

"I'd need to check my calendar but I think there is a rodeo outside Dallas in a couple of weeks we are scheduled to participate in. I'm only off every other weekend usually so we go when we can."

"That's cool. Maybe I'll come by and watch sometime."

"Why don't you tell me about your family?" Amy asked. "How many siblings do you have?"

"One brother and two sisters. I'm the eldest."

"I bet that puts a lot of responsibility on you."

"Yeah, but its okay. I enjoy spendin' time with my family. How about you?"

"I have two sisters. One is in Oregon, near Portland and the other lives up by Seattle. I don't get to visit them much since I live here now. I try to go once a year."

"How did you end up in Dallas, then?"

"I don't know. I got tired of the crap on the West Coast. You can't buy property because everything is so expensive and they offered an awesome job at the hospital in Dallas, so I took it."

"Let's cut back through the trees here. The river isn't far."

The tinkle of a trickling stream met her ears soothing her like nothing else could. She loved the water and missed going to the coast and just listening to the ocean wave's crash over the jagged shoreline.

Tanner took the lead as they rode toward the sound and broke into a small clearing near the rippling stream.

"Oh wow! This is beautiful!" The good sized pool at the base of the rocks reflected their images almost like glass. Trees, thick with leaves, shaded the spot and the sunlight filtered sporadically through the foliage, cooling the area from the summer heat.

The two dismounted and Tanner dropped the reins of his horse without tethering it. Pulling off the saddles, they let the horses' wander nearby.

"We don't need to tether them?"

"No. They won't go far. We can eat now, or in a while, if you want to fish first." The slight southern drawl tickled her ear. She'd heard it before, but right now, with it rippling on the breeze around her, it sent shivers down her arms. She was such a sucker for an accent.

"Later on is fine. I'd like to find out if the fish are biting." She grinned as she took the fishing pole from his fingers. "Did you bring bait or are we digging?"

* * * *

A smile rippled over his mouth. Surely she wouldn't get on her hands and knees to dig worms. "We're diggin'."

Shrugging, she said, "Okay. Works for me."

She took the small shovel he handed her, dropped to her knees and started to scoop some dirt out of a hole. Her tight jeans revealed a nicely rounded backside to his appreciative stare.

Lifting her head, she flashed a triumphant smirk in his direction as she pulled out a worm and placed it in the small can.

His breath caught in his throat. *Lord, I want to kiss her so bad.* Desire pooled in his groin as she knelt on the ground. Images of her naked before him raced across his mind and he groaned.

"I've got about a dozen worms in here. Think that's enough?" She looked up at him, holding the can out for his inspection.

"It should be plenty to start with. I'll grab the poles if you bring the bait.

There is a big log juttin' out over the river where we can sit." He held out his hand to help her stand.

She pulled her hand from his grasp once she stood and brushed the dirt from her fingers on the legs of her jeans. She motioned for him to show the way as she said, "All right. I'll follow you then."

They walked for several hundred feet to the area that Tanner pointed out. They both kicked off their shoes and socks before they stepped across the log and sat down, side-by-side.

"This is fantastic! Are there lots of fish in here?" Amy peered into the pool of water beneath her.

"My dad keeps it stocked with catfish and trout all the time so there are always somethin' to catch."

He handed a pole to her, watching her keenly. She grabbed the bait can, digging her fingers into the soft dirt and pulled out a nice fat wiggly nightcrawler, threading it onto the hook. She turned, flashing a gorgeous smile at him and skillfully cast the line.

"Not the least bit squeamish, are you?"

The dubious expression on her face made him chuckle as she said, "I'm a nurse. I deal with blood and guts all the time. Do you think a little worm is going to gross me out?"

"Yeah, pretty dumb thought, huh." He sent his own line sailing into the water.

The warm summer breeze brushed the hair from her neck and she tipped her head back, letting it fall out of the way as she closed her eyes.

"This is perfect," she whispered.

His breath caught in his throat as she bared her neck to his eyes. Unable to pull his gaze away, a groan rumbled in his chest and he started to squirm uncomfortably on the log, causing the wood to move slightly.

Her eyes popped open, and she turned her head. "Something wrong?"

He cleared his throat as his cock grew painfully behind the ridged fly of his jeans. "No, but do you have any idea how much I want to lick that spot on your neck where the pulse flutters against the skin?"

A dreamy smile spread across her lips. "Do you?"

His mouth lifted at the corners as he answered, "Oh yeah."

"Here, hold this." She handed him the fishing pole, turning on the log and straddling the expanse with her legs. Scooting closer, they both laughed as the log jiggled with her movements, threatening to spill them both into the water. When she got close enough, she threw her legs over his thighs, her breasts almost touching his chest. *Holy shit!* His breathing hitched sharply as his heart slammed against his ribs.

Sweeping her hair over her shoulders, she leaned back on her hands and arched her neck, she said, "Now you can reach it."

He accepted her invitation, tucking the fishing poles under their legs and leaned forward, lightly touching the hollow of her throat with his tongue. He almost groaned out loud at the salty taste of her skin.

"I love the way you taste and smell," he whispered softly and she started laughing.

He sat back, startled at her giggles, not quite understanding what was so funny. She laughed so hard, she almost doubled over, putting her hands on his shoulders to keep from falling. As she continued to chuckle, the log began to shake and they both tumbled off, landing in the cool water below.

Surfacing not far from her in a spot where he could stand, she came up out of the water still laughing and he joined her. They chuckled for several minutes as they looked at each other, until he noticed how transparent her white T-shirt appeared. The bra beneath did nothing to hide the pert nipples that strained against her shirt. He stepped closer as the laughter died on her lips and his hand came out of the water to skim across her shoulder.

He ran his fingers along her jaw, letting his thumb whisper over her bottom lip. She released a soft sigh and closed her eyes. He let his hand move to the back of her neck and pulled her closer as he slipped the other one around her waist. He bent forward and captured her mouth, softly at first, but after only a moment, desire took over and he deepened the kiss, pressing his tongue insistently against her lips until she opened for him with a groan.

When he finally lifted his head and he stared into her eyes, he let his palm slide over her breast and she gasped. "God, I want you Amy, but not here, not like this."

A blush crawled up her neck and splash across her cheeks as she dropped her gaze. "I'm sorry. I didn't mean for things to happen this way. I don't want you to get the wrong impression."

He lifted her face so he could look into her eyes. "Don't be sorry. I don't want to make love to you for the first time in the creek or on the slope of the grass, where anyone can see us." He kissed her softly, before grasping her hand and pressing it to his straining, throbbing erection. "I want you, make no mistake about that, but not here, and I don't relish tryin' to get those wet jeans off of your hips."

She laughed. "Me either. What's going to suck is riding back to the house in them." Reaching inside her shirt, she lifted a small fish out of her bra and they both chuckled.

A smile rippled across his face. "Yeah, it will and bein' hard enough to hammer nails with my dick, makes it so much worse."

Giggling softly, she said, "If you'd like, I can take care of your problem for you."

He groaned at the thought. "Very temptin', but I don't want this to be one sided. I'll survive until we can do this together." He grabbed her hand in his, leading her out of the creek to where they'd dropped their shoes and the picnic basket.

He pulled sandwiches and potato salad from the saddlebags and handed her everything as he settled back on the blanket. She chewed the sandwich as she looked out over the water.

When her tongue flicked out to capture a small spot of mayonnaise that rested on the corner of her mouth, he almost whimpered. *Damn! It's going to hurt ridin' home.* "If you like, we can ride along the river for a while after we are done eatin'. The trip is prettier, but a longer way back to the house."

"That would be cool. It took us, what, about an hour to get here?"

"Yeah. If we travel down by the river, it will take about two hours to get back."

"Do you ride out here a lot?"

"Sometimes. Between helpin' my parents on their place and playin' at the bar, I don't have much time for myself."

"What are your plans for the future?"

"Why?" He grinned.

"Curiosity, I guess." Her shoulders lifted in a shrug. "I assume you don't expect to work on your parents' place all your life or playing just at Pete's."

She shifted on the blanket, lying on her side with her hand beneath her head.

"No, I reckon not. I hadn't thought too far ahead yet, not much past the next couple of years. I'm hopin' to get a recordin' contract someday. I'd love to be able to perform for a livin', but it's such a cutthroat market, you never know. We don't do so badly with what we have, but I won't get rich that way." He let his eyes caress her face then settle on her lips. "What about you?"

"I'm happy at the hospital, with my job anyway. My love life sucks at the moment, but hopefully it won't stay that way."

Frowning, he asked, "Why does your love life suck?"

"I just haven't had much luck with relationships lately."

"I know what you mean. I've had my own troubles."

"A nice looking guy like you?" She appeared not to believe him and he laughed.

"Yeah. It's not easy when you play in a band. There are usually women that like to hang around, you know, but you are never sure exactly what they are after."

"I guess I understand."

"What I mean is, you saw those girls hangin' around at the bar last night, right?" He shifted, folding his arms across his knees.

"Yeah."

"Most of them have slept with half of my band members."

"But not you?" She squinted as she looked at him with a questioning raise of her eyebrow.

"No. I don't like sloppy seconds. Its one thing if I dated them first and they moved onto someone else, but I don't share well. They want to be with someone they think may have money in the end." Turning the conversation back to her, he asked, "What about you? A pretty girl like you isn't married?"

She gave him a sideways grin. "No, never. I guess I haven't found the perfect person for me yet. I've had a few serious relationships, but nothing that has gotten to the point of marriage. Have you?"

"Yeah, once," he replied.

"Been married?"

"No, almost, though. It wasn't a pleasant experience and one I'd rather not talk about."

"Sorry."

"No problem," he replied coming to his feet and holding out his hand to help her rise. "Shall we head for the house?"

* * * *

Confused at his sudden turn of demeanor, she let him help her to her feet. Reaching for the remnants of their lunch, she helped pack everything away as the now uncomfortable silence stretched between them. Slipping their shoes and socks back on, they re-cinched the saddles and prepared to mount, while she examined him over the horse's back. He sure did not want to talk about his almost marriage, but now it bothered her. What was she like? Was she pretty? Was it one of those women at the bar? No, she did not think so by the way he acted last night. He obviously knew them, but he wasn't uncomfortable around them like she assumed he might be around someone he almost married.

They checked to make sure nothing had been left behind, remounted and slowly walked the animals, following the riverbank.

Tanner talked about everything other than his engagement while they rode. He asked more about her job at the hospital and he told her some of his plans for the band. They finally reached his house about five, heading the horses toward the barn.

"Are you hungry?" he asked as they dismounted and pulled the saddles off.

"A little."

"Where would you like to go for supper?"

"Doesn't matter to me. I'm not a really picky eater, but I love red meat."

Giving her a quick, sexy grin, he said, "A girl after my own heart. How about steak?"

"Sounds good, but I need to shower before we go anywhere. I like the scent of horses, but not on me."

"All right. I'll take care of them if you want to head back to Chris' place. I'll pick you up in about an hour."

"I like that plan. I'll see you then." She glanced in his direction as she left the barn, a small smile gracing her lips.

* * * *

Chris pulled the little black dress out she had purchased yesterday. "I can't wear that!"

"Why not? It's gorgeous on you."

"That's one of those dresses you put on when you are thinking of possibly getting lucky or want to knock the guys' socks off."

"This isn't your first date, and well, aren't you?"

"Aren't I what?" Amy said absently, searching through the things she brought for something suitable to wear.

"Hoping to get lucky or just knock his socks off."

Her shocked expression must have been hilarious as Chris laughed. Heat curled up her neck and splashed across her cheeks, giving away the secret of her growing attraction to Tanner.

"I knew it!" Chris exclaimed.

"Stop, for crying out loud. I've only known the guy for a couple of days."

"I still think you should wear the dress."

With a heavy sigh, she agreed. "I didn't bring anything else that seems appropriate. I hadn't expected to be going on a date."

"I knew you'd see it my way. Here." Chris laughed and handed the dress to her. She took it into the bathroom, slipping the dress over the black bra and panties. She touched up her makeup, splashed on a bit of some of her favorite perfume, pulled her hair up on her head, letting a couple of tendrils tickle her shoulder, and she was ready.

"Well?" Amy asked buckling the shoes she'd bought as well.

"I suspect he will be speechless when he sees you. You look awesome!"

"Thanks, but I'm not doing this to impress him. I don't want to be the pretty thing on someone's arm anymore."

"Nothing wrong with looking beautiful, Am. Tanner is a simple guy, but I'm sure he appreciates a ravishing woman." They heard the doorbell ring down the hall. "Must be him."

Her stomach tightened, her heart jumped in her breast and her palms started to sweat. She sucked in a steady breath, pulled the door of the bedroom open and walked down the hall into the living room. Catherine had already invited him in and he stood with his back to her, talking with Robert.

"Ah, there she is," Catherine said as Amy walked through the doorway. When Tanner turned around, the appreciation in his eyes was worth every minute she had spent in the bathroom.

Dressed much as he had been the night before at the bar, his starched white shirt had small blue stripes running down the front, pressed jeans and brushed clean boots, along with the standard stark black cowboy hat, he was a sight to be seen. *Damn! He's gorgeous.*

"Wow! You look fantastic!" He quickly walked to her side and tucked her hand into the crook of his arm. "All set?"

"Yes, just let me grab my purse." She reached over and picked up her small bag from the table as they approached the door.

"Make sure you have her home by midnight, young man," Catherine said sternly. As both sets of eyes turned in her direction, she laughed. "I'm kidding!"

The couple smiled and Tanner opened the front door, ushering her outside and closing it behind them.

Once she sat comfortable inside, she watched from behind the windshield as he moved around to the driver's side, her heart beating wildly in her chest. He swung open the door and slid onto the seat. He started the engine and graced her with a devilishly sexy smile.

Silence prevailed in the truck as they drove down the now darkening road toward town. The hair stood up on her arms as her heart continued to hammer against her ribs when she thought of being alone with him.

"What do you want to do after supper?" His voice broke the silence enveloping them. "We could go to Pete's if you'd like."

"You don't have to play tonight?"

"No. The other guy and I switch off. That way we both aren't tied up durin' the whole weekend. I'll be playin' on Wednesday night this week."

"Ah. Pete's is fine."

"Good. I can dance with you again," he said with a smile.

She smiled in return, giving him a sideways glance. They continued to the restaurant in silence. Once he had parked the truck, he walked around, and opened her door, taking her hand in his as she slid out, tucking her fingers into the crook of his elbow.

Once inside, a waiter met them. "Hey, Tanner. How's it going?"

"Good, Matt. How have you been?"

"Not bad, working a lot. Who's the pretty lady with you?"

"This is Amy Russell. She's a friend of Chris Robins from Dallas."

Tanner smiled at her, the dimple peeking out of his cheek and appreciation clear in his eyes.

"Nice to meet you, Amy. Let me see if I can find you two a special table." Matt moved toward the podium with the restaurant seating sketched out. "This way. I have the perfect one." Matt grabbed two menus and pointed the way for Tanner and Amy to follow.

Acutely aware of the man next to her, all six feet of him as they walked side-by-side, she proudly lifted her chin, noticing the many stares of the other women in the restaurant. The scent of musk and man reached her sensitive nose, making her feel all liquid inside, as her heart thumped to its own excited tempo.

Matt led them to a little area sitting in the back secluded corner of the room. A small candle burned, illuminating the quaint space and Amy noticed a single white rose lying across the placemat. The table was obviously reserved. She did not quite understanding why Matt seated them there until Tanner pulled out the chair where the flower rested.

Raising her surprised gaze to his, she said, "What's this?"

"Call me a romantic. I thought you'd like it." He shrugged.

"It's beautiful," she whispered, her eyes getting a little misty. None of the men she had ever gone out with before thought to do such a small thing and the tender gesture quickly raised Tanner to the top of her list. "Thank you."

"You are welcome, but it wasn't anythin'." Tanner blushed as he took the seat across from her.

You have no idea how much this means.

"Order whatever you like. The rib-eye is good."

Picking up the menu and setting the rose to her left, she tried to focus on the selection of food. She kept peeking over the top of the laminated pictures to look at the man before her, unable to decide if he was real. If she didn't know better, she might think he had just walked out of one of her romance novels.

Once their selections were made, Matt took their order and disappeared toward the kitchen.

Tanner sipped the water sitting in front of him. "Pete's is usually pretty busy on the weekends. Are you sure you want to go there?"

"Whatever is fine. I'm here to enjoy your company, nothing more." She traced the water droplets on her glass, peeking at Tanner through her lashes.

The corners of his lips turned up and she had the insane urge to suck his bottom lip into her mouth and nibble. Lost in her steamy thoughts, she almost missed what he said.

"That's fine with me."

Matt arrived at the table with their salads and drinks. Amy picked up her fork and stabbed at a piece of lettuce. The tang of the Italian dressing danced on her taste buds as she chewed, the aroma of seared meat wafting in the air, making her mouth water.

Gazing across the table, she wondered what he was thinking as his eyes twinkled in the dim light, almost like he knew the images racing across her mind. Her sight moved down his freshly shaven chin, down his throat as she contemplated running her tongue along the column, licking and sucking on the soft skin into her mouth. His shirt opened at the collar and the curling hairs of his chest peeked out, daring her to run her fingers through them.

"Does your family visit you in Dallas at all?" His question brought her thoughts back to their present location, instead of the steamy encounter she had begun to imagine.

"Not very often. Dad has a hard time sitting with his bad knees so it's easier for me to visit them."

"I can imagine." He smiled across the table and her heart skipped a beat as heat rushing through her blood, making her shift uncomfortably in the chair.

"So, what department do you work in?"

"Chris and I work in the critical care unit. We take care of patients on ventilators, or people fresh out of open-heart surgery. Ours are the sickest of the sick."

"I imagine your job is rewardin' though."

"Sometimes, but other times things get rough. If we lose someone we've been taking care of for a while, it's bad. It's really hard when there is a wife or husband. To see such love between two people and then their other half is gone so quickly..." Her voice trailed off to a whisper, and she dipped her head to hide the pain.

"I bet you tend to wear your heart on your sleeve."

He picked up her hand in his, turning it over and kissing the inside of her wrist. The soft kiss sent a tingle all the way up her arm and settled itself in her belly as their eyes met.

The moment disappeared as Matt returned with the rest of their food and Tanner let go of her hand. She slid the appendage back onto her lap, trailing her finger over the spot he had kissed.

The food tasted wonderful. The steak was prepared perfectly, slightly pink in the middle, a delicious marinade kept the meat moist and tender – almost tender enough to cut with a fork. Tanner told her stories of growing up in Brenham and by the time they finished eating, she laughed so hard, her stomach hurt. "Okay, stop." She giggled, holding her side. "I can't take it anymore."

* * * *

Tanner's mouth curved into a smile. Her laughter strummed his heart strings and his chest ached for the sound. He could easily picture spending the rest of his life with her.

"You two sound like you are having a good time over here. Anything else I can get for you?" Matt asked as he laid the bill onto the tabletop.

"I think that's it." Tanner reached behind him and slipped the wallet out of his back pocket, laying some money on top of the check.

"Great. I'll be right back with this," Matt replied as he left the table.

Amy grasped her purse, intending to leave the tip, but he stopped her. "I've got it."

"Let me get the tip at least, Tanner." She grabbed ten dollars from her wallet, intent on leaving some money for the waiter.

"I said I got it. My treat, Amy. I asked you out, remember?"

Shaking her head, she gave him a small smile. "All right, but next time, it's my turn."

"Next time?"

Blushing as she realized what she had said, she shrugged. "Yeah. You never know when we might run into each other again."

He smiled, fully aware of how evasive her answer sounded. She wasn't going to give him an inch, he realized. "Ready?"

"Yeah. I'm so full I don't think I could eat another thing for the next week."

He held out his hand to help her to her feet and she slipped her palm into his, as he laced their fingers together. He relished the feel of her by his side as they walked out to his truck and he inhaled her intoxicating scent, letting it wrap around his senses.

Once they were seated and he turned over the engine, he said, "Pete's is not far."

"Perfect."

He pulled the truck out in traffic, drove the few blocks to the bar and stopped in an empty spot.

"You weren't kidding when you said the bar was just up the road." Amy looked out the window at the multitude of cars in the lot.

"Told you," he responded, opening his door.

Once he had opened her door and she stepped out, he closed it, placing his warm hand on the small of her back to guide her as she shivered under his touch and he smiled.

* * * *

They reached the doors, as the twang of the latest country song met their ears. The night breeze blew slightly, rustling the trees overhead. Standing next to him, made her completely aware of the handsome man by her side. His body heat penetrated her entire being and she sighed, shifting as her panties rubbed against her clit. *Amy, you are getting in way too deep, way too soon with this.*

He opened the door, ushering her inside while she scanned the crowd for an empty table.

"To the left," he murmured in her ear, directing her attention to the open spot several feet away.

"What do you want to drink?" he asked.

"Beer is fine."

"Be right back." Her gaze followed him as he weaved through the crowd, headed for the bar. *Yummy.* It took several minutes for him to return to the table. "Sorry, I got waylaid."

Her lips curled up in a smile as he sat next to her. "I noticed."

Tanner moved his arm behind her, placed his hand on her shoulder and pulled her close to his side. The warmth of his skin caused a shiver to race down her back, settling in her between her thighs. She pressed them together to calm her racing desire and he whispered in her ear, "Cold?"

Shaking her head no, she took an unsteady breath, trying to calm her overheated body. His finger traced little circles on her shoulder, making her very aware of the man next to her and the wetness of her panties.

After several minutes, he turned and nuzzled the hair near her ear with his nose, sending another shiver down her arms. The warm breath on her neck made her want to tip her head and let him lick, nibble, bite, whatever he wanted to do, until she creamed right in front of everyone.

"You were right about the smell of horses. I like this smell much better."

She closed her eyes, her breath catching in her throat as his whisper flittered in her ear and she tried desperately to put the thoughts of him between the sheets out of her mind. No one had ever had this effect on her before and it drove her crazy. Oh, she had been with a few men in the past, even men who knew exactly what to do and what to say to turn her on, but never like this and *damn it*, he wasn't even trying.

"Are you all right?"

She knew the bright rose color on her cheeks gave away the heat radiating from her core at his very touch. *I wonder if he can smell how hot I am? What I wouldn't give to have him fuck me right on the seat of his truck?*

"I'm fine, but I need to make a trip to the ladies room. I'll be right back." She stepped away from his hand and hurried off toward the door marked 'women.'

Once inside the safety of the bathroom, she placed her purse on the ledge over the sink. She bent her head and took a few deep breaths to try to calm her racing heart. She heard a couple of girls moving toward the door so she raised her head, grabbed her purse and disappeared into the bathroom stall. The two women chitchatted for several minutes before disappearing. Her desire better under control, when they were gone, Amy stepped out of the stall, fluffed her hair a little and opened the door. As she headed back toward their table, the same group of women from last night stood by Tanner's side and a spark of jealousy zipped down her back. When she stopped at his side, she slipped her arm around his waist and he draped his over her shoulder. He softly kissed her on the temple, much to her delight and to the horror of the women around them.

"Amy, this is Laurie, Marie, Janice and Alice." Amy tipped her head and smiled in greeting. "Ladies, this is Amy."

Alice said hello in return, but the other three grabbed her arm and without a word, disappeared back to their table.

"Okay then," Amy grumbled.

"Don't worry. Bitch comes to mind when you think of those three."

She laughed.

"Let's dance," he took her hand, leading her to the middle of the floor. "I'd much rather this be a slow song, but two-steppin' will have to do for now."

Scooting around the dance floor, her hand resting on his shoulder and his caressing her waist, did nothing to cool her ardor. She followed his steps as he led, their bodies moving together in a sensual rhythm reverberating in her head. The song changed to Rascal Flatts crooning Cool Thing and Tanner shifted, drawing her closer to his chest. She fought a moan when her breasts brushed against him and her nipples puckered under her clothing.

"Much better," he whispered, nuzzling her ear. "Watchin' you on that bull last night, all I can say is *totally hot.*"

Moving back so she could see his eyes, she said, "I'm glad you liked it."

"The kiss afterwards got my attention, too."

"Did it?"

"Most definitely." His nose brushed hers as he said, "Even more than the first one. Of course, I'd much rather kiss you without interruptions."

"We'll have to work on that."

The song ended and he dropped his arm, but grabbed her hand and moved toward the table.

For the next several hours, he managed to be the most attentive man she had ever dated. He stayed by her side almost constantly as they danced, drank, and laughed with his friends. He rode the bull, but chuckled when she refused, pointing to the fact that she wore a dress even though he suggested pulling it up.

"But I can enjoy your legs if you do."

"So would everyone else in the bar," she giggled, leaning closer to his side.

"True, scratch that."

His dimple peeked out of his cheek and she wanted so badly to run her tongue over that tempting indentation.

"What are you thinkin'?"

The corner of her mouth lifted in a half smile as she leaned over and whispered in his ear, "How much I want to lick your dimple." His breath came out in a short burst, ruffling the hair by her neck. "I think it's sexy as hell."

"God, woman. Do you have any idea what you're doin' to me?"

Her fingers brushed down his chest until she reached the waistband of his jeans. "Shall I find out?" she murmured and he groaned as she let her finger nails graze against the obvious bulge in his jeans.

"Let's go somewhere a little more private," he said as she gave him her saucy smile.

She stood saying, "I need to make a trip to the ladies room before we go anywhere. I'll be right back." She picked up her purse from the chair, kissed him quickly on the lips and moved through the crowd.

The bathroom crowd stood from wall to wall, leaving very little room to maneuver inside, but she managed to find an open stall. She shut the door and slipped the lock as the words from outside her stall reached her ears.

"Did you see Tanner? Damn, that's one fine looking man."

"I know. Laurie sure is one lucky girl."

Laurie? Who the hell is Laurie?

"She knows it, too. They have been seeing each other for such a long time."

"Well, I'm sure one of these days she'll get him to the altar. It's just a matter of time."

Their footsteps retreated and the conversation changed as it faded.

Shock reverberated through her as their words sank into her mind. Surely they weren't talking about her Tanner, the Tanner she had just spent the last several hours with. She must have heard them wrong. Her mind, being the logical one chimed in. *How many guys do you know with the name Tanner?*

Anger and betrayal seethed through her as she ripped open the stall door and hurried to the sink to wash her hands. *I'm going to find out about this right now. If he's just playing with me, it will be the last time.*

She pulled open the bathroom door and walked briskly in the direction of where her date stood leaning against a pole.

When she arrived at his side, Tanner went to slide his arm around her again, but she shrugged him off, taking several steps in front of him.

"Amy?" He caught up with her as the question reached her ears.

Giving him the most dangerous glare that she could muster, she moved away from him again. She wasn't going to discuss things in front of the crowd. She would save it for when they got in the truck.

Tears burned behind her eyes and a lump formed in her throat, choking off any words she might have said, even if the only thing she could think of happened to be *bastard.* Tanner caught up with her, but didn't say anything as she fought to hold her emotions together. He opened the door for her, and without a word, she slid into the passenger seat, grabbed the handle and pulled it shut.

"Do you want to tell me what's wrong?" he asked when he got in. The question hung in the air between them as she waited for him to start the truck. She continued looking out the windshield but shook her head, afraid if she said something now, she would burst into tears. He grumbled under his breath as the engine turned over. After several minutes, she realized they weren't heading back to Chris'.

He took a side road to the right, bouncing along over the dirt and gravel leading back into the trees, but she wasn't going to ask where they were going. She trusted him, Lord only knew why, but she did, knowing he wouldn't hurt her, not physically, anyway.

When he finally stopped, the most beautiful view of the town below, greeted her. The lights twinkled in the distance like stars, but in a varying color scheme that took her breath away.

She watched as he angrily pushed open his door, slammed it shut behind him and stomped away. He pulled his hat off and ran his hands through his hair. Taking a deep breath, she opened the door and followed him out. Her anger now deflated, she knew she had to give him a chance to explain. If she thought he lied, she would just have him take her back to Chris' and be done with it and him.

* * * *

Damn, she can tie me up in knots. He stared out over the bluff wishing he knew what had pissed her off now, but she wasn't talking, at least not yet.

As she walked up beside him, he stiffened. Shooting a glance in her direction, he saw her watching the lights below. She didn't appear to be angry anymore, or at least not as mad as before. Wanting to let her start the conversation, he kept quiet. When she finally started to speak, he turned so he could see her face.

She sighed heavily and said, "I'm sorry."

"Sorry?"

"Yeah. I shouldn't be mad at you for something you have no idea about. At least, you should have the chance to explain."

"Okay. What have I done that I have no clue what you're talkin' about." *Damn, she is making this hard.*

"Who is Laurie?" The question whipped on the wind as her frustrated stare dared him to lie.

Chapter 5

"Laurie? I don't know what you are talkin' about. Why?" Confusion rippled across his face.

"I guess I should put it this way. Are you seeing somebody that lives here in Brenham?"

"No. I'm not seein' anyone, no one but you."

"You haven't been in a long term relationship with someone named Laurie?"

"I told you, I haven't been seeing anyone, much less anyone named Laurie, but I do know, what a minute. Did somebody give you the impression I'm seein' someone else?" She dropped her gaze, avoiding his searching stare. He stepped close, putting his fingers under her chin and raising it so he could look her in the eyes. "Amy?"

"Yes," she whispered.

"I had hoped you trusted me, but I guess not." His disappointed in her lack of trust, shone bright in his eyes.

"I'm sorry, Tanner. I've been burned so many times in the past with guys who tell me one thing and do something else that it's difficult for me to trust."

"Do you believe me?"

For some reason, she knew he didn't lie to her. "Yes, but who is Laurie?"

"The only Laurie I know is the black-haired girl from the bar. That's Laurie and you don't have to worry, I wouldn't date her."

I should have known. I should have trusted him or at least given him the chance to explain before I blew things out of proportion. She stepped back and turned to peer over the bluff at the lights. "I guess I should have given you the benefit of the doubt."

"You could have at least asked me before you jumped to conclusions."

"I know." Totally embarrassed by her behavior, she blushed. She knew she had trust issues with everything that happened with Jack, but it wasn't fair to hold Tanner to the same standard. He was one of the good guys, wasn't he? Changing the direction of the conversation, she asked, "Did you plan to bring me up here anyway? It really is beautiful."

"Actually, yes. This is one of my favorite spots. I come up here a lot to think. I've written several songs up here, actually."

"Really?"

"Yeah." He kicked the dirt under the toe of his boot nervously. "Maybe I'll play one for you sometime."

"Cool. I like to listen to you sing."

"I'm going to turn the truck around so we can sit on the tailgate. I'll be right back."

He backed up so the rear of the truck sat near the edge of the bluff.

When she saw what he carried, she raised a questioning eyebrow. "A blanket?"

"This thing will hurt your butt if you sit on it too long. At least the blanket will pad things a little." He spread it out on the bare metal and she sat down.

"Perfect," she said, slipping off her shoes and leaving them in the grass as she started swinging her legs.

Tanner sat beside her, staring out into the night as the music from the radio drifted on the breeze to their ears. She hummed along, hearing one of her favorite songs.

"You can sing pretty well yourself." He grinned as he glanced back at her.

"Yeah, right. I can't sing to save my life, although I used to in the high school choir, but that encompassed at least fifty other people. I could lose my voice in theirs."

Smiling, Tanner said, "We all have to start somewhere, I guess."

"Does anyone else in your family sing? I mean professionally?"

"Not really. My dad and my uncle play some and mess around, but it's not like they have attempted a career or anythin'."

"Where have you traveled with the band?" Curiosity about his life here got the better of her, although she wasn't sure why. Her body was acutely aware of his, and by asking, it kept things on a lighter note than replaying his kisses in her mind or imaging his cock between her legs.

"We've done gigs all over, but mostly here in Texas. Things are pretty steady at Pete's. I usually play at least one day every weekend, and one or two days during the week. The crowds are excellent those nights."

"That's good. It gives you some steady income. I'm sure it helps the fan base, too. You seem to be pretty popular with the locals or at least the women, anyway."

A bit shyly, he dropped his head to hide the blush on his cheeks.

"You're blushing!" She laughed as she placed her hand on his forearm. His eyes focused on her hand for a moment, before he lifted his gaze to hers and the raw desire reflected there took her breath away.

The first notes of Clay Walker singing Hypnotize the Moon reached their ears, as she whispered, "This is one of my favorite songs."

He scooted off the tailgate and held out his hand. "Would you dance with me?"

Not saying a word, she placed her hand in his as her bare feet touched the soft blanket of grass under them. Holding his gaze, she stepped into his arms with a satisfied sigh.

He pulled her close, near enough her breasts brushed his chest as she heard a groan rumble in his throat. Her cheek came to rest against his as she felt the whisper of his breath at her ear and she shivered. Her fingers touched the softness of the hair at his nape, making her fingertips tingle.
Their bodies moved as one, with the lyrics of the song drifting on the breeze and settling in her heart.

Oh lord, Amy, you are in trouble now. His lips touched her skin where the collarbone and shoulder met, infusing her with heat that settled between her thighs in a heady pool. The little straps of her dress did nothing to shield her from the softness of his kiss. Her legs got weak as his tongue darted out, capturing the salt as she moaned softly.

When the song ended, she pulled back in his arms just far enough she could see his face. His eyes had turned to a deep, chocolate brown, and as they skimmed over her, her cheeks heated as her body grew warm from his look.

When his gaze settled on her mouth, her lips parted in silent invitation, and a small sigh escaped. She knew he had every intention of devouring her mouth under his in a kiss that would knock her socks off, just like the others.

As his stare moved back up her face and she watched a small smile cross his lips right before he took hers. The kiss was soft at first, but when she accepted him, he deepened the caress, moving his lips over hers. She felt him groan deep in his chest as he wrapped his arms around her, as if he couldn't get close enough. The kisses before had been fantastic, making her want him like no other, but this one, this one kiss held all of the wants and needs of his heart in one touch.

Oh God, she thought, right before his tongue touched her lips, seeking entrance into the soft cavern, and all logical comprehension left her mind. Her lips parted, allowing him access to the moist inside of her mouth as her own moan reached the surface.

Their tongues danced, each wanting something from the other, but not exactly sure what. Their breathing came in a short, rapid tempo as desire spiraled out of control. Breaking the kiss, Tanner put his forehead against hers, closing his eyes.

When he opened them again, her own need rushed through her as she almost threw caution to the wind at the heat in his gaze. She watched a small, wry smile cross his lips as he brought his fingers up to skim gently across her jaw. She closed her eyes to his touch, wanting more as she snuggled against his hand.

"We need to stop this before it gets out of control," he whispered against her parted lips, nibbling at the corners.

"I know," she moaned in return, a shiver running down her spine as his lips touched hers for the second time.

"I didn't bring you up here to fuck you until you scream, although the thought has crossed my mind several times since I met you," he murmured, lifting his head. His hand moved to cup her breast and she pushed her now taut nipple against his palm, craving the friction of his caress. She tasted the passion in his kiss, as desire raced along her veins like she had never experienced before. *You want him, Amy. You want to know what it would feel like for him to do exactly what he suggested, fuck you until you scream,* her heart whispered as her body reacted to his touch.

A moment later, he pushed away from her.

Bewildered, she looked at him, wondering what the hell just happened.

* * * *

As the desire between them zinged out of control, he felt the cell phone in his pocket vibrate. He pushed Amy back as he reached into for it. His breaths came out in rapid pants when he looked at the screen. Tanner groaned out loud as he heard Amy ask who it was.

"Chris." He seethed. *I'm going to personally kill her.*

Amy took a few steps away from him as he flipped open the phone. "What do you want, Chris?"

"I'm checking on you two since I couldn't reach Amy."

"Her cell is in the truck I imagine."

"Let me talk to her." Amy reached for his phone. He handed it to her, right before he turned to walk near the bluff.

Use this to cool off, Tanner. You need to get yourself under control before something happens that you'll both regret. He stared out at the lights as the murmurs of the conversation reached him

"Hi, Chris," Amy said with a shaky voice.

He laced his fingers behind his head, breathing deeply, trying desperately to bring his raging desire to a tolerable level.

"As Tanner said, it's in the truck inside my purse."

Amy walked a little closer, close enough he could smell the sweet scent of her perfume.

"Somewhere overlooking the town."

Chris must have asked where we are.

"Yeah, I guess so."

Maybe it wasn't such a good idea to bring her up here.

"Bye." The phone clicked shut and Amy walked over, touching him on the shoulder, bringing his attention back to her as she handed it back to him.

"Chris told me to tell you to behave yourself." Amy tried to joke as he stiffened.

"Did she?"

"Yes. She also said this is make-out drive?"

"They do call it that around here." He chuckled.

"Every town has one."

"Probably so." He shrugged as he said, "I guess I shouldn't have brought you up here."

"Why not?"

"I don't want you to get the idea I was trying to come on too strong." Their desire cooled as he put distance between them and stuffed his hands in his pockets. "I'm sorry. I didn't mean for things to get that out of control. Make no mistake, you are a very attractive girl, and I'd do it again in a minute."

Blushing, she dropped her gaze to her feet. Stepping near her, he put his finger under her chin so he could look into her eyes as he asked, "Are you okay?" She nodded as his gaze moved back down to her lips. *Don't to it. If you kiss her again, it will be over and you'll be fucking her in the back of the truck.*

She sighed in what sounded like disappointment as he murmured, "I should probably take you home."

She stepped back. "Yeah."

"I'll get the blanket if you grab your shoes."

* * * *

Shivering now in the cooling night air and the loss of his body heat, she picked up her shoes and moved around to the passenger side of the truck. Opening the door, he grasped her chin and quickly kissed her on the lips. After she slid into the seat, he gave her that melt-your-heart-in-a-puddle smile, closed the door and walked around to the driver's side.

Without another word, he started the truck and popped it into gear, pulling out of their parking spot onto the dirt road.

Afraid to read anything into what happened on the bluff, Amy kept quiet, but snuck a peek at him several times during the ride. It wasn't far from where they had sat overlooking the town back to Chris' parents' house, but the ride seemed to go on forever, then wasn't long enough.

She didn't want him to leave. She feared she would never see him again once he left her at the door. Insecurity clouded her mind and rose to incredible levels the moment he pulled up to the front of the house. She stared out the window as he shut the truck off. He reached across the expanse between them, brushing his hand against her shoulder and taking a tendril of hair between his fingers. The sensation of having his hand so near, but not really touching, drove her crazy. She was such a sucker for the smallest, intimate touch, always had been, but no one, until now, had brought on this raw hunger in her. She would be totally lost should he decide to rub his fingers around her ear. *That* would be her undoing, no matter what the consequences of her actions might be.

She turned to look at him across the truck and gave him a tentative smile, wanting to rub her cheek against his hand.

"When are you going back to Dallas?" The soft whisper of his voice sent shivers down her arms.

"We have to leave Monday afternoon. We both have to work on Tuesday morning."

"Ah..."

He didn't move, just stared, watching her and waiting as she craved his touch.

Taking a deep breath, he pulled his hand back and turned to open his door. Shocked by his retreat, Amy sat stunned. He closed the driver's door and walked around the front of the truck to open hers. Feeling totally confused, she grabbed her purse and climbed out of the opening, moving to the side so he could shut the door behind her. Not sure what to make of his sudden change, she started toward the front of the house with him walking beside her, but not touching.

As they reached the porch, she moved toward the door and turned right before reaching it, putting her back to the wall.

"Thanks for supper—" Her words were cut of as he took her mouth with his. Both hands bracketed her head as his lips caressed hers softly.

When he finally lifted his head, she almost moaned at the loss of contact as he gave her wry smile. "I didn't want you to think I wasn't gonna kiss you good-night."

"Well, I had begun to wonder." Her lips burned where he touched them.

"Can I see you tomorrow?" His fingers slid through a small piece of hair that had come loose as his warm breath fanned her face.

"Um, sure," she whispered in return. "Do you have something specific in mind?"

His sexy grin returned as his eyes moved over her face and settled on her lips. She held her breath when the words *fuck you until you scream* zinged through her thoughts and she almost whimpered with need.

"I'm sure we can think of somethin'," he whispered against her mouth, right before he pulled away. "I'll pick you up about six."

She smiled as he stepped back, giving her just a little breathing room. "Six is good."

"I'll wait until you get inside and lock the door," he told her, his voice a little breathless.

Always the gentleman. She turned to pull open the screen, his warm gaze caressing her back. She pushed the door and went inside, but as she went to shut it, she peeked out and smiled. He obviously wanted to make sure she was safely inside before he left. She didn't hear him leave the porch until she had shut the door firmly and slid the lock.

She leaned back against the hard wood with a deep sigh as she brought her fingers to her lips where they still tingled from his kiss. He could have taken advantage of her obvious willingness, but he didn't. He wanted her. That much she could tell, but she also knew for a man that didn't mean anything other than physical attraction. She pushed away from the door as his truck started and pulled out of the yard. She let a small smile drift across her lips before she headed toward her temporary quarters and the soft bed awaiting her.

Chapter 6

She woke the next morning more sexually frustrated than the night before. Tanner, his kiss and the thought of what comes next, to the point she had to take a cold shower, had haunted her dreams. The way her body reacted, one would think she hadn't been with a man in more than a year, which wasn't the case.

After spending several minutes under the cool water, washing away the desire-filled thoughts that plagued her, she pulled herself out of the shower and managed to dress. She wanted to find out about Chris' date. Even though she hadn't mentioned her destination, Amy knew that's where she went the night before. Catherine had let slip when Amy had returned to the house to change for supper with Tanner.

"Good morning," Amy said, walking into the kitchen.

Catherine greeted her with a hearty, "Good morning to you. Did you have a fun night with Tanner?"

Night? Oh how I wished it had been the night. Good grief! I need to pull my head out from between my legs!

"We had fun. We went to Pete's for a while then he showed me the lights of the town from the bluff."

"It is very pretty up there at night." Catherine sighed.

"Is Chris here? I didn't hear her come in unless she came in before me."

Frowning, Catherine said, "No, Chris isn't here. She rarely returns for the night if she goes out with Rob."

Amy cocked her head to the side at the negativity in Catherine's voice. "Don't you like him? Chris seems rather fond of him."

"Chris hasn't told you about Rob?"

"No. I never knew he existed until the other night when I met him at the bar."

"She and Rob have been a sort of couple for years. They started dating after high school, but every time I imagine they might be getting serious, Chris avoids him for several months. Don't get me wrong, he's a nice boy, and I think he's the right one for her, but they can't seem to get together, I guess."

"I'm kind of surprised that she's never mentioned him to me, but then again, she's been too busy trying to hook me up with some guy here that she thinks I would like."

"Sounds like Chris."

"I know, matchmaker to the lonely hearts of the world."

"What are your plans today?"

"Um, well, I'm not sure now. I thought maybe Chris and I would go do something, but she's not home."

"Did you bring your bathing suit? You are welcome to use the pool in the back, if you like to swim."

"I love to swim! And just my luck, I brought my bikini."

"Well, it should be warm enough now. Why don't you go for a swim?"

"I think I will. Thank you!" Amy leaned over and kissed the old woman on the cheek before she scooted off to change.

Several moments later found her standing at the edge of the most wonderful basin of water. Chris' parents had built the area around the pool to resemble a desert landscape with a cool waterfall and a lovely pond.

She pulled her suit cover over her head, kicked off her sandals near the lounge chair and dove headfirst into the shimmering water. Surfacing several feet away, she turned on her back and floated as the warm sun hit her face. She stayed in the water for over an hour, swimming back and forth, floating some and sitting under the cascading stream from the falls.

When she finished, she easily glided toward the steps near where her towel lay warming in the sun. As she started up the stairs, she heard, "What's this? I sure don't see fins."

She shaded her eyes enough to be able to spot Tanner standing next to the gate that enclosed the pool. He leaned against one of the poles with his arms crossed over his chest, watching her, a wicked smile curving his lips.

"Hi," she said as she moved toward the towel.

"Hi, yourself. How's the water?" He straightened from his position and stepped closer.

"Nice and cool."

"Too bad I didn't bring my trunks or I'd join you."

Raising one eyebrow questioningly, she gave him a half smile as her gaze skimmed down his nicely muscled legs, encased in his Wranglers.

"Don't look at me like that, ma'am," he murmured, his eyes getting darker as he came closer.

"What look would that be, sir?" Amy questioned breathlessly.

"The one tellin' me you might like to see what's under these jeans," he whispered against her mouth once he reached her side.

"Um...maybe. One can always hope. Your suggestion from last night sounded pretty appealing." She grinned in return, hoping he would take her mouth with his, but when the sliding door of the house opened, he stepped back.

"Tanner, how nice to see you." Catherine smiled, joining them.

* * * *

Tanner almost groaned as Chris' mom walked toward them. The splashing he had heard as he worked with a mare in the round pen piqued his curiosity and he couldn't help coming over. The sleek, tanned view of Amy as she swam in the cool water, heated his blood to a roaring temperature. Standing near the gate as she rose from the shimmering water, his heart felt like it had stopped in his chest.

"Nice to see you, too," he replied, his voice a little higher pitched than before.

"Did you bring your trunks? The water looks very appealing."

"No. I wasn't aware Amy was in until she got out. Maybe some other time."

"Would you two like some lemonade? I have some fresh made."

"Um, sure." He hoped that would get Catherine back in the house so he could at least kiss the beautiful girl his body craved. He shifted uncomfortably under Catherine's scrutiny.

"I'll be right back, then," she replied, moving back toward the house.

He knew there had to be a pained look on his face as he tried to get the raging desire racing through him under control. He saw Amy hold her side, trying not to giggle as he asked with a laugh of his own. "What?"

A huge smile spread across her face as she said, "You. You look like you could chew nails."

Giving her a wide grin, he replied, "She always had the most impeccable timin'."

"Well, I guess I'll wait until later for that kiss."

"Mmm…maybe not." He moved next to her and quickly took her lips with his. The searing kiss left them both breathless as he stepped back with a smile.

"I better get back to work. I'll see you later," he murmured, running his fingers along her cheek in a caress.

* * * *

He turned on his heels, disappearing from sight through the gate just as Catherine returned with the lemonade.

"Where did Tanner go?"

"He said he had to get back to work," Amy replied, her stare fixed on where he had vanished.

"Okay. Well, here." She handed the glass to Amy. "We'll enjoy the lemonade without him."

"Thank you," Amy said, taking a sip from the refreshing liquid. "This is perfect."

The two women sat in the sun, chatting about mundane things until the rumblings of a car pulled up in the drive.

"That might be Chris. I'll be right back."

Catherine disappeared through the sliding glass door into the house. Several minutes later, Chris joined her on the patio and Amy grinned.

"Where have you been?"

"Out," was the evasive reply.

"Obviously, since you didn't come home last night. Care to explain what's between you and Rob?"

"No."

"Come on. You've been driving me nuts over the guy you want me to meet here, yet you don't tell me about Rob. We've known each other how long, Chris?"

"There isn't anything to tell. Rob and I see each other when I'm home, nothing more." She changed the subject. "How did things go with Tanner?"

"Not good after your call."

"Sorry, Amy. Did I interrupt something?"

"Not really," Amy replied, blushing.

"Bull shit! I can tell by your face, something happened. The way your voice shook on the phone and Tanner sounded upset gave you both away. So fess up."

"He kissed me."

"Kissed you." Chris repeated. "That's all? Why don't I believe you? Either that, or it was one hell of a kiss."

Avoiding Chris' inquisitive eyes, Amy whispered, "A hell of a kiss."

Chris shouted, "Yes!"

Amy frowned, wondering exactly why Chris seemed so happy. "Why are you so happy he kissed me other than the two at the bar?"

"I knew you two would be perfect together." Chris laughed gleefully.

As realization hit her, she said, "Don't tell me! Tanner is the guy you've been trying to hook me up with for months?"

Chris didn't have to answer as a huge smile crossed her face and Amy groaned.

"I didn't even have to introduce you two. You found each other without much help from me at all. I just had to get you two in the same town."

She rolled her eyes, knowing Chris spoke the truth, but it still didn't sit well with her. She couldn't deny the attraction between her and Tanner as flashes of memories from the creek and his attention the night before crossed her mind and warmed her body. Still, it bothered her.

"I can't believe you set me up. I take that back, yes I can." She frowned as she realized she had walked right into this situation with her eyes wide open.

"Come on, Amy, you can't deny your attraction to Tanner. I saw the way you two looked at each other at the bar the other night. You sure didn't seem to notice anyone else in the room and you didn't even know him yet."

A small wistful smile crossed her mouth as she remembered dancing with him and his heart-stopping kisses. Attempting to hide the blush that rose on her cheeks, Amy turned her head away from Chris.

"See!"

"All right. No, I can't deny I'm attracted to Tanner. He's one hell of a gorgeous guy, but its not like things could or would go anywhere, Chris. We live four hours apart. You know as well as I do, long distance relationships don't work."

"You never know."

"Well, I do and I'm not about to try. Besides, I told you before, I don't need another man in my life, especially a cowboy."

"We shall see."

* * * *

"Chris, will you stop, please? We are only going out to dinner," she complained.

"For a girl who said 'I don't need another man in my life,' you've sure been spending a lot of time this weekend with a particular cowboy we both know."

She sighed as she heard the doorbell ring in the background. "I need to finish getting ready," she hinted, trying to get Chris to leave her alone.

"All right," Chris replied, holding up her hands in defeat. "I'll go bug Tanner."

Amy finished getting ready as she continued to hear murmurs from the other room. A few moments later, she walked in only to have her breath catch in her throat and a blush rise on her cheeks.

Tanner stood in the center of the room wearing a magnificent smile and holding a dozen red roses.

Stunned, she stopped in her tracks as he walked to her side and said, "These are for you." He kissed her cheek and handed her the flowers.

"They're beautiful. Thank you."

"Let me get a vase and some water." Catherine stood and walked toward the kitchen.

Knowing roses weren't cheap, she felt guilty he had spent so much. Other men she dated had given her flowers, but it never touched her heart like Tanner taking his hard-earned money to buy her roses. After all, he was just a hard-working man helping his parents on their farm and playing at the bar on the weekends.

"Ready?" Tanner asked, taking her hand in his, lacing their fingers together intimately.

"Yes," she replied as the warmth of his touch, crept up her arm.

When they had settled onto the seats of his truck and he had started the engine, she said, "You shouldn't have done that."

"Done what?"

"Bought the flowers. Don't get me wrong, they're gorgeous and roses are my favorite, but I know they had to be expensive."

"Amy, I may not be rich, but I can afford to buy you flowers if I want to," he grumbled.

"I didn't mean to make you angry."

Tanner pulled over, putting the truck into park and turned to look at her.

"You didn't make me angry, baby," he said, sliding his fingers along her jaw. "I don't want you to think I can't do nice things for you every now and then."

"It just makes me realize I don't know you very well," she whispered, still afraid she had angered him.

A small smile crossed his lips as he looked at her, his fingers caressing a piece of hair. "I tell you what. Instead of going out somewhere where tons of people are, how about we grab a pizza and go back to my house? We can watch a movie, play Monopoly, play cards, you name it, and you got it. That way we can get to know each other better."

Amy smiled, realizing he would change his plans to make her feel more comfortable. "Or talk?"

He flashed a heart-stopping smile as he said, "Or talk."

"Okay. Sounds like fun," she replied, watching him pull his hand back almost reluctantly.

"I know a good take-out pizza place. We'll grab somethin' and head back to my house. The pizza place is around the corner from here," he said, putting the truck into drive. "What do you like on your pizza?"

"I'll get just about anything but anchovies." She laughed.

"Good. I hate anchovies, too." He smiled as he slid a glance in her direction.

* * * *

They pulled into the pizza place a few moments later and he frowned when he noticed a silver Honda, two spots over from where he parked.

"Maybe we should go somewhere else," he said, his eyes fixed on the vehicle.

"Why? This looks fine. Let's get it here and we can leave. No big deal, right?"

"Right," he murmured, opening his door and walking around to open hers.

"Is there something wrong?"

"No. I hope that they aren't too busy."

As they walked into the building, several pairs of eyes fixed on the two of them. One particular pair met his before he turned away and headed for the counter.

Shit! I don't need her making trouble. He tried to focus on the menu and the pretty girl next to him.

"How about a supreme pizza?" He shot a glance over his shoulder.

"Sounds good to me." When his gaze came back to hers, she asked, "Are you sure there isn't anything wrong?"

"Yeah," he said, giving her a smile before he turned to order their pizza. "How about if we sit over by the wall while we wait?"

"Okay."

He moved in the opposite corner of where the green eyes were attempting to get his attention. He sat next to Amy, threading her fingers through his and putting them both on the tabletop.

* * * *

The glares from across the room spent a shiver down her arms, as they took a seat.

All right, Amy, he's probably had several girlfriends around here and you two are bound to run into someone he's dated. He fidgeted uncomfortably in the seat.

A few moments later, a beautiful blonde walked to the edge of the table where they sat. Dressed to the hilt in her tight leather outfit, with pants hugging her hips and tapering down her slim legs, and a satin chemise emphasizing her unbound breasts, Amy thought she looked like a hooker.

Tanner stood as she approached, attempting to intervene before she reached their table.

"Tanner," the woman purred.

"Diane," he replied through clenched teeth.

"Who's your friend?" The blonde raked Amy with her green eyes.

"What do you want?"

His impatient, almost rude response gave Amy pause.

"I thought I would stop by and say hello," she murmured, running her manicured fingernail down Tanner's chest. Amy wasn't sure, but she could have sworn he shivered. "It's been a long time."

"Not long enough."

She frowned, watching the exchange. She wasn't sure she liked how this was going down.

"Number 42." The intercom blared and Amy stood, moving to stand next to him and slipping her hand into his.

"That's ours."

"If you'll excuse us, Diane, our order is ready."

"Of course, sugar. I'll see you later." She winked.

"Not if I can help it," Tanner replied, putting his arm around Amy and moving toward the counter to pick up their food.

She didn't say a word and Tanner seemed lost in thought as they left the building. Silence prevailed on the drive back to his parents' house and Amy didn't know what to think about their encounter with the blonde. *Obviously there is a history between the two.* She felt the green-eyed monster of jealousy creep along inside her, waiting to rear its ugly head.

Tanner pulled the truck up in front of the barn instead of the house.

"I thought we were going to your house?"

"We are. My place is above the barn. It's not much, but I don't have my parents breathin' down my neck over here and a lot more privacy."

He smiled at her, the first one since their encounter at the pizza parlor and she relaxed a little. She had a terrible feeling about the woman's relationship with Tanner and his reaction to her presence gave her doubts.

Once he had taken the pizza from her lap and they headed up the stairs, he pulled out a key, slipped it into the lock and opened the door. He reached over and flipped on a light switch, illuminating the entire apartment and she gasped. Wasn't much? The apartment was awesome.

"Tanner, this is really fantastic. I thought you said it wasn't much. It's quite impressive." Her eyes surveyed the room, taking in everything.

"I'm glad you like it. You can put your things over the chair, if you want. I'll get some plates for the pizza," he said, moving toward the kitchen. "There are DVD's in the cabinet if you want to pick somethin' out."

The cabinet stood against the wall, beckoning her. She pulled open the door and began to read the titles of the movies he had accumulated as several hundred titles met her eyes.

"What would you like to drink?"

"Milk, water, beer, whatever you have is fine."

Grabbing two bottles of beer, along with the plates that he had placed the pizza slices on, he walked into the living room and set everything down on the coffee table.

"Find anything?"

"Maybe. I'm sure you've already seen all these otherwise you wouldn't have them here, but I haven't," she replied, picking a movie from the shelf and walking over to sit on the couch. "What about this one?" She handed him the box.

"That's a good movie. I'm surprised, though," he said, cocking his head to the side. "Most girls don't like action flicks."

"I do," she smiled, picking up the pizza and taking a bite.

"The more I learn about you, the more you surprise me."

Amy sipped the beer as she watched him slip the movie into the player, fascinated by the way he moved, so graceful and sexy.

The light blue, long sleeved shirt he wore fit snuggly across his chest and open at the collar. Chest hair peeked out of the opening of his shirt. *I wonder if that hair is as soft as it looks.* She brought the bottle back to her lips. A small drop of the liquid rested on her lip and when he turned around, her tongue flicked out, capturing it. All the sudden, the temperature rose thirty degrees and sweat began to run down her back, tickling as it moved. Their eyes met across the expanse of the room and she could see the same heat in his gaze that rushed through her. Unable to take her eyes off him, her lips parted, as he moved closer.

Standing over her, he bent his head, capturing her lips with his in a kiss she thought would surely set the place on fire. His mouth slid over hers as his tongue sought entrance into the warm recesses of her mouth. She moaned when he took possession, pushing her against the hard surface of the couch, his hand moving up and around, to cup the back of her head. He slid onto the seat next to her, wrapping one arm around her and pulling her close.

"Shit!" He stood up rapidly and looked down at the front of his jeans.

The fog lifted slowly when he moved, but when she shifted her eyes downward, she began to giggle uncontrollably, holding her side as she laughed. His jeans were soaked with beer.

"I'm sorry," she whispered in a giggle.

Grinning, he said, "Its okay. I've never had to cool down like that before, and I would rather not repeat the experience. I need to change. I'll be right back."

He turned and headed to what appeared to be the bedroom as he disappeared through a doorway. Tempted to follow him, she stood up, but she thought she had not for the time being. Instead, she walked into the kitchen to find something to clean off the couch.

He returned a few moments later, wearing clean, dry, jeans. She had cleaned up the mess and sat waiting for him on the couch, finishing her pizza.

Curiosity getting the better of her, she wanted to ask about the woman at the pizza parlor. She figured that she might as well jump in with both feet.

"Can I ask you a question?"

"Sure," he answered, sitting beside her.

"What's between you and that girl?"

* * * *

Tanner took a deep breath before answering. He wanted her to know the truth, but he didn't want her to think feelings still existed for Diane. Their relationship ended some time ago to him, and Amy was his here and now.

"Nothing anymore," he said. "She and I dated."

"You did?"

"Yeah," he cringed, before he continued, "and we were engaged at one time."

"Engaged?" *She must have been the one he mentioned before, the one he almost married.*

"It's over Amy. I caught her in bed with one of my friends about two months before the weddin'. She didn't quite understand why I called it off."

"I'm sorry, Tanner. I know how that type of betrayal feels and it cuts deeper than any other." Amy touched his arm.

"Do you?"

"Yeah, actually I do. I've been cheated on in the past."

"Do you want to tell me?"

She closed her eyes for a moment as tears slid down her face, before she said, "I saw Jack for about six months. He is a bull-rider. I thought I had it made. He even told me he loved me. Unfortunately, I believed him. I planned to meet him at a rodeo one weekend as a surprise, but I'm the one who got the surprise when I caught him in bed with someone else."

Tanner took her in his arms and held her close. He could see the pain in her face, and he knew it had to be the same pain that he had seen earlier. This guy hurt her badly, but he wanted to be the man to pick up the pieces, if she'd let him.

Chapter 7

After a few moments, she moved back and he pulled out a handkerchief from his pocket, handing her the soft linen.

"Thanks," she whispered, dabbing at her nose and eyes. "Can I use your restroom?"

"Sure. Back through that doorway and to the left," he answered, pointing to the opening he had passed through earlier when he had gone to change his jeans.

"I'll just be a minute."

When she reached the room, she peered in the mirror, trying to fix her makeup. His bathroom held a certain curiosity. She scanned the room, noting the shaving cream on the counter, the toothbrush in the holder and the comb nearby. Everything in its place. The cologne sitting next to the sink drew her attention and when she picked up the bottle and brought it to her nose, the scent wrapped around her senses. She loved the combination of musk and male resting on his skin.

After a few moments, her composure recovered so she headed back toward the living room. She walked through the doorway as she heard him talking.

"What do you want?" he growled into the phone, his back to her.

Amy heard murmurs, but she couldn't make out the words.

"Wasn't it enough that you slept with Greg before our weddin'? Now you want to destroy everythin' for me?"

Obviously he is talking with the girl from the pizza parlor.

"I couldn't care less what you want, Diane. I'm a lot happier now that I ever was with you and you hate the thought."

More murmurs filled the silence.

"It doesn't matter who I had with me tonight and it's none of your business who I'm seein'. This conversation is over. Goodbye."

Tanner hung up the phone and ran his fingers through his hair in frustration. She walked up behind him and put her arms around his waist, resting her head on his shoulder. He rubbed the hand resting on his stomach before turning around to cup her face with his hands.

"I'm sorry," she whispered.

"For what?" He pushed his hands into her hair and she closed her eyes for a moment, loving the feel of his fingers on her scalp.

"For the hell she put you through. I guess we've both been hurt pretty badly."

"I'm not lettin' her hurt me anymore. She's not worth the trouble," he murmured, pulling her to his chest. "This is what's important now, not her."

They stood in each other's arms for what seemed like hours. Tanner stroking her back as she clung to him, daring to hope somehow he wasn't too good to be true.

She stepped back slightly as she whispered, "Tanner, I think—"

His lips on hers stopped the flow as he took possession of her mouth, blinding her to whatever she planned to say. Desire raced through her veins like a match to dry grass, while his lips brushed against hers as light as a feather. She had always been a sucker for soft kisses and Tanner's drove her crazy. He moaned as she pushed her breasts against his chest. His tongue dove inside her mouth, swirling within, dancing with her own as he swallowed her answering whimper.

After a moment, he pulled away and ran small kisses down her neck to her shoulder as he whispered, "I love the way you taste. Your skin is so soft, I could touch you forever." He finally dragged his mouth from her and put his forehead against hers, as their rapid breathing mingled. "We should stop. I didn't bring you over here to try to get you into bed with me."

"But, I don't want to stop," she murmured, holding his gaze with hers.

He closed his eyes as she shifted to run kisses along his jaw and down his neck, nibbling at the skin beneath her mouth.

"Amy," he whispered, trying to step back, but she followed. "Amy, please. We shouldn't do this, not yet."

"Why?"

"We should get to know each other better before we jump into havin' sex."

She looked into his eyes. "I want you. Right now, I don't care how well I know you. You said something about fucking me until I scream." She heard him groan at her words. "Show me." His breathing hitched, coming out in little panting breaths as he fought for control. Goose bumps flittered along his arms while her lips trailed kisses down his chest, unbuttoning his shirt as worked her way down.

Cupping her face with his hands, he tugged her back up, the heat in his eyes intense and scorching. "Are you sure this is what you want?"

She let a small smile flitter across her lips. "Oh yeah."

He looked almost afraid as he whispered, "God, I need to fuck you so bad."

"What's stopping you, cowboy?"

He swooped down, taking her lips in a desperate kiss, his tongue gliding across until she opened her mouth. A deep moan rumbled in his chest, slipping from between his lips as she captured it with her own.

His hands were everywhere, wrapped in her hair, along her shoulders and down her arms, raising goose bumps on her skin. She wrapped her own in the hair at the nape of his neck, sliding the silky strains through her fingers. He released her lips as their rapid breaths mingled and he reached for the hem of her tank top before he slipped it over her head. His lips skimmed over her cheek to her ear, nipping at the earlobe with his teeth for a moment, prior to continuing his journey down her salty neck, nibbling at the soft skin. One hand palmed her breast, pinching the sensitive nipple through her bra and she gasped as longing zinged straight to her aching clit. Both hands moved lower, grasping her ass and pulling her tight against him until he cradled his erection to her. One hand slipped up her back until he reached the snap of her bra, unhooking the piece of silk with quiet efficiency and slid it off.

He lifted his head and met her gaze. She shivered as he whispered, "You are so beautiful."

She closed her eyes and tipped her head back when his tongue slid along the top of her breast before slipping lower until he took her nipple between his lips. Moaning softly, she felt him run the rough pad of his tongue over the sensitive tip, before sucking the hard nub into his mouth. She whimpered her need as she held his head tight against her.

He worked the button loose and slid both hands into the waistband of her pants, before cupping her ass and molding it to his touch. He pushed the rough material off her hips and she stepped out of them, kicking them away. A soft smile lifted the corners of her mouth as she whispered, "My turn."

Her lips dipped against the hollow of his throat, nipping at the skin until he hissed. His skin quivered under her touch as she smoothed her hands down his chest, pushing his shirt out of the way so she could run her lips over the hard muscles. Her mouth found his male nipple, licking and biting as he moaned her name. She worked the belt buckle at his waist loose before she slipped the button free with her fingers, rasped the zipper out of her way and slid inside his boxers. Wrapping her hand around his erection, she heard a tortured groan come from between his lips. *Holy hot damn!* "Wow."

He chuckled and she blushed. Her kiss followed the path of hair south to his groin, while she worked the jeans off his hips and down his legs. Her tongue darted out, softly licking the pre-cum from the tip as he wrapped his hands in her hair and whispered, "Oh God."

She opened her mouth and took the head of his penis inside as he hissed above her and rocked his hips. She sucked his cock, taking all of him inside the warm cavern while she cupped his balls, kneading with her fingers, until he pulled her by the shoulders and growled, "Stop."

She smiled as their eyes met and he kicked his jeans off. Standing in front of her, he reached out and he ran his palm over her breast, before slipping behind her and pulling her to him. He lifted her up in his arms as she wrapped her legs around his waist, before he moved toward the couch. He sat her on one of the cushions then knelt on the floor at her feet. Not sure what he was going to do, she waited.

His lips blazed a trail from her ankle to her knee, nipping and licking until she was left squirming on the soft leather beneath her ass, groaning softly.

He nudged his nose closer to her clit as he whispered, "I want to taste you."

Whimpering softly, she opened her thighs and closed her eyes as his soft lips grazed the inside of her leg. His tongue touched her throbbing pussy lips, before sliding between them and licking from her vagina to her clit in one long stroke. She almost climbed out of her skin when he blew softly against her wet clit, sending shivers up her body before racing back down.

"You taste so good."

"God, Tanner, please. Fuck me now."

He chuckled tenderly as his tongue found her clit, toggling until she whimpered and begged, the words coming out in panting sighs. Her climax hit her like a wave, curling from her toes, up her legs and crashing over her as she moaned his name.

When she finally stopped trembling, she opened her eyes slightly to see him reached for his pants and pulled out a condom. The slippery piece of latex enclosed his jutting cock and he moved between her thighs. Taking her mouth with his, he slid inside her as their moans mingled. Pulling his mouth from hers, he clenched his jaw as he rocked slightly, pushing himself completely inside her.

"God, you feel incredible," he murmured against her lips.

He began to rock his hips, slowly at first, but gaining speed when she pleaded, "Harder".

Her orgasm built again as she wrapped her legs around his hips, urging him to move faster and deeper with her heels against his ass. When her climax rolled over her, she arched her back and screamed his name as she felt hot cream seep from inside her and roll down between them. Pounding his pelvis into hers, his own orgasm spiraled out of control as he groaned. "Oh God."

Several hours later, his soft snores brought a wistful smile to her lips as she slipped out the door of his apartment, shutting it softly behind her.

* * * *

Later that morning, she stood outside her car loading the suitcases in the hot sun. She hadn't seen Tanner again since she left his apartment the night before, after their wild sex, and she wasn't sure she wanted to. She'd given in to her attraction for him and the fantasy she created for herself in his arms, but now she had to get back to the real world. Her life waited in Dallas.

Sighing heavily, she headed back toward the house to get the last of her things. Grabbing her shopping bags, she walked out the door only to find the object of her fascination standing next to her car. Her steps slowed as her eyes met his across the expanse of the yard. He leaned against it with his arms crossed over his broad chest, just staring, like he couldn't get enough of looking at her. She stopped at the trunk of her car to put the bags in as he moved toward her.

"Were you going to leave without saying goodbye?" His question hung in the air between them.

"I really didn't think it necessary."

"Can we talk?"

"There isn't anything to talk about."

Running his hand through his hair in frustration, he replied, "Well, I need to." He took her arm and led her around the side of the house, away from Chris' prying eyes.

Once out of earshot, she pulled her arm out of his grasp. "Whatever you had to say could have been said in front of Chris."

"I don't think so, Amy. Why did you leave without even wakin' me?"

She shrugged, dropping her gaze to the boots on her feet. She couldn't let him work his way into her heart. If she did, she'd never recover. He put his fingers under her chin, forcing her to look at him. "I didn't think it was a big deal."

"You're kiddin', right?"

Her lips turned down at the corners in a frown. "No. Don't get any ideas, Tanner. It was just a weekend thing, you know. I have my life in Dallas and you have yours here. Once I drive away, I'll more than likely never cross your mind again."

"If you really believe that, I am definitely not doing somethin' right."

"It doesn't matter. We probably won't see each other again, anyway. I'll go back and you'll be here, working on your parents' farm and playing at the bar." She squared her shoulders, shoring up her pride. She wasn't going to let him hurt her. She had already let him get too close and it would be better if she stopped this before she lost her heart.

"But I want to see you. I don't want this to end. I haven't even had a chance to get to know you very well. Are you cuttin' this off before it even gets started?" He stepped closer as she stepped back.

"It was fun while it lasted, but we live too far apart and—"

He quickly backed her against the wall of the house and took her lips with his. His tongue swept between her parted lips, invading her mouth and she whimpered under his onslaught. She pushed against his chest for a moment before giving into the sensations he caused and wrapping her arms around him. She allowed her tongue to dance with his as she felt him soften the kiss.

Tanner pulled his mouth from hers as his rasping breath caressed her cheek. "Don't tell me you aren't as attracted to me as I am to you. The way you screamed my name as you came around me, the softness of your lips against mine with every kiss and each caress, I know you hunger for me as much as I crave you. Once won't be enough."

She opened her mouth to protest, but snapped it shut when his mouth hovered over hers, almost touching. She couldn't argue with what he said.

"This isn't finished. It will never be over between us. There is too much at stake," he growled and stepped back.

Without another word, he turned and walked away.

* * * *

The ride home was miserable. Chris tried to pry out of her what had happened, but she wasn't talking.

They reached Chris' apartment and Amy opened the trunk for Chris to get her things as she said, "Amy, are you okay?"

"I'll be fine, Chris. I just want to get home. I've got laundry to do and I need to clean my apartment. We have three days of work coming up so I won't have time."

"I meant about Tanner."

"What about Tanner?"

"You looked like you were getting along great when I peeked around the side of the house, but then he came back toward the car madder than a wet hen."

She shrugged, studying her nails as if they were the fascinating thing on this earth. "There is nothing to tell. I'll probably never see him again, and I told him as much."

"Don't you want to see him again?"

"I don't know. It just seemed like the whole thing would be a lot of work. He had old relationships getting in the way and so did I. I told you before. I don't want or need another man in my life right now."

"I think Tanner would be good for you."

She rolled her eyes and said, "I'm going home. I'll see you at work tomorrow."

She put the car in gear and pulled out of the parking lot, heading toward her own apartment. *My life seems to have changed so much in less than a week. First, I find out Jack cheated on me and then I meet Tanner. Oh lord, it would be so easy to fall in love with him, but long distance relationships just don't work. He lives four hours away and our lives are so different. I'm just not going to hold out a lot of hope.*

Finally reaching her apartment, she popped the trunk to retrieve her belongings as her cell phone rang. She didn't recognize the number, but when she answered it, she wasn't surprised to hear Tanner's voice on the other end.

"How did you get my number?"

"I called Chris' mom and got Chris' number who in turn gave me yours."

"Remind me to chew them out tomorrow," she grumbled.

"Why? You didn't want me to have it?"

"I guess I didn't think about it. I figured if you really wanted my phone number, you would have asked me." She had reached the door of her apartment and pushed it open, laying her suitcase and bags on the couch. The red light blinked on her answering machine.

"I didn't get a chance to."

"Only because you walked away."

"It doesn't matter I guess. I wanted to make sure you got home all right."

"I just walked in the door. I've got some cleaning to do and laundry before work tomorrow."

"I guess I'll let you go." Silence. "If I drive up one weekend, can I see you?"

She wanted to see him again, but then she didn't. She missed his kiss and it had only been five hours or so since she'd seen him. Things had gotten way too deep already, but she couldn't seem to stop herself.

"I suppose so. We can see a movie or something."

"When is your next weekend off?"

"Two weeks from now, but I have a rodeo I'm riding in, so I won't be home."

"Where is the rodeo?"

"In Forth Worth. Not far for me, but I will be gone on all weekend."

"Oh. Well, maybe next time. I'll let you go. I know you've got things to do. I'll talk to you soon."

"Bye, Tanner," she whispered.

"Bye."

Amy hung up her cell phone, wishing they hadn't left things unsaid between them. She laid the phone down next to the answering machine and hit the button, listening as the messages started to play.

She smiled as her mom's voice filled the silence in the room. "Hi, sweetheart. I just wanted to call and see how you are doing. I haven't talked to you in a while. Call me when get this if it's not too late. Bye." She would have to call her later, she decided as she erased the message.

Jason's deep baritone met her ears. "Hey, Am. I thought I'd call and find out if you wanted to do something this weekend, but I guess you're busy. Don't forget about rodeo in a couple of weeks. I'll see you at work. Bye."

She erased Jason's call and her heart sank when she heard Jack's voice next. "Amy. It's Jack, sweetheart. I need to talk to you, to explain things. I love you. Call me when you get this please."

Feeling completely overwhelmed with everything, she sank down on the couch, laying her head against the back and closed her eyes.

Her last encounter with Jack at her work left a bitter taste in her mouth. He had parked near her car and almost forced her to listen to his pleas of 'I love you.' She had come to realize in the last week or two that he only said those things and never meant any of them. He was a player and she didn't want anything more to do with him.

The phone rang, bringing her mind back to the present. She didn't want to talk to anyone. Her love life seemed to be on the rocks at the moment and she was desperately afraid she had lost control. Her attraction for Tanner felt like a tangible thing and her disdain for Jack's treatment sent her anger through the ceiling. Squaring her shoulders she decided, she would just play things by ear and not read too much into this thing with Tanner.

She flipped on the radio and started sorting her laundry.

Chapter 8

The next two weeks, went by at a snails pace. Tanner called once or twice, but the conversations felt strained and clipped. She missed him, more than she should, but at least she had the ability to admit it. Her dreams wrapped around him and his brown eyes, hot with desire, raking her from head to toe. The heat of his last kiss and how her body hummed with each caress of his fingers left her breathless and wound up tighter than a spring when she woke each morning.

She barked at her coworkers almost constantly, until one day Chris confronted her. "You need to knock it off, Amy. Are you PMS-ing or what?"

"No," she snapped. Dipping her head, she apologized. "I'm sorry. I don't know why I'm in such a bitchy mood lately."

"Well, you need some Xanax or to get laid. I'm not sure which, but it better happen soon. You're driving all of us nuts."

"I don't need comments from the peanut gallery."

"Your moods sure seem to have gotten worse every day. What's your problem anyway?"

"Nothing. I'm just short-tempered I guess."

"You could say that." Amy was afraid her friend knew more about her bad mood than she wanted her to. "Heard from Tanner lately?"

"No, and I don't care if I do or not," she grumbled.

"That explains it."

"What's that supposed to mean?"

"I didn't mean anything. It just seems like your temper has gotten shorter and shorter the more time we have been away from Brenham, that's all." Chris' knowing smile had her grinding her teeth.

"Tanner has nothing to do with my short temper, all right?"

"Well, you need to get over it, whatever *it* is. Aren't you riding this weekend with Jason?"

"Yeah. We're riding outside Fort Worth tomorrow. Since we are off the weekend and I'll be gone, you won't have to put up with me."

"Thank the Lord," Chris prayed, as the call button went off in one of her patients' rooms. Giving Amy a deliberate wink, she turned headed down the hall.

* * * *

Early the next morning found her at the stable waiting for Jason.

His white pickup pulled in beside her, stopping next to where she stood with her mare ready to load. "Hey, Jace."

"Are you ready to go? I'm glad this competition isn't far."

"Let's get Misty loaded and we'll get moving. What time is our ride?" Amy asked, unhooking the back of the trailer.

"We're due up at eleven."

"We better hurry, then. I hate to ride right after unloading them."

"No problem," Jason answered, hopping out of the truck.

When the animals were settled, they pulled out of the stable. The comfortable chatter eased her mood. Talk centered on things going on at the hospital, Jason's lack of a significant other and Amy's busy work schedule.

"Are you still seeing Jack?"

"No." She didn't elaborate. *It isn't any of his business, anyway.*

"Good." Amy shot him a confused look at his terse words and he asked, "What?"

"Why do you say that?"

"He's an asshole, that's why. He's not good enough for you."

"Thanks, Jason. You're good for my ego."

No more time for talk as they reached the fair grounds and he parked near the other trailers. They unloaded the horses and gear, tying them to the trailer to allow them to graze on the tall grass while they registered. The scheduled ride time wasn't for an hour.

"I need food." Amy's stomached growled in protest.

"Yeah, me too."

"Let's hit the breakfast line."

The final piece of pancake found her mouth and she groaned in protest.

"I love their pancakes, but we need to get saddled and ready."

Plates hit the trash barrel and aimed themselves in the direction of the trailer.

Qualifying at hand, they backed their horses into the shoot, but her thoughts drifted to Tanner. The soft timbre of his voice ricocheted in her head. The lack of conversation stretched on for several days and left a hole the size of Texas where her heart normally lay in her chest. *Does he think about our weekend together at all? What if he wished it never happened?* Uncertainty and self-doubt clouded her mind. To her, each passing day without talking to him, meant he could care less.

The clang of the gate hitting the dirt snapped her thoughts back to the task at hand. The cow shot out with Jason hot on his heels. He threw his lasso, looping the horns precisely on target. For Amy, her daydreaming threw off her timing and she missed her throw.

"Shit!" She pulled her rope in, frustration lacing her words.

Jason trotted back around to her and shouted, "What the hell was that?"

"I missed," she yelled back.

"You never miss."

"Well, I did," she grumbled, reining her horse back toward the gate.

They trotted back toward the trailer without another word. *Get your shit together, girl. You need to pull your thoughts off Tanner and back to this ride, or you'll lose the competition.*

When they reached the truck, they dismounted and Jason stopped in front of her, blocking her retreat. "What's up with you?"

"Nothing. I lost my concentration. I'll be fine on the next ride."

"You had better figure out what the problem is before that," Jason demanded, his own anger evident in his voice.

"I've got something on my mind breaking my concentration. Chill out."

"Something or someone? You aren't still torn up about Miller, are you? Hell, you jumped in head first and he used you, but you need to move on."

"No, it's not Jack," she murmured as she turned away. Explaining to Jason meant opening her heart to the disappointment she harbored. She closed her eyes for a moment, trying to regain her composure as tears burned behind her eyelids. When she reopened them, the next thing she focused on was Tanner walking toward her with a sexy grin and flashing that dimple in his cheek.

"Tanner," she whispered, taking a couple of tentative steps in his direction. She broke into a dead run when she realized he was real, and not her randy imagination conjuring him up out of nowhere.

Meeting halfway, she threw her arms around his neck and hugged him as he pulled her close. The scent of musk and male drifted to her nose and she sighed.

Jason reached interrupted several minutes later, clearing his throat. "Amy?"

Jason's question hung in the air, but she chose to ignore it for the moment. She needed to drink in everything about the man holding her close as she melted against him, resisting the urge to nibble his neck and mark him as her own. She pulled back in his arms slightly asking, "What are you doing here?"

"You said you were ridin' this weekend. I wanted to see you, so here I am."

A thrill of excitement zinged along her nerves and she smiled. "I'm glad you came."

Hearing Jason clear his throat again, she turned around and blushed. "I'm sorry. Jason, this is Tanner. He's...a friend of mine. Tanner, this is my riding partner, Jason."

The two men sized each other up and frown lines settled between Jason's eyebrows as he said, "I'm going to see when we ride again." He turned to head back toward the judging tables without another word.

She watched him leave with a frown of her own as she murmured, "Sorry, Tanner. He's usually not rude. I wonder what's wrong with him."

Tanner slipped an arm around her waist as he asked, "Don't you work together at the hospital?"

"Yeah. He's one of the radiology techs. We've been friends for a long time," she replied absently, still watching Jason's back.

* * * *

When Amy threw herself into his arms, his world righted itself. He had missed her something terrible over the last couple of weeks, but he knew she needed time. The parting in Brenham left him frustrated and angry. He knew he'd botched things as he confronted her outside of Chris' place, and he wanted to make things right.

Standing next to her with his arm around her waist, watching her friend disappear, he knew exactly what the guy's problem appeared to be. Jason thought of him as competition for Amy's affection and he didn't like it, but Tanner wasn't about to tell Amy. She thought of Jason as a friend and she would never accept the fact that her work buddy wanted more than friendship, but he knew. Jason's attraction to Amy shone bright in his eyes. The other man's eyes had narrowed into slits, daring Tanner to come after the woman they both obviously cared about.

"So what are your plans?" Amy snuggled up to his side, wrapping her arm around his waist. Her warmth sent images of naked bodies zipping through his mind.

"I thought I'd spend the weekend with you, here at the rodeo or at your house."

"You aren't playing at the bar?" The twinkle in the blue depths of her gaze delighted him.

"No. I switched with the other guy so he's playin' both nights this weekend, and I'll do both nights next weekend."

"We might be staying overnight here, though. If we win today then we don't have to stay."

"That's fine with me."

Sure he knew the thoughts running through her mind as color splashed across her cheeks, he bent his head and whispered in her ear, "You're blushin'."

She tried to hide her face against his shoulder, just as Jason returned.

"We ride again at two."

The almost purple hue to his rival's face made Tanner grin. *Boy, the guy is angry.* Tanner almost laughed as he asked Amy, "Are you hungry?"

"Not really. We just ate about two hours ago, but if you want to get something, I'll go with you. Jason, you can come, too, if you want."

"No, thanks. I'd rather not."

"I'll be right back. I want to check out something on the roster. Do you want to stay here? It will only take a minute."

"Sure. I'll be right here keepin' Jason company." The doubtful expression on her face as she walked away goaded Tanner into irritating the other man. His presence alone provoked a confrontation.

"You want to tell me what's going on between you two?"

"No, but I will anyway, just because you need to be made aware. We're friends, but I have every intention of becomin' more to her. What's it to you?"

"Don't hurt her. If you do, I'll be there to pick up the pieces. Trust me, I won't give them back." Jason's warning sent apprehension down Tanner's spine as he watched the other man's eyes narrow into slits.

"I have no intention of makin' her unhappy, so you'll have no reason to pick up the pieces." Tanner let his gaze rake over Jason, sizing him up as he wondered about the relationship between Amy and her so called friend.

"I've been through enough relationships with her and seen way too many assholes break her heart. You're going to be just another tear she sheds in the long run."

"Don't count your chickens. I'm in this for the long haul."

He could see Amy walking back toward them as the strained conversation came to an end.

"Shall we go?" Her questioning gaze moved between him and Jason as if she could feel the tension in the air.

"Yeah. My truck is parked over there. We can take it and get somethin' in town."

"Are you sure you don't want to come along, Jason?"

"No, I'm good. You go on. I'll watch the horses."

"Okay. We'll be back in a bit. It shouldn't take long."

As they headed toward his truck, she asked, "What were you two talking about? You both looked like two dogs ready for a fight."

"You."

"Me? What about me?"

"How close are you and Jason?"

"We're friends, nothing more. Why?"

"Just curious. He acted pretty possessive, that's all."

"He's been a friend for some time. I guess he's a little protective of me. He's been through a lot of relationships as my backup and sounding board."

"Maybe that's it. He wants to protect you." *My ass! He wants you for himself.* They reached the truck and he opened the passenger door for her.

"Did he say something to you?"

"Not really. Where do you want to eat?" He wanted to avoid getting into a big discussion with her about the relationship between her and Jason at this point in time. Soon, though, he would find out what was really existed there, if anything, before he revealed his own feelings toward the woman next to him.

* * * *

Amy and Tanner took a seat in the stand to watch the competition after returning, and she smiled as he laced his fingers with hers. The intimacy of his touch closed the hole in her chest and sent her hopes soaring into the clouds. *Maybe this will work out after all.*

Her attention returned to the arena as she sighed wistfully. Almost all of the other teams qualified without difficulty and she knew she and Jason had their work cut out for them. Hopefully, since her pre-occupation with the handsome cowboy next to her had been taken care of, her concentration would return. Making stupid mistakes like the one earlier went completely against her competitive nature.

When their turn came, she and Jason backed their horses into the shoot as Tanner watched from the fence. He gave her a sexy smile and a wink just as the cow shot out of the gate.

Jason nailed the horns with perfection with Amy only tenths of a second behind him, looping the hooves without missing a beat. The crowd went wild when the time flashed on the board. Tanner cheered from his place at the rail.

She rode next to the fence and Tanner almost swept her off her horse as he grabbed her, placing a passionate kiss on her mouth before letting her go. Stunned for a second, it took a moment for her to kick her horse and move toward the gate. Tanner met her on the other side and as she reached the trailer and dismounted, he swept her up in his arms, twirling her around in a circle, before placing her back on her feet.

"Awesome!" His excitement evident in his voice as he continued, "I didn't realize how good you really are!"

"Thanks, but we've done better."

"You're kiddin', right?"

"No. Actually that time was only our third best. We've shaved two seconds off that time." She turned to Jason as Tanner released her from his possessive hold. "When's our next ride?"

"In about thirty minutes."

"I want to go watch the last two qualifiers. Care to join me?"

"Of course. This should be interestin'. I wouldn't miss this, for the world," Tanner replied.

"I'll be back in a bit, Jason." She let her horse loose in their makeshift corral, before closing the gate behind them.

"No problem," he grumbled and Amy looked at him a bit confused. Shrugging, she walked away with Tanner by her side.

The pair sat on the fence watching the next two teams make their run. Both pairs put up pretty good times, but not as well as Amy and Jason's. Each qualifying time came up short by at least a second.

"Now the hard part." She hopped down from the rail as he landed beside her.

"What do you mean?" Tanner slipped his arm around her waist, resting his hand possessively on her hip as they walked back toward the trailer.

"If we nail this next ride, we win. If we don't, we are back tomorrow in the loser's bracket."

"Ah, well, I have confidence in you. I think that you'll do great, maybe even do better than your best time."

"I hope so," she murmured, watching his lips, wishing he would just kiss her and get it over with. The kiss after their last ride wasn't nearly enough. She wanted one of those curl-your-toes, all tongues, hot, mesmerizing and almost make you come in your panties, kisses. Her frustrated exhale did nothing to ease the hum of need between her legs.

Amy retrieved her mare, and walked her out next to the truck so she could check her straps. *The last thing that I need is a loose strap.*

"Go get 'em, baby." That sexy smile graced his lips, making her sigh in sexual frustration.

Jason and Amy got into position while the first team rode and Tanner positioned himself back on the fence rail to watch. She did her best to ignore him, even as he winked and smiled. Her stomach flipped over and the friction of her panties against her clit did nothing to ease her discomfort. *Concentrate, need to think—no daydreaming. Horse, cow, rope*—she caught Tanner's seductive grin again—*damn!*

Finally, she managed to ignore him for a moment and focus.

Anticipation burned in her gut and sweat beaded on the back of her neck, rolling down her spine as the sun beat down on their heads. She pulled her cowboy hat down low on her brow and squinted, watching the first team's time, whistling softly through her teeth.

The first team put up an awesome time. They needed to beat them by at least a whole second to stay ahead and that wasn't going to be easy.

Jason and Amy rode into the arena, backing their horses into the shoot, as the crowd grew silent. A pin drop in the dirt would have been loud as all eyes turned, anticipating, and waiting for the cow to move. As the gate dropped and the animal charged out, Jason took off with Amy right on his heels, watching him nail the horns. Within a split second, Amy threw her rope, easily looping the rear hoofs as her horse did what she had been taught, stopping on her haunches and pulling the rope tight.

The silence stretched on for what seemed like a lifetime as everyone waited for the time to be posted on the board. A roar went up as the numbers appeared. They had beaten the first team's time by two seconds.

Tanner came off the fence with a whoop and a holler, pumping his fist in the air in triumph and Amy laughed. She met Jason in the middle of the arena, giving him a high-five before they turned to head out the gate.

Once they reached the trailer, Tanner stood waiting. She dismounted and laughed as he swept her up in his arms, hugging her tight. The inferno blazing in his eyes as he let her slide down his body scorched her with heat. His gaze settled on her lips seconds before he took them with his own in a softly possessive kiss. A moan escaped on a sigh as she opened for him and his tongue slipped between her lips. Pulling her mouth from his reluctantly, she opened her eyes and smiled, stepping back from his embrace.

"We shouldn't celebrate yet," she whispered. "There are still two more teams that need to ride. We could still lose."

"Um…somehow whether you win the competition or not, we'll both win later," he whispered, brushing her lips softly with his again.

She hesitantly pulled herself away from him, stepping back to put some distance between them. Being that close to him did really wonderful things to her insides, but it played hell with her peace of mind and her concentration.

"We better go watch the others riders," she whispered.

"Yeah. I guess so."

She turned away to walk toward the arena, but he quickly caught up, sliding his arm around her waist. They reached the side of the enclosure as she heard the gate snap open and the next team began their ride. The next two qualifiers missed beating the leading time by at least a full second. The last team backed into place and Amy held her breath. The cow shot out like a bullet, the riders fast on his heels. The header nailed the horns with a time better than Jason's and she groaned. The heeler needed to miss his throw for Amy and Jason to win.

The whole scene moved in slow motion as the second rider spun his lasso over his head and with a flick of his wrist, let it go. The rope slipped under the cow's rear hoofs, but only hooked one as his horse pulled the rope tight and the cowboy cursed a blue streak.

"Too bad guys," the announcer said over the intercom. "That's a full second penalty."

Amy let out a triumphant yell, grabbed Tanner and hugged him as she jumped up and down.

Chapter 9

Amy and Tanner walked to the trailer, prize money in hand.

"How about you ride back with me?"

She let what she hoped to be a sexy smile flitter across her mouth as she glanced at him from the corner of her eye. "May—be. What do you have in mind?"

"I told you I wanted to spend the weekend with you, but now that you are done with your ride, we can head back to Dallas together."

"I might be able do that." She grinned, slipping her arm through his as they walked.

When they reached the trailer, she told Jason she would be riding back with Tanner, and she asked if he would return her horse to the stable.

"Why?" Jason asked. "Never mind. It's none of my business what you do."

"Can I talk to you a minute?" She moved a short distance away from Tanner. She wanted a little privacy to talk to Jason. "What's your problem?"

"Nothing." Jason studied the tree off to the right for a second, avoiding her gaze.

"You sure aren't acting like it's nothing. Tell me what's bothering you. Is it Tanner?"

Angry rippled across his face. "You and I have been friends a long time. I've seen you get your heart broken on several occasions, and I'm afraid you are in for another fall. That cowboy is after nothing more than a quick lay and you are ripe for the picking."

"How dare you! You may be my friend, but who I choose to go out with, or go to bed with for that matter, is none of your business." She shook with anger as the air crackled with tension.

"If that's how you feel, fine, but don't come crying on my shoulder when he breaks your heart." Jason's words of dismissal caught her by surprise before he stomped back toward his truck, leaving her standing alone.

Her mare stood in the trailer, already loaded when she returned. Jason ripped the door open and climbed into the cab. He jammed his key into the ignition, firing up the engine just as Amy reached the window.

"Just put her in her stall and give her some hay. I'll put the check into our account and take my half."

"Fine." He refused to look at her as he put the truck in gear and pulled away.

* * * *

Tanner reached her side, sliding his arm around her. The stiffness in her shoulders and the ridged posture of her spine, communicated her anger even though her body quivered under his touch.

"Everythin' all right?"

"Yeah. He's only being the overprotective friend, I guess." Jason pulled out onto the highway, leaving a large cloud of dust in his wake.

"Well, he doesn't have anythin' to worry about."

Tanner hated the way the other man affected her and he hoped the emotions scrambled inside her and reflected on her face, were not going to be a problem between the two of them. *Hell, I wish he wasn't even in the picture.*

Climbing into the cab of his Ford, he said, "You'll have to give me directions since I'm not that familiar with Fort Worth."

"No problem. Turn left out of the parking lot. It takes you toward the interstate. We'll head for my apartment and go from there. We can stop and eat something on the way."

Giving her a questioning raise of his eyebrow and letting a sexy smile ripple across his lips, he said, "Whatever you say."

On the way back, they talked of things they had been doing over the last couple of weeks. Her work, the mare he had been working with, the band, and his parents' farm, anything but the feelings between the two of them.

He glanced at her on the other side of the truck as he wondered what the coming evening would bring. The time spent apart did nothing to cool his attraction. He craved her touch, her smile, her laughter and not talking to her had driven him crazy.

"How come you didn't call me the last week or so?"

The question whipped through the air, putting him on the defensive. He wanted to call her, had even picked up the phone on several occasions to do just that, but hung up before he dialed. "I didn't want to come on too strong. We had a good time and all, but I was afraid you might not want to see me again."

"I already told you about what happened with the last guy I saw. I'm just not sure I'm ready for any type of relationship, Tanner, and I don't want to give you the wrong impression."

"Don't worry about it. Whatever happens, happens," he replied, taking her hand in his, he brought it to his lips and kissed the inside of her wrist.

As he pulled the truck into the parking lot of her apartment complex, he whistled softly. "Nice buildin'," he said, looking up.

"Thanks. It's secure and I've got a fantastic view from my balcony. I guess you could say the one luxury that I've afforded myself is a nice place to live."

"I can't wait to see inside."

He followed her through the lobby and toward the elevator as a large black man, sitting behind an even bigger desk, called out, "How are you, Ms. Amy?"

"I'm good, George. How are things with the wife and kids?"

"They're doin' fine," he tipped his hat as he glanced at Tanner. "Evenin', sir."

"George, this is my friend, Tanner. Tanner this is George. He's the best security guard we have and a nice guy, too."

"Nice to meet you, George."

"You, too, young man. Any friend of Miss Amy's is a friend of mine."

They reached the elevator and she pushed the button. After a few moments, the glass doors opened and they stepped inside.

"What floor are you on?"

"The seventh."

"Then we have a minute or two." He grinned, stepping in front of her, bracketing her shoulders with his hands. Bending his head, his lips touched hers softly. She leaned into his kiss, moaning under his mouth as his tongue grazed the crease and she opened for him. He stroked the inside of her mouth, deepening the kiss until they were both breathing heavily.

The doors of the elevator opened and she pushed against his chest, breaking the kiss with a grin. "We're here."

"Damn," he murmured pulling back slightly. "I was beginnin' to enjoy that."

He followed her down the hall, enjoying the view of her ass, until the door of her apartment loomed in front of them. Once they had stepped inside and she shut the door behind them, the most spectacular view of the city from her living room window, reflected off the glass. "Wow," he said as he moved closer.

"It is pretty cool, huh?"

"And I thought the view from the bluff was nice, but it's nothin' like this."

"I like it, but I thought the view overlooking Brenham was perfect, too," she whispered, slipping her arms around him from behind and resting her hands on his abdomen.

Bringing her fingers to his lips, he placed a small kiss on each one. She moaned softly behind him when he took one in his mouth and sucked. Turning around, framed her face with his hands and bent his head to take her mouth. His tongue slipped between her parted lips, dancing with hers as he wrapped his arms around her and pulled her tight against his chest. She slipped her hands up to his shoulders as he deepened the kiss and slid his thigh between hers. A moment later, he pulled his mouth away as their rapid breathing mingled. "God, I want you. One night wasn't enough. I've hungered for you since you left. I came to see you because I need you like a man needs water to survive. I've been in a constant state of hard-on for the last two weeks, wantin' to love you again," he whispered as his eyes held hers.

Pain registered on her face as she pulled out of his arms. *Holy shit! What did I say?*

"I don't go around fucking men I just met, Tanner. Not on a regular basis, anyway. I hadn't been with a man in awhile and I wanted you, but if you think you can just waltz back into my life for a quick lay, forget it. The couch is comfortable enough. I'll get you a pillow and blanket. You can sleep here tonight, but tomorrow, I want you gone. I'm not going to be your port in a storm."

"Amy," he sighed but she had disappeared. He could have punched the wall. *I sure stuck my foot in my mouth with that one. Now she thinks I only came here to get her into bed again. How am I going to explain?* Lacing his fingers behind his head, he fought the desire still racing through his veins.

When he heard the water switch on from the living room, he groaned as his imagination went wild. He could almost see the water running down her body in rivers of clear liquid mixed with soap, making her skin slick to the touch. He could just imagine her running the bar of soap across her breasts and down between her legs as she washed. The blood pooled in his groin as he moaned and shifted his hard cock in his jeans to relieve some of the pressure. Just the thought of her could make his blood boil and he couldn't stand it anymore. He needed to make her understand he wanted more from her than sex.

The water sounded louder when he stood in the doorway. He pushed the door open and he could see the sliver of light coming from the bathroom. Past the point of no return, he moved toward the light, aching with need.

He reached for the handle just as she shut off the water and the shower slid open. He turned the knob in his hand slowly and the steam rolled out as she stood silhouetted in the light from the bathroom.

She lifted her leg onto the side of the tub to dry it, giving him the most luscious view of her ass as a groan rumbled in his chest. Her skin, almost translucent in the light, made his fingers tingle and ache to touch where the fluffy towel soaked up the water.

* * * *

Anger made her tremble and tears burned behind her eyelids while the hot water sluiced over her head. *I want him so bad I ache for him to be inside me, but I want more. I deserve more than a quick fuck.* Face the facts. You are half in love with him already.

"No. No, I'm not. I refuse," she said out loud, her logical mind fighting with her heart. *Then why does the thought of him only wanting sex disturb me so much? Do you really think he drove all the way up here for sex?* He could have gotten that at home. "I'm sure he doesn't want for sexual partners," she grumbled. *Am I really going to turn him away? You want him as much as he wants you.*

She stepped out and toweled herself dry, wiping the water from her legs as she placed her foot on the toilet and bent over. She wasn't sure when she knew he was there. Presenting him with her back, she slowly dried the front she shortly before she felt his lips on her shoulder.

"I don't want it to be all about sex between us," he whispered softly. He turned her around in his arms, the towel trapped them.

"Neither do I."

"I need you so bad, I ache, but there has to be more. We have so much more ridin' on this." He kissed her nose, across her cheek and down her throat. "Please say you want me, too."

"I do. God, Tanner. I want you so much." She sighed heavily as he ran kisses up to the side of her neck. She tipped her head to give him better access as a shiver rolled down her spine. Goose bumps flittered across her skin. She dropped the towel that hung from her fingertips between them, revealing her breasts to his seeking eyes. His stare moved from her eyes to her mouth and down to her breasts as his hand skimmed down her arm. He cupped her breast in his palm and as he rolled the nipple between his fingers, she sucked in a ragged breath.

"You are so beautiful," he whispered against her skin as his head dipped and he kissed her chest. He moved lower until he finally took the areola in his mouth and sucked, drawing the tip deep inside. Twirling his tongue around the hard tip before swiping the rough pad across the engorged bud, elicited a tortured moan from her mouth.

She took a shaky breath, tipped her head back and wound her fingers through his hair. She pushed his head harder against her, arching her back, making little mewing sounds in her throat as he suckled and pulled, before moving to its mate.

Her legs trembled as he feasted on her and skimmed his hand up her thigh toward her aching, throbbing pussy. His fingers finally sliding into wet cunt, she moaned and grasped his shoulders, praying he wouldn't stop.

"Don't stop—please don't stop. I'm going to come."

She whimpered when he pulled his fingers from inside her. "Not without me." He finally stood and captured her mouth with his, his tongue diving inside to stroke her own.

Running her hands up his sculpted muscles, she worked the buttons loose on his shirt. She tore her mouth from his, kissing the skin as she revealed the hard pectorals to her seeking lips. His flat male nipples puckered when she grazed them with her teeth and he sucked in a ragged breath. She smiled as a moan rumbled in his throat. Her hands moved toward the belt buckle he wore, working it loose, before she got to the button of his jeans, slipping it free. She grabbed the zipper and pulled it down, moving her shaking hands insides his pants to skim along his cock as she heard him moan again.

"Amy." Her name on his lips drove her desire out of control. He wrapped his hands in her hair and pulled her mouth back to his.

"Fuck me, Tanner. Right here, right now," she whispered against his mouth as he crushed her to him, his heart beating a rapid tempo against her breast.

He smiled. "I love it when you talk dirty."

"Then do it. Make me scream."

He pushed the pants down his lean hips and off his legs, tossing them across the bathroom as the florescent light threw shadows across the hard planes of his muscles. Wrapping his hands around her back, he grasped her ass in both hands and lifted her onto the vanity behind her. She leaned back as he ran his tongue down her breasts, laving her nipple, before moving down her belly and dropping to his knees. His tongue touched her engorged clit softly and she almost screamed as pleasure rocketed from her toes to center in her groin. Delicious sensations all built on one another as he licked, slowly at first then harder, sucking the swollen nub between his lips. Each caress, every nibble sent her passion skyward. His hands held her hips in place as he pleasured her, his tongue alternating between spearing her vagina to toggling her clit, even when his own husky moans of satisfaction mingled with hers. On the edge of coming apart, she wiggled her hips wanting more pressure on her aching clit, begging without words. "Oh yes. Oh God, yes!" Thick cream rolled from inside her, coating his tongue as he swiped every last drop. The tremors ceased and Tanner stood, reaching for his pants laying on the floor a few feet away and pulling out a foil package.

She took the condom between his fingers. "Let me." Tearing the package open, she grasped his cock in her hand as he hissed above her. She rolled the slippery latex over him until he was completely encased. "I want you inside me," she murmured, guiding him as he slipped into her hot vagina and they both moaned.

Lips fused, breaths mingled as the heat rose. Slowly rocking his hips, his rock hard erection dipped in and out of her damp cavern. The tempo of his thrusts increased and their breathing escaladed until the air around them filled with lusty moans.

"Fuck yes! Harder, please." The sound of flesh against flesh, his cock filling her to the hilt sent her desire completely out of control.

* * * *

He wanted her to come again, needed to make sure she enjoyed this as much as he did. "Oh God," he moaned, pulling his mouth from hers as he sought control. Gasping breaths rattled his frame when he started to move. Her tight pussy gripped him, sucking everything from inside him as he rocked. "Jesus, you are so tight." Her little whimpers echoed loudly in the bright room as she brought her hips higher, wrapping her beautiful legs around his hips, locking them behind him, wanting him deeper.

"Tanner, please, fuck me, fuck me hard."

Knowing she was close, his hips ground into hers, faster and deeper until he heard her cry out and he took his own pleasure with a moan torn from center of his soul. He rested his head against her shoulder as their breathing slowed and she stroked his back.

He kissed her hair as he whispered, "Are you okay?"

She smiled against his skin. "Perfect," she whispered, snuggling as close to him as she could get.

They groaned in union as he slipped from her warmth. He grabbed the full condom and stripped it off, before he dropped it into the trashcan nearby. Her eyelids drooped in contentment and he smiled. Both of his hands slid around her as he lifted her off the vanity into his arms. She giggled when he headed toward the bed and dropped her in the center. Scooting toward the headboard, she yanked the covers back and crawled under the sheets as he slipped in beside her. Contentment wrapped him in a warm cocoon as he slowly relaxed, her head resting on his chest. He knew now that each time he held her, she continued to wrap his heart around her little finger. He could have sworn that she purred as she snuggled closer. Within minutes, her breathing became regular and she slept, leaving Tanner to think about what just happened as he drew little circles on her arm. When sleep finally claimed him, he snuggled next to her and curled his body around hers.

Chapter 10

When they woke the next morning, confusion rippled through her mind as she realized a warm, brown arm lay draped across her abdomen. Memories flooded back of the night before, and how Tanner had made sweet love to her. A wistful smile crossed her lips as she rolled over to see his sexy grin and brandy colored eyes.

"Good mornin'," he whispered, his hand slipped slowly up her flat belly so his fingers could rest beneath her breasts as his gaze moved down to her parted lips. A heavy sigh escaped her mouth when his calloused palm rasped over the bud already standing straight up, wanting more. Her eyes closed on a moan when his mouth took the place of his fingers, his tongue swirling around the hardened nub, pulling and sucking.

Her palm came up to rest at the back of his head, tangling her fingertips in the hair at his nape, while her breath hitched in her throat.

His free hand skimmed down her belly, through the curls guarding her quickly swelling pussy lips, to dip between the folds and slide easily inside. The moan held in her throat escaped and she felt him smile against her skin. Her legs fell apart to allow him better access as he finger fucked her vagina and his thumb toggled her clit, driving her to distraction.

"Tanner," emerged from her lips on a gasp.

"Yes?" He lifted his head and removed his fingers from her warmth as a strangled whimper left her throat. "Something I can do for you?"

"You are rotten," she complained.

He smiled again. The blush of desire rose on her cheeks and her breaths came in rapid, gasping pants as his fingers moved back inside.

Deciding to take control for a moment, she rolled over, pushing him to his back and lying half on top of him as she started kissing his chest. She moved her mouth to his flat, coppery disks to nibble and tease as his eyes slowly closed to the sensations she aroused. His semi-soft cock rose to the occasion as she raked the surface of her tongue across his nipples, ripping a groan from his throat.

Another moan rumbled in his chest while he tried to control the desire as it raced along his nerve endings, heightening them to her every touch. His skin quivered as she licked and her tongue found each ridge of his washboard abs. She continued to move lower as a deep, almost painful groan slip from between his lips. Reaching his steel hard cock standing at attention, she wrapped her warm hand around him and his hips surged against her touch. The thrill of desire rippled through her, knowing his need came from being with her. He almost whimpered as her hand started to stroke and her tongue rasped against the tip. She laved at the pre-cum glistening on the end of his penis.

"Oh God, Amy," he sighed, as her tongue darted out, running behind where her hand had just been, licking the soft skin. Up and down his hard cock she skimmed, until she finally took the tip fully into her mouth and sucked. "Suck me baby. Yes, perfect." His balls tightened in her hand as his hips rocked and his cock bumped the back of her throat. "Okay, stop. I wanted inside you when I come."

With a groan of torture, he pulled her up by the shoulders so she straddled his hips. He settled her over his engorged erection and pushed his full length into her. Her slick, wet pussy closed around him, taking everything he had to offer.

A heavy moan escaped her lips as her eyes slid shut, the shear sensation of having him there almost sending her over the edge. She braced herself on his chest, his hands rested on her hips and they began to move, each seeking what the other had to give.

* * * *

Soft groans mingling in the morning light streaming through the window, they rode higher and higher, until he felt her body climax above him. Her slick cream rolled down between his legs, coating his balls. With several more strokes of his cock, his jaw clenched as he reached his own climax, shooting his seed deep within her before he realized they had forgotten a condom.

His groan of satisfaction mixed with a moan of realization. "Son of a—"

Unable to stop, his hips continued to move until his climax ended.

As their bodies cooled, she rolled off to lie next to him, running her hand through the hair on his chest, as he threw his arm across his eyes.

"God, Amy, I'm sorry," he whispered, unable to meet her eyes.

"It's not your fault."

"But I should have protected you," he groaned, moving his arm so he could see her face.

"We are both adults. I'm just as responsible as you are," she returned with a smile. "Besides, I know I'm clean."

"I'm sure you are," he murmured. "I wasn't worried about that. But what if we made a baby?"

"No worries. I'm on birth control," she told him, continuing to run her fingers across his chest, as another strangling groan rose in his throat and he grabbed her hand to forestall the motion. "What's wrong? Not up for more?"

"I think I've created a monster," he murmured, his cock stirring against his belly. "I thought maybe you might be hungry."

"Actually, yes, I'm starving." She laughed and vaulted from the bed.

She paraded across the bedroom toward the bathroom while his hot gaze followed. When she returned, she had slipped on a t-shirt and underwear and stopped to lean against the door jam, his clothes dangling from her fingertips as she dared him to come after them.

Answering her challenge, he rose from the bed in all his male glory as she sucked in a shaky breath and a flirty smile lifted the corners of her mouth. When he reached her side, he slipped an arm around her waist and pulled her tight to his naked chest, his rough clothing trapped between them. He took her lips with his in a heart-stopping kiss, pressing her hard against the wood behind her.

He finally lifted his head, pressing his forehead to hers as he moaned. "We'll have to continue this later."

"Promise?"

"Definitely." He slipped on his underwear and jeans, before he followed her toward the kitchen.

* * * *

A heavy sigh escaped her lips. She suspected she would need lots of caffeine to keep up with him, but the idea of a repeat performance, already had her panties wet as her pussy throbbed.

"How about I make breakfast?" He pulled open the refrigerator as she watched him survey the contents.

Her startled expression must have been hilarious as he laughed out loud.

"Don't look so shocked. I can cook. Do you like omelets?" His gaze moved back to the refrigerator and its contents as he cleared his throat. "Let's see, you have cheese, eggs, and ham. Perfect."

She watched him pull the ingredients from her refrigerator, placing everything on the counter, her mouth still hanging open. After he set things down, he reached over, pulling her to him, sliding his finger under her chin to close the opening and then kissing her soundly on the mouth. Once he raised his head, he murmured, "A pan?"

Breathlessly she answered, "In the cupboard, next to the sink."

Releasing her with the promise of more in his eyes, he bent to retrieve the skillet from the opening. As he puttered around the kitchen, grabbing the things he needed to make breakfast, she stood in stunned silence. *He cooks, too? Holy shit!* Jack had never even suggested making her anything, much less after they had sex. She either cooked or they went out to eat.

The more she learned about this handsome cowboy, the more he trapped her heart and wound the disobedient organ around his finger. Last night, he had made her body sing for his, plucking and strumming her nerves in a way no one else had ever done. A flush crept across her cheeks as she watched him through her lashes. Taking a deep breath to calm the desire racing through her blood, she turned to grab two cups as the coffee maker spit and spattered.

"Do you take anything in your coffee?"

"Yeah, cream and sugar."

She put a couple of spoons of each in his cup and set it next to him on the counter. She grabbed the hot chocolate from the cupboard above her head, spooning some into her cup before pouring her own.

The omelet in the pan was almost ready as he asked, "Where are your plates?"

"Above your head to the right."

"Can you put some bread in the toaster? This one is almost done."

"Sure."

The toast popped out of the toaster as Tanner placed the omelet on the plate.

"That one is yours. Mine will be ready in a minute," he said, handing her the dish.

"I'll wait for you. That way we can eat on the balcony if you want."

"That's fine with me, but you might want to put somethin' over your underwear," he grinned, his hot gaze sliding down her bare legs. "I really don't want to share those gorgeous legs with your neighbors."

Blushing under his stare, she retreated to the bedroom to slip on some shorts before she returned to his side. "Better?"

"Not for me," he whispered, placing a kiss on her mouth. When he lifted his lips from hers, he whispered, "I kind of like you with no clothes on, but that's probably not a good idea on your balcony. Then again..." His eyes darkened at the suggestion and a sexy smile graced his mouth, as shivers rolled down her spine. She wasn't the exhibitionist type, but letting him fuck her on her balcony held a certain appeal.

His omelet now done, Amy watched him put it on another plate along with the next batch of toast, and grab his coffee as they moved outside. She took the seat across from him and when she cut into the soft, cheesy eggs and stuck a bite into her mouth, she sighed as the flavors blended on her tongue.

"This is fantastic," she told him after the food slid down her throat.

"I'm glad you like it," he whispered as she saw his eyes fix on her mouth, watching her tongue slide across her lips to capture the cheese that lingered there.

"You need to stop looking at me like that." Her words came out in a breathless whisper.

Taking a bite, he asked with a raised eyebrow, "Why?"

"Because if you don't, we will never make it out of the bedroom for the rest of the day."

"I don't see the problem," he replied as she watched a sexy grin return to his lips.

Swallowing hard against the lump that formed in her throat, she tried to focus on the food in front of her and not on the heat that pooled in her groin, making her wet and ready. *Good Lord! I can't believe I'm reacting to him this way.* She tried to calm her racing pulse as she wiggled on the seat and rubbed her thighs together in a vain attempt to still the throb.

Once they were finished, she sat back with her coffee cup near her lips, watching him over the rim as scenes of the night before flashed across her mind. She felt her cheeks flush at her thoughts and the grin on his face grew wider.

She drank the last bit of her coffee and quickly stood, grabbing her plate and cup to take back into the apartment, attempting to catch her breath. He followed close on her heels, and by the time she put her dishes in the sink, he stood right behind her.

Feeling a little self-conscious, she placed her back to the sink and stammered, "I think I'll go take a shower. Then we can decide what we want to do this afternoon." *This is silly. I've already had wild sex with him, oh, at least several times. Why am I being nervous around him now?*

"All right. I'll do up the dishes."

She scooted by him, but as she headed toward the bedroom, she peeked over her shoulder, watching him turn on the water.

She took a steadying breath once she reached her bedroom and shut the door, putting her back against the hard surface. After a moment, she grabbed some clean clothes and went into the bathroom, flipping on the shower as she shucked her clothing.

Showering quickly, she dressed in some casual clothes, not sure what the rest of the day would bring. When she returned to the living room, he had already cleaned up the kitchen and sat back on the balcony with another cup of coffee.

"How was your shower?"

"Good," she replied shyly, not quite sure why she wanted to be so evasive with him now. After all, he had already seen everything she had to offer. "It's all yours."

"Thanks. I could probably do with one myself." He sniffed his arm and grinned.

"There are clean towels in the cupboard next to the toilet."

"Okay, I'll be right back." She returned his smile, before he disappeared into the apartment.

A heavy sigh escaped her lips. Her attraction to him confused her. She had never been this distracted by any man before, and fear gripped her insides as she realized her feelings ran deeper each moment around him. She couldn't talk to Chris her feelings, since her friend had been trying to get the two of them together for months.

She looked at the distant skyline as the sun continued to rise in the morning sky, before she peeked behind her and hoping he would be in the shower for at least fifteen minutes. *I'll call Angela. I need to talk to someone who doesn't know him, but knows enough about me and my past relationships that can give me some sound advice.*

She darted inside the apartment to grab her cell phone and slipped back out the patio door, leaning on the railing. She hit speed dial, putting it to her ear as she heard the first ring.

The sleepy voice, grumbled. "Hello?"

"Angela? Hey, it's Amy."

"Hey, Amy, what's up? I haven't heard from you in a while," Angela replied.

"I'm good. Listen, I need to ask you for some advice, and I don't have a lot of time."

"Okay, shoot."

"To make a long story short, I've met this guy," Amy began. "I went out to one of my friend's parents' house. He lives next door to them. Anyway, we've kind of hooked up. In fact, he's here at my apartment now."

"Damn! You move fast, girl! Weren't you just seeing that rodeo guy, not long ago?"

"Yeah, but I caught him cheating on me."

"Sorry, Am, that sucks."

"Never mind that."

"So what's up with this new guy?"

"He's about my age, a real, honest to God cowboy. I mean, he breaks horses and everything. He's gorgeous, dark brown hair, brown eyes, nice chest, rock hard abs—"

"So what's the problem? He sounds great! I'm assuming you are attracted to him, so when are you going to bed with him?"

"That's just it, Ang. We already have, several times in fact. You know I don't normally go to bed with someone I just met, but damn Ang, we had sex within the first couple of days knowing each other. I couldn't keep my hands off him." She captured her bottom lip between her teeth nervously.

"So was it good?"

"Rock my world good."

"Exactly why are you calling me then instead of being with him?"

"I'm afraid I'm getting in way too deep already, Ang. He's perfect. Too wonderful to be true, I think. He even cooked me breakfast this morning and did the dishes."

"You better hang onto that one, girl. He sounds like a keeper."

"But I've only known him like two weeks."

"So? He sounds like the type to take home to Mom, you know? There aren't many of those around anymore. Usually the gorgeous ones are married or gay."

"Don't I know it," she grumbled.

"Well, my advice would be to play things through 'til the end. Take everything there is to take, but be careful. Don't fall in love with him. Then again, that advice might be a little too late from the sound in your voice."

"That's what I'm afraid of. I think it probably is, Ang. It would be so easy to fall in love with him without even trying."

"Just be happy, Am. You deserve to be after the jerks you've been seeing. If you think he's the one, then go for it."

"Thanks, Ang. You've been a ton of help. I'd better go. He'll be out of the shower soon." She turned around only to be met by Tanner's questioning gaze as he leaned against the door jam and she stammered, "I gotta go, Ang. Talk to you later." She shut the phone with a click, her gazed riveted to the handsome man standing in the doorway.

Chapter 11

"Hi." He grinned as he leaned against the door jam with his arms across his chest. His clean light blue T-shirt fit snuggly over his taunt pectorals and the standard pressed Wranglers complimented his long legs and lean hips. Wet hair combed off his forehead, curled at his neck and fresh shaven face gave her the urge to rub his cheek with hers and let his unique scent fill her head. *Oh crap! How much of that conversation did he hear? Probably much more than I wanted him to.*

"Hi," she replied, not meeting his gaze.

"Was that Chris?"

"Uh…no. I called a friend of mine out in Oregon."

"How's the weather out there?" His non-committed comments confused her as he slid into the chair across the table.

"Rainy, of course."

"Did you decide what you wanted to do this afternoon?"

"No, not really. What about you?"

"I don't know, either. We could just stay here and watch a movie. That is unless you want to go out somewhere."

Although not exactly sure why, she was a little panicked at the thought of spending the entire afternoon alone with him in her apartment. *A little too domestic, maybe?* Just having him this close drove her to distraction. "I need to run by the hospital and pick up my pay check."

"Cool. I can see where you work and meet some of your co-workers."

"I'd like to hit the farmer's market today and get some produce. Did you bring your guitar?"

He grinned and said, "Always. Like the American Express card, never leave home without it."

She laughed and shook her head. "Why am I not surprised?"

"I thought you would have known me well enough by now to guess that one."

"Anyway, Gilley's has open mic night tonight if you'd like to go."

"You're kidding me."

"No. I'm perfectly serious. You might be able to do a song or two."

"That would be awesome!"

"I know of a nice spot for a picnic near the market. We could get some chicken, pack a lunch and just relax under a tree."

"Anything is fine with me as long as it lets me spend time with you."

"It's a date. Let me grab a few things from here to take along and we'll go."

He stood as she neared him, taking her hand in his to stop her, placing a quick kiss to her lips and a caress to her jaw.

"This should be fun," he grinned. "At least I can get to know you better this way."

She grabbed her sandals, a blanket and a couple of small pillows. She figured it would be better if they stopped somewhere and bought something to take for their picnic. She really didn't have a lot of food in the house, since she wasn't sure if she would be home this weekend with the rodeo.

They took his truck and Amy gave Tanner directions to the hospital. He wrapped his arm around her possessively while the elevator moved from the parking garage to the floor where she worked.

Approaching the nurses' station, several pairs of eyes settled on the gorgeous guy next to her and jealousy stabbed at her heart like a hundred bees stinging the vulnerable organ.

"Hey, Amy. What are you doing here today?" Virginia sat perched on her chair, but Amy knew from the interest in her eyes, the other woman's gaze was riveted to Tanner.

"I needed to pick up my pay check. Are they in the drawer?" Amy moved from Tanner's side to a spot around the other side of the desk. None of the four taking up space in the immediate area even noticed her movement.

"Yeah, same place as always. Hey, aren't you going to introduce us to your friend?"

Amy almost groaned as the sexy, flirty, you-know-you-want-to-fuck-a-cowboy smile graced his lips.

"Girls, this is my *boyfriend," I guess I can call him that since we've had sex,* "Tanner. Tanner this is Virginia, Allison, Katie and Veronica."

He tipped his hat and Amy could have sworn all four women melted on their chairs as he drawled, "Howdy, ladies."

Katie, with her love 'em and leave 'em attitude said, "Where has Amy been hiding you?"

"We haven't been seein' each other all that long," he answered.

"Back off, Katie," Amy growled in the other woman's ear as she walked past her.

"Touchy, touchy," Katie whispered, grinning at Tanner like she wanted to lick him up, from the tips of his pointed boots to his kiss-me lips.

"I'll see you all in a few days."

"Have fun and don't do anything we wouldn't do."

"I know what you would do, Katie."

The four women laughed as Amy took Tanner's hand and moved back toward the elevator.

Once inside, he wrapped his arms around her and pinned her to the wall behind them.

"You don't have to be jealous," he whispered against her lips.

"I'm not jealous."

His disbelieving chuckle grated on her nerves. "The daggers being thrown at your friends say differently."

"All right, so I'm a little. I don't appreciate other woman coming on to my guy."

"Your guy? I think I like that."

"Good, me too," she murmured as the doors slid open to the parking garage.

They stepped out of the elevator and through the glass doors, as the heat from outside instantly caused sweat to gather and roll down her back. His hand caressed her ass, not enough anyone would notice unless they happened to be paying attention, but she did. Heat licked at her insides and her pussy filled with need as his fingers followed the seam of her shorts down the crack of her ass while they walked. Once they reached the passenger side of his truck he stepped behind her and trapped her along the side, breasts squashed by metal as her butt cradled his impressive erection.

"Sweet Jesus! I want to bury my cock in your ass," he whispered, his tongue flicking along her neck, gathering the beads of sweet glistening on the surface.

His hand moved around the front of her shorts, flipped the buttons open down and slid inside. His finger found her swollen clit and massaged as she whimpered with need.

"Someone's a naughty girl." Warm breath caressed her ear, sending shivers racing along her spine. "Open the door and put your foot on the running board," he growled in her ear as he pulled the digit out of her cunt.

I can't believe I'm doing this. Her hand fumbled with the handle.

As if reading her mind he murmured, "It'll be good, I promise."

Once in position, the door blocking the view from any passerby, he slipped in fingers back inside her panties. "You're so wet." The device of torture came back, rasping from her vagina to her clit and she almost screamed. "Do you want to come?"

Her hips rocked forward as she whimpered, "Oh God, yes."

"Right here, right now?"

"Don't tease me anymore, please."

He chuckled in her ear, but he must have decided to let her off the hook as his finger began to toggle her clit with increasing force. Heat built from her pussy outward as she laid her head back on his shoulder and he kissed her neck. He whispered in her ear as she started to pant, "Come for me, baby."

His command released her from her torment as she bit her hand to keep the screams of completion muffled. Cum flooded her center, wetting his fingers and her panties beneath as goose bumps skittered across her flesh. When the tremors ceased and she could focus, she groaned, "My God."

"Good?"

"Yes, but I can't believe I let you finger fuck me in the garage at my work." Heat crawled up her chest to splash across her face as she fixed her clothing.

"I'd do more than that, but we aren't in a secluded enough spot in here."

She contemplated the thought before brushing it away. His way too sexy grin tempted her and she blushed further. "I can't believe I'm even considering your suggestion."

He kissed her soundly on the lips, flashing a grin before walking around to the drivers' side. "Where to?"

"Would you think badly of me if I said my house?"

His sexy as hell smile graced his mouth. "We'll take up where we left off later."

A tortured sigh escaped her mouth. "Okay. Take a left out of here, and we'll head to the market."

Always the attentive one, Tanner kept a possessive grip either on her hip or holding her hand as the walked around the market. The smells bombarded her senses, wafting through the air as fans whirled overhead. Ripe strawberries, raspberries, tomatoes, squash, beans, peppers, any kind of fruit or vegetable grown in the area had the proud display from each local vendor. Flowers of every imaginable color hung from rafters or graced long tables as all the dealers haggled over prices. Amy bought several different vegetables, clicking off ingredients in her mind on her mental recipe list for dinner. Tanner found a bright bouquet of mixed flowers and against her protest, purchased them and presented the exquisite arrangement to her with grand flourish and down on one knee, much to the delight of various onlookers. She blushed to the roots of her hair as the crowd clapped and laughed, especially after he stood, wrapped his arms around her and gave her one of his heart-stopping, melt-your-heart-in-your-chest kisses. Always the showman, he waved to the throng as she buried her red face in his chest.

"Let's get out of here. I'm tired of sharin' you," he chuckled in her ear. "Besides, we need to finish what got started earlier."

"I thought we were going to eat."

"I'd like to eat somethin'."

"Damn. You are incorrigible." She laughed as her face burned from embarrassment. "There is picnic area with a small lake not far from here."

"Perfect."

She directed him to the lake where several families milled about with children in tow. Grabbing the blanket and picnic supplies, they found a shady spot not far from the water and sat down.

"Are you hungry?"

With a wicked grin, he replied, "Not for food."

Blushing, she dropped her eyes from his as her heart did a little flip in her chest.

He scooted across the blanket, brought his finger under her chin, forcing her to look into his eyes. "What's wrong?"

"Nothing. I…" her voice trailed off, as she tried to decide what to say.

"You can tell me," he murmured, bending his head to brush a soft kiss across her lips.

When he finally lifted his head again, she felt like she had lost herself in his eyes. He had become very important to her in such a short time, she almost couldn't remember her life before he had become a part of it and they had only known each other for three weeks.

He waited, caressing her jaw with his fingers, sending shivers down her spine, and making little goose bumps rise on her arms. She closed her eyes to the sensation, trying to get her body under control before she threw herself into his arms and begged him to fuck her right there on the blanket.

Her skin burned where he touched as moistness settled between her thighs, making her wet and wanting.

* * * *

He took her mouth, his lips sliding across the softness as a small moan rose in his throat. Her hands skimmed across his chest and inched their way up, curling around the back of his head as he deepened the kiss, his tongue finding hers. Pulling away from her just slightly, he gasped for air to fill his burning lungs, his chest rising and falling as he tried desperately to control the need racing through him. *What is it about her? Hell, I can hardly control myself when I'm around her.* He pulled farther away from her. He needed to put some distance between them, and quick, if the passion in their kiss was any kind of indicator. Otherwise, he would take her right there and to hell with anyone that saw.

Clearing his throat and shifting uncomfortably, he said, "We'll have to continue that later. Now is probably not a good place."

She opened her eyes when he moved away. He saw her glance around as embarrassment flushed across her cheeks. Thankfully, no one seemed to notice the passionate embrace as they set up their own picnics and the children raced to the river's edge.

She put her palms to her cheeks as she murmured, "I'm so embarrassed."

He pulled one of her hands away as he asked, "Why?"

"Because! Who knows what people saw?"

"Amy," he whispered caressing her cheek. "They saw two people kissin', nothing more."

"If you hadn't stopped..." She flushed again.

"We are just going to have to learn to control ourselves, I guess. It's going to be hard, though. When I'm around you, all I want to do is pull you into my arms and..." his voice lowered as he whispered, "lick every inch of you until you come in my mouth and scream my name." Her blush deepened when she heard what he said and he pulled back with a smile.

An older couple walked up behind them as they headed toward the water and a picnic table that sat nearby. As they moved passed Amy and Tanner, the woman sighed, "Oh, to be young and in love again."

"Don't you still love me, Sylvia?"

"Of course, I do. Being married to you for sixty years hasn't changed that."

Watching the couple move closer to the water, Tanner's gaze caught Amy's and his grin just got bigger. He knew what he did to her, and he liked it. It kept her off guard and that's exactly how he wanted her, hot and ready. Now that they had already made love on several occasions, he knew he'd ever get enough of her.

"How about we eat some of this food we brought. I don't mind cold chicken, but its better warm," she said, pulling open the bag.

"Sure. I could use something to eat." He winked and she flushed.

"Will you stop doing that?" she whispered, blushing more.

"Doing what?" He grinned, running the tip of his finger along her forearm.

Pulling her arm back, she said, "That!"

She handed him a plate of food as she settled back with one of her own and she started to talk. He could tell he made her very nervous and obviously when she was nervous, she talked. She told him about her parents and two sisters, the farm in Oregon, how her dad had been a bull rider and bronco rider in the rodeo, until he had gotten hurt and had to stop. How she had gone to nursing school shortly after she graduated from high school, following in her mother's footsteps.

"So, did you always want to be a nurse?" She licked her fingers and his groin tightened painfully.

"Yes. My mother is a nurse, too, and she used to tell me stories about the patients she took care of. She made it all sound so glamorous and helpful." She shrugged as he watched her look around.

"And how did you hook up with Chris? You two seemed to be opposites. You're down to earth and come across as a simple country girl. Chris is all wrapped up in the high life of Dallas. It's just the opposite of life in Brenham."

"Maybe that's why we get along so well. I guess I keep her a little grounded, and she prods me to do more of the wild things."

"Could be. What kind of wild things has she gotten you into?"

"Nothing illegal or anything. She drags me off to some of the bars and stuff. She's always trying to hook me up with someone. She hated the guys I've dated and she loves to play matchmaker."

"How many did you date?" It seemed like a simple question to him, but she paused like she was nervous telling him.

"How many cowboys?"

"Yeah."

"One, not including you. The last guy happened to be a bull rider. I try to stay away from rodeo men. I'm not into temporary relationships and usually that is what you get with a rodeo guy."

"I can see your point."

"They travel so much all the time and unless you travel with them, you don't see them very often." She shrugged. "I haven't found the right guy yet, I guess."

"You aren't hard to get along with, are you?" He hoped his teasing would put her more at ease.

"No, or at least I don't think so."

"Well, so far, I don't think you are, either." His finger caressed her arm again as the goose bumps rose along the surface under his finger.

"I just seem to find the guys that don't have time for me, for one reason or another. I've dated cops, fireman, cowboys, they all had other priorities."

The pain in her heart reflected brightly in her eyes.

Frowning, he said, "I just hope you aren't disappointed that I don't have a lot of money."

"Why would I be?"

"I don't make a lot from just the bar. I do all right for myself, but I don't have a fancy car or lots of nice things."

"It doesn't matter how much money you make or have in the bank. I like you just the way you are."

"I'm really glad Chris brought you home with her," he said, capturing her gaze.

"Me, too."

He folded her fingers into his, pulling her down so he could take possession her lips, sprawling her across his chest.

"We shouldn't be doing this here," she murmured against his mouth.

"I know, but I can't seem to keep my hands off you."

* * * *

She smiled, glad he seemed to be as attracted to her and she was to him. *I just pray he doesn't break my heart.* "How about we head back to my apartment? It's not private enough here." The tryst in the parking garage only whet her appetite for him. She wanted him, needed him to make love to her again as desire rippled through her when she felt his hand slide up her side to slip his fingers under her breast. Her breath caught in her throat as a moan escaped her lips.

He murmured against her mouth, "Shall we go?"

Not giving him an answer, she pushed herself up and stood. He started putting their food away in the bag as she helped. They quickly gathered their belongings and walked back toward his truck.

Amy looked over her shoulder to see the older woman smiling at her and giving her a knowing wink. She smiled wistfully before she turned away. *I hope I find that kind of love someday.* Tanner slipped his arm around her waist. *Maybe you already have,* her heart whispered in return.

They reached her apartment in record time, quickly saying hello to George as the walked toward the elevator. Once the doors had closed behind them, Tanner pulled her to his chest and locked his lips with hers, groaning as their tongues danced.

Lucky for them, they were alone in the elevator, but when the doors opened on her floor, an older couple met them and the woman exclaimed, "Good grief!"

Amy felt the heat crawl up her neck and splash across her cheeks before she bowed her head and pushed past the couple on the way to her apartment with Tanner on her heels.

"They should just get a room, for crying out loud."

"You are only jealous, Maggie. Especially since we haven't done anything like that in years," the man grumbled and Amy smiled.

The couple had been her neighbors for a long time, and she had to admit, she rarely heard that kind of activity coming from their apartment.

When they reached her apartment door, she fumbled with her keys, anxious to get inside. She pushed the key into the lock, turning it as she felt Tanner's warm breath on her neck, sending shivers down her spine.

Once the door opened, she didn't bother with the light, but she tossed her purse on the couch. Tanner shut the door behind her and flipped the lock. Amy walked to the center of the room and turned around as the late afternoon sun cast shadows across the floor of the living room. The look in his eyes made her toes curl, her pussy fill and throb insistently. He stepped toward her while that sexy smile he liked to give her graced his mouth. When he reached her side, she brought her hands up to his chest, sliding them up to wrap them around his neck, twisting her fingers in the curls.

He groaned deep in his chest as she pressed her breasts against him and he dipped his head, taking her soft, waiting mouth with his. His hands grasped her hips, pulling her tight to him as his tongue slipped between her lips to find her own.

Her desire rose ten-fold as her groin cradled his cock through their clothing. She brought her hands back down to his chest then down to his waist, pulling his t-shirt from his jeans and bunching it up between them. She wanted to feel his skin, needed the heat of his body against her.

Amy pulled her mouth from his as her rasping breath tore at her lungs. The t-shirt disappeared over his head, leaving his chest bare to her touch. She nibbled at his collarbone, before she worked her way down. She kissed the surface, finding each male nipple with little nips of her teeth as she heard him inhaled sharply, his hands on her shoulders and a moan on his lips. Amy grasped his belt buckle and worked it loose, before finding the button at his waist. She slipped it free and slid her hands beneath the waistband of his jeans as she felt his skin quiver under her touch. She started to work the pants off, but he grabbed her hands and brought them back to his chest.

* * * *

"My turn," he whispered, kissing her fingertips then taking each one between his lips, caressing them with his tongue.

Finally, he let go of her hands and ran his own down her arms until he could reach her side and slide his fingers beneath her breast. He watched her eyes close as she pushed her breast into his palm, a soft moan rising to her lips.

She had tipped her head back and whimpered low in her throat when he let his tongue follow the dip of her collarbone. When he finally raised his head, she slowly opened her eyes.

He whispered against her mouth, "Do you want to take this in the other room?"

She whispered softly as he moved his lips across her cheek. "I suppose we should."

"How about we take a shower? I would love to see you in there with water runnin' down your breasts makin' your skin slick. Just the thought almost makes me come."

"Sounds fun. I've never had sex in the shower before."

"First time for everythin'." He wiggled his eyebrows and she giggled.

He grabbed her hand, leading her toward the bathroom.

Facing her once they reached the other room, he ran his fingers across her cheek. "Do you have any idea how much I want you?"

"Probably only half as much as I want you."

He smiled, reaching for the strings holding her top at her shoulder, and pulled it loose. He let his eyes wander over her breasts when the shirt slipped down.

"You are so beautiful." His hand reached for her, rasping his palm against the nipple as it beaded into a hard nub and she moaned. His head came down, kissing across her chest and moving toward the areola.

"Please," she whispered. Her skin quivered under his touch and a tortured moan slipped from between her lips when his mouth finally settled on her breast. He sucked and nipped at the pert tip beneath his lips, flicking it with his tongue as she pushed his head harder against her.

He rose in front of her again, his mouth settling on hers as his hands worked at the button on her shorts. He slipped them off her hips, taking her satiny underwear with them until they both rested at her feet and she kicked them off. He quickly shed his jeans as he saw her rake his body with an appreciative glance before she turned to start the water. As it reached the perfect temperature, she walked into the stream as he followed. She tipped her head back, wetting her hair, letting the water run in rivulets down her chest as his gaze roamed over her enticing form.

She grabbed the soap and began to lather it up, but he took it from her hands saying, "Let me."

With a sexy grin gracing her mouth, she handed him the soap. Once his hands began their torturous exploration of her taut nipples, she tipped her head back "God, I love what you do to me."

He kissed her neck as his hands slid over her soap-slickened breasts, teasing and taunting, before moving down her belly to explore between her thighs. Her legs got weak as he ran the callused surfaces up and down, around her hips to grasp her buttocks and pull her hard against him. He stepped back with her so the water could run over them, washing away the soap as he continued his exploration of her ass.

He took her nipple in his mouth again as the water ran over his head and down between them. One hand slid between her thighs as she parted them. Sliding two fingers, knuckle deep inside, her pussy closed around him, as she whimpered and rocked her hips.

* * * *

Her whole body shook from the intense desire racing through her. She moaned as his fingers slid into her, stroking her clit at the same time, stretching, her need making her slick to his touch. His mouth moved down her body, raining little kisses down her belly. A moment later, he knelt in front of her and pushed her onto the shower seat.

"Open your legs, baby," he whispered.

He spread her thighs with the width of his shoulders and ran butterfly kisses up the inside of her leg as he got closer and closer to her aching clit. Her whole body shook with need, and when he settled his mouth on her, sliding his tongue against her, she almost slid off the seat, but his hands on her hips stopped her.

"Oh God, Tanner," she groaned, gripping his shoulders.

His mouth moved over her, pleasuring her with his tongue as she quivered and moaned, her back arching against the side of the shower. When release finally came, she felt like her insides had turned to liquid and it all centered between her legs as hot cum slipped out and he lapped it up like a kitten after fresh cream. His mouth continued to play until the tremors stopped.

He pulled her to her feet, bracing her against the side of the shower. Lifting her until her legs straddled him and her pussy lips were open and waiting for him, he prodded her opening slightly as she moaned. Unable to wait any longer, she begged for him to take her as he pushed into her slick crevice, rocking until he was fully encased.

She could tell he was trying to hold himself in check as his jaw clenched tight while he fought for control, and he growled when she wiggled her butt. A tortured moan rose to his lips as she held onto his shoulders and kissed his neck, sliding her tongue along the length of it, sending goose bumps along his skin.

Gripping her hips, he pushed her against the wall of the shower as he began to move. Their moans mingled, filling the air as the hot water rolled over his back and down between them. The walls of her vagina gripped his entire length as the spasms of her climax rippled through her. She heard him groan as he released the stranglehold he held on his own need, flooding her womb with his seed as shuddered.

They stood there for several moments as their desire cooled. She rested her head against his shoulder, holding on until she felt him slip from inside her and release her so she could try to stand. Her legs rubbery and weak made it difficult, and Tanner kept an arm around her until she knew she could hold herself up.

"We'll have to shower again now." He grinned, his gaze sliding down her still flush body.

"Mmm, yeah, I guess we will," she whispered as her own eyes took in the view. "This time, we just wash."

"Oh, you aren't any fun," he said, soaping up his hands to help her.

Chapter 12

They stood in the center of the bathroom, and Tanner slowly dried her off, running the fluffy towel over her breasts and down between her legs.

"You are torturing me," she whispered, closing her eyes. Drying off had never been so titillating.

"Yeah, I know." He grinned.

Amy grabbed another towel from the rack and dried him off, too, enjoying the flush of desire that painted his cheeks as he closed his eyes. She loved how quickly his body reacted to her touch, rising to the occasion without much stimulation at all. Jack took several long minutes, if at all, to get hard again after a good fuck. *Why in the hell am I comparing Tanner to Jack? They are nothing alike.*

He wrapped his arms around her, bending his head to take her mouth. Tanner traced her lips with his tongue, she moaned when he slipped it inside.

She finally pulled back with a groan, giving him a sexy smile and toward the bedroom. A moment later, she felt a stinging snap on her buttocks, and she spun around. "Ouch! That wasn't very nice," she screeched, rubbing the welt.

"I'll kiss it and make it better, I promise." Giving her a wicked grin, Tanner threw the towel onto the floor.

"You better," she replied, backing toward the bed as he followed. When the mattress hit the back of her knees, she sat down and rolled over.

When he saw the red welt he had left on her ass, he traced the outline with his finger before his warm lips took its place and she slowly closed her eyes. *Good lord, he can make me hot and wanting with little more than a touch.* A groan rose to her lips when his tongue traced the welt. Her knees fell apart, giving him better access, while his hands traced the inside her thigh, moving higher and higher until she felt them slide inside her wet cunt.

Her knees came up on the bed, lifting her buttocks when she felt his fingers replaced by his tongue.

"You are driving me crazy, Tanner."

"Good. I hope you want me as much as I want you."

"Oh God, yes," she whimpered, as the wetness flowed from inside her. He continued to pleasure her with his mouth and his fingers as she trembled, her clit swelling with blood as she rode his hand.

Once the tremors ceased, Tanner stood, bringing her down off the bed so she could stand in front of him, but he wouldn't let her turn around. "Ever had a man in your ass?"

"No," she whispered, shivering at the thought.

"Will you let me?" he murmured, his mouth trailing across her shoulder to her ear.

"Now?"

"It's up to you. I want you so bad, I ache." He licked her neck and she trembled. "I would love to have your ass grip me so hard, squeezing my cock as I come inside you."

"I want you to, but you'll have to show me, teach me."

"God baby, are you sure? Don't do this only because I asked."

"I've been curious before, but I didn't want just anyone to initiate me into the intense part of sex. I need you to show me."

* * * *

The thought of fucking her ass drove him past the point of no return as he brought her hips back toward him and ground them against his groin. "Do you have some kind of lubricant? I don't want to hurt you."

"Is it going to hurt?"

"Probably, but I'll make sure you are as ready as I can make you."

She trembled as his lips moved down her back. "In the night stand."

He retrieved the tube from the drawer and returned to her side. "Are you sure?" He trailed his hand over her shoulder and she shivered. She nodded her head 'yes' and he sighed.

"Come here then." He pushed her down on the bed and positioned a pillow under her hips. "Just relax. Let me do the work." His kissed her back, down her spine, licking and nibbling the soft skin as she moaned softly. He forced her to widen her stance as he dropped to his knees. Slipping his hands slowly up her legs, he spread her pussy lips and slipped a finger inside. Her vagina gripped him tightly as he curled the finger up under her pelvic bone to stroke her G spot. When he started stroking her from back to front, the rough pad of his tongue flicking her clit as he slid the digit in and out of her pussy, she moaned.

He wet his fingers with her pre-cum and slipped one past the ring of muscles in her ass, stroking her anus as she rocked her hips. She shifted her pelvis, pushing her clit harder against his tongue as he licked and sucked. Her breathing hitched in her throat for a second and she almost screamed, her thick juices flooding his mouth while he continued to lap at her center and fuck her ass with his finger.

She sagged back on the bed as he rolled her over and moved behind her.

"That's cold," she whispered as he dropped slick lube on her ass before sliding his finger back inside in anus, spreading and stretching. He kept up his pace for several long minutes and didn't stop until she started to moan and wiggle.

"I'll warm it up. I promise." He stood behind her and spread her legs, his cock nudging her back entrance. "Relax, baby."

"I'm trying."

"I know." He licked up her spine as he continued to push against the tight ring until she hissed.

"It burns."

"Only for a minute." The head of his penis penetrated her ass and he fought for control as his balls screamed for him to slam inside her and fuck her hard.

She let out a high pitched groan as she whispered, "Oh. My. God."

"Pretty intense, huh," he groaned.

"You aren't kidding. That's incredible."

"You're going to feel full so relax and enjoy. I'm almost all the way inside," he growled.

"Just do it."

He slowly slid the rest of his cock in as he hissed.

"Fuck me hard, please. Oh God, please."

Pulling back until he almost slipped out, before he pushed back inside, he whispered, "You are so unbelievably tight. I'm tryin' to make this last."

She wiggled her backside against his groin. Gritting his teeth, his jaw starting to ache, he began to move. He drove into her, harder and faster, making her whimper beneath him as her own climax neared. Her sex quivered, sending shock waves to his toes as her ass gripped him and he couldn't hold back any longer. Driving into her almost wildly, they climaxed together, their heavy moans rising to an almost fevered pitch.

He kissed her back and ran his tongue up her spine to the nape of her neck, as goose bumps rose along her skin.

"Mmm..." she moaned, a shiver running down her spine.

As he pulled out of her, they both groaned heavily. She sank onto the bed, as he went into the bathroom to clean up. Tanner brought a warm washcloth and told her to roll over as he moved to sit on the bed next to her and softly cleaned her off.

Once she had dried off, he lay down beside her and she rolled over so she could rest her head on his chest, tracing the hair down his belly almost to his groin.

"We should probably get dressed."

"Why? I kind of like this." He smiled against her hair.

"Me, too, but I thought we might do something else besides just have sex this afternoon."

"Sounds like a good plan to me."

* * * *

She liked this. It felt good to just lie with him and talk. During her relationship with Jack, their time together had always been limited, so she didn't have the pleasure of enjoying his company, other than in bed, for more than a couple of hours. Aware now of what had been going on, so many things made sense.

"This is nice," she murmured, but smiled when she heard his stomach rumble.

"I guess maybe we should get dressed after all. Sustenance could be required if we are going to continue this later," he teased.

"Um, probably," she laughed, pulling away from his side and standing so she could retrieve some clothes.

He rolled onto his side as she moved about the room, a wicked smile gracing his mouth.

"You need to stop looking at me like that or there won't be any food for a while." She sighed as her pussy started to throb and swell.

"But I like the view."

"Me, too," she said, raking his still naked body with her eyes. "You had better get dressed, though, while I go make something for supper."

"Oh, all right." Sighing exaggeratedly, he rose from the bed to find his clothes.

Her heart did a little flip in her chest as she was given the most amazing view of his ass. Her own heavy sigh reverberating through the room, she turned to retreat to the kitchen before she did something like forget food and just crawl back onto the bed with him.

A few moments later, he walked out of the bedroom dressed in his jeans and t-shirt as she watched from the kitchen, a small smile on her mouth. *Damn, he's easy on the eyes.* She sipped a glass of wine she had poured.

She raised her glass. "Care for some?"

He wrinkled his nose as he said, "I'm not much into wine. Have you got a beer around?"

"Sure," she said, pulling one from the refrigerator. "Spaghetti okay with you?"

"Sounds good," he replied. He took the beer from her hand and lifted the long neck to his lips. A moment later, he slipped an arm around her waist, pulled her tight against his chest and planted a quick kiss on her lips.

She sighed heavily once he pulled away, missing his warmth and wishing she didn't as frown lines settled between her eyes.

"What's wrong?"

"Nothing," she said as she turned back around to get the sauce from the cupboard.

He took her arm in his grasp and forced her to look at him as he asked, "Amy?"

"It's nothing, Tanner."

"Then why are you frownin'?"

"I just remembered that I forgot to do something, that's all."

"Are you sure? You make me nervous when you frown right after I've kissed you. You're makin' me self-conscious that way, woman."

His teasing banter lifted her spirits slightly as she tried to smile to reassure him. *Be careful, he's becoming way too important to you and you are going to lose your heart,* her head warned.

"It's fine, really. Why don't you go out on the balcony while I finish supper?"

"Okay." Her phone rang as he moved toward the sliding glass door.

"Aren't you gonna answer?"

"No. It's probably a telemarketer anyway." She stirred the sauce in the pan as they listened to the machine kick on with a beep.

"Amy, its Jack. I know you're home. I'm sitting outside the apartment and your car is here in the parking lot. Pick up." Her eyes met Tanner's across the room before she quickly walked over as she heard again, "Come on, Amy. Pick up the phone. I need to talk to you."

She grabbed the receiver as he watched from near the door, curiosity written across his features.

"What Jack?"

"Can I come up?"

"I don't want to see you."

Her eyes met Tanner's across the room as fear gripped her heart.

"But I love you, and I want to be with you," Jack said on the other end.

She turned her back to Tanner, whispering into the phone. "I don't care if you say you love me. You cheated on me for God's sake. Why can't you leave me alone? You aren't going to be faithful, so just stop this."

"I want to see you."

"No, Jack."

Her voice quivered as she tried to keep Tanner from hearing what she said.

"I love you. I miss you."

"I—"

"Just for a minute, Amy, please? I'll come up so we can talk."

"I'll talk to you later, Jack. I can't talk about this right now. No, don't come up here. I need to think and I can't do that with you here. I'll call you tomorrow," she murmured. "Bye."

She turned back around to face Tanner. "I'm sorry," she whispered.

He walked over to her and put his arms around her, pulling her to his chest. "It's all right."

"This isn't fair to you," she said, shaking her head. "You shouldn't have gotten involved with me. I'm afraid I'll end up hurting you in the end and I don't want to do that."

He ran his hands up and down her spine as she wrapped her arms around his neck. She pressed her face to his shoulder as tears burned the back of her eyes.

"I knew you had just gotten out of a relationship when we met. I didn't think things would happen this fast between us, not that I'm complainin'. I won't pressure you."

Her heart clenched at his words. *I wish I'd never met Jack Miller.* "I wish I had met you first," she whispered against his neck, before her lips traced along the column. She desperately wanted to reassure him, but her heart felt split in two.

"It probably wouldn't be a good idea to start that now. Dinner on the stove, remember?"

"Oh crap! I forgot!" She stepped back from him and headed back into the kitchen.

* * * *

He smiled as he saw her bustling around the stove, but then a frown settled on his face. He really didn't like the idea of her talking with this guy, Jack. She sounded too vulnerable on the phone, vulnerable to persuasion.

"I'll be right back. I want to get somethin' out of my truck." He pulled on his boots and headed for the door.

"Okay. Supper should be ready in a few minutes so don't be gone long."

He grabbed his keys, walked out the front door, and headed for the elevator. The doors opened and he stepped in, punching the button for the bottom floor. With any luck, this Jack character would still be hanging around outside. He wanted to have a little conversation with him.

The elevator opened and he walked toward the front doors. George talked with someone who appeared to be agitated. The man yelled and argued with the guard, his belligerent tone reaching Tanner before he had even got close to the desk.

"I'm sorry, sir, I can't let you go up there without permission from the resident."

"Why the hell not? It's not like I haven't been up there before and you know I have. You've seen me with Amy on several occasions." Tanner's steps slowed as he got near the man. At the mention of Amy's name, curiosity got the better of him, and he walked closer.

"I'm sorry, Mr. Miller. You can't go up to Ms. Russell's apartment without her permission," George reiterated.

The condescending tone he gave the security officer made anger race through Tanner. No one deserved to be treated like that, especially someone hard-working and only looking out for the residents of the building.

He walked up behind the man saying, "Hi, George."

"Well, good evening, Mr. Lewis," George responded, tipping his hat to Tanner.

"I'm going to run out to my truck for a minute, before I head back up to Amy's. I'll be right back," Tanner said, making sure the man standing in front of the security desk knew who he meant.

"Amy? You mean Amy Russell?" Jack grabbed Tanner's arm before he could turn away.

"Yeah," he growled, pulling his arm out of the other man's grasp, suppressing the urge to wipe off Jack's touch.

"Who the hell are you?" Jack yelled in his face.

"The man who will be lyin' next to her tomorrow mornin'." They stood toe-to-toe as Tanner balled his hands into fits at his sides, trying to keep his temper in check.

Raking Tanner with his gaze, Jack replied, "Well, well. She's hooked up with some nobody, has she? A step down, I'd say."

"At least I'm not about to cheat on her."

"You bastard."

"Actually, no. My parents were married at my conception. What about yours?"

Jack stepped back, apparently looking to take a swing as Tanner growled, "I wouldn't if I were you."

Jack dropped his fists and took a couple of steps back as he snarled, "Stay away from her."

"Not on your life," he snapped, his chest heaving from the tight rein he held on his temper.

"She's mine."

"Correct me if I'm wrong, but you weren't the one sharin' the shower with her several minutes ago." He smiled at the look of shock that rippled across Jack's face. *Let him wonder.*

Jack lost control of his temper, and swung but missed connecting with Tanner's face. The younger, more agile one, he sidestepped and brought his fist up, placing his well-aimed knuckles against Jack's chin. The other cowboy hit the floor, skidding across the tile several feet before he was out cold. Tanner stood over him waiting, hoping he would move so he could hit him again, but he lay silently in the same spot.

"Mr. Lewis, you had better go on back up to Ms. Amy's place. I have to call an ambulance and the police. I don't want you to get into trouble. I'm aware he swung first, but I'm sure there will be a stink."

"Thanks, George." He smiled at the security guard as his anger dissipated and he flexed the knuckles of his hand. "Let me know if the police want to talk to me."

"No problem. I like Ms. Amy, and I didn't like seeing her with this no good guy in the first place."

He stuck out his hand and George took it in a firm handshake before he headed back for the elevator and the beautiful girl he'd left upstairs. When he reached her floor and the door slid open, she stood on the other side.

"Where did you go? Timbuktu?"

Tanner smiled as he grabbed her around the waist and dropped his head so he could take her lips with his. He needed to feel her against him, wanted to feel her respond to him like she'd done before.

"No, just downstairs for a minute."

"It took you long enough. The food is ready."

"Good, I'm hungry," he said, following her through the door.

She had already set the table with two plates and dished up the food, setting a beer down for him and some wine for her. He pulled out her chair and after she sat down, she picked up her fork.

Tanner moved to his own chair, grabbed the beer and took a long sip before setting it back down.

When she saw the blood across his knuckles, she asked, "What happened to your hand?"

"It's nothin'."

"It's not nothing, Tanner, you're bleeding." She stood and went back into the kitchen, returning a moment later with a wet paper towel and some ice.

"Amy, its fine." He could tell by the look on her face when she realized what he had done.

"You met Jack downstairs, didn't you?"

"I don't know what you mean."

Releasing a heavy sigh and rolling her eyes, she murmured, "Men! You knew he was downstairs and you just had to go down and confront him." She tenderly wiped the blood from his hand and placed the ice across his knuckles. "I should kick your butt for doing this," she murmured. "Why did you do that?"

"Because I care about you and he hurt you," Tanner replied, wondering how she couldn't understand. *Doesn't she realize how much I care about her?* "You said you were going to call him later."

"You don't need to get involved in this, Tanner. This is between me and Jack."

"Bullshit!" The look on her face almost enough to make him laugh, almost. "Do you love him?" He pulled his hand out of her grasp.

"I don't know, Tanner. I'm confused." She stood and walked over to the sliding glass door.

"After all he's done to you and you still care about him?" He stepped behind her, putting his hands on her shoulders.

"I don't know what I want anymore."

"I can't help you make up your mind. I care about you, but I won't try to compete with him for your affections. We're good together."

"Don't you think I know that? Don't you think I know he's not good for me? He cheated on me and abused me."

"What do you mean, he abused you?"

"I didn't tell you this before, but he smacked me around a little. I got tired of it and when I found out he had been sleeping around, that just sealed the deal and I left."

"How can you think about being with him?"

"I don't know. I wish I did."

"I wish I knew what to say. He used you. He took your love and crushed it." He slid his hands down her arms, making goose bumps raise along the surface.

"I wish I'd never met him. I know I shouldn't ever want to see him again, but…" she whispered, turning so she could look into his face.

"I think I should go. You don't need me here complicatin' things." He dropped his hands and turned to leave.

"I don't want you to," she murmured. "Please stay."

God, the look on her face tore him up inside. He knew what it felt like to love someone who ripped his heart to pieces and didn't care where the tattered remains landed. Diane had done that to him. He was beginning to care for Amy more than he wanted to, but she didn't know what she wanted.

"I think its best I head for home. You need to decide what you want before anythin' more happens between us. I'll call you when I get there," he said, gathering his belongings. He almost changed his mind when he heard Amy whimper behind him, but he didn't, he couldn't. She needed to figure things out and as long as he stayed, he was afraid it would sway her one way or the other. If she decided she indeed wanted to be with the other guy, it would hurt.

"Please don't go."

"I can't stay, Amy. You need to decide what you want."

He grabbed his bag and headed for the front door as she followed on his heels. As he reached the opening, he turned and pulled her to his chest, wrapping his arms around her before stepping back.

Caressing her face with his eyes, he whispered, "I'll call you when I get home." The door shut behind him, but he could hear the heavy sobs on the other side. Forcing his feet to move, he moved toward the elevator as he resisted the urge to turn around.

As he reached the main lobby, the police were finishing up their report so he stopped and gave them a statement. They didn't hold him after he supplied them his phone number and address, since George corroborated his story of self-defense.

He felt like his heart was breaking in two as he looked up at the black windows of Amy's apartment complex before he started his truck and pulled out onto the dark highway.

Chapter 13

True to his word, Tanner called her when he got home but the conversation came out short and clipped with frustration.

"I guess you're home." Her voice sounded curt and hoarse from crying, even to her own ears.

"Yeah, I just rolled in."

"I'm glad you made it okay. The drive wasn't bad, I guess."

"No."

"Maybe I can drive down myself in a couple of weeks."

"I suppose," he answered, noncommittal.

"If you don't want to see me, say so." Her voice rose as the anger built in her chest.

"I want to, but I think you need to take some time away from me and from your other friend. You said you are confused about your feelin's for him and I assume for me, too."

"I care about you, Tanner. I don't want to lose what we started."

"But I don't want you to be with me on the rebound. If you are in love with him, then you need to do what you need to do."

"I'm not in love with him."

"That's not what you said."

"I didn't say I'm in love with him, either. I said I'm confused. I know I'm tired of being used. He just wants a plaything, and I don't want to be his toy of the week. I want someone who cares about me for me. Can you be that guy?"

"I can be anythin' you need me to be, but I'm not gonna be your second choice. Give it a couple of weeks. Okay?"

"All right, I won't call you or anything." A lump formed in her throat as she choked on tears. "I miss you already."

"I know. I miss you, too. I'll talk to you in a couple of weeks."

"A couple of weeks. It's going to be hard."

"Well if it's meant to be, then two weeks isn't too long."

"Yeah…well, I better go. I've got a lot of thinking to do. I'll talk to you later."

"Okay. Bye."

"Bye," she whispered. The tears came again as the final click echoed in her ear, signaling the end of their conversation and maybe the end of their relationship, too. She hoped with all her heart it wasn't the latter as the silence stretched into the darkness of the night.

* * * *

She avoided Jack like the plague until she ran into him at a rodeo her and Jason competed in a week after Tanner left, sporting a huge bruise to his jaw. Amy didn't ask him about it, but she smiled behind her hand, knowing Tanner stood up for her. Having that hunky cowboy on her side, felt wonderful.

Chris rarely went with her to shows, but this competition, her friend tagged along. Amy shivered as Jack sauntered by and gave her a wicked grin on his way to the arena.

"I really hate him, but it makes me wonder how he got that big bruise on his chin."

"Tanner gave it to him."

"You're kidding, right?"

"No." She went on to tell Chris about the incident, filling her in on the details.

"I'm confused. You didn't see what happened?"

"No, but that's the impression I got."

"Wait, a minute. Tanner spent the weekend with you?" Amy blushed. "Ah."

"Don't read more into this than there is. We aren't serious or anything."

"Sure. I can tell by the blush on your cheeks. You two slept together, didn't you?" Chris questioned and Amy's blush deepened. "It's not something to be embarrassed by, Am. I'm glad you two hooked up."

"I don't want to hurt him, Chris, and I'm afraid I'm going to." She pulled at the cinch strap under the belly of the horse.

"Why would you?"

"I'm confused. I don't know what my feelings are for Jack and now things have gotten complicated between me and Tanner."

"I thought you didn't want anything more to do with Jack."

"I don't or at least I don't think I do. Hell, I'm not sure what I want anymore. No more talk of him. Let's go check out the competition."

The two women sat in the stands for a while, enjoying watching the bronco riding event until Amy made a trip to the bathroom before her and Jason's had to ride. As she approached the restroom, Jack stepped out from between two vehicles.

"Amy, I need to talk to you."

"I don't want to talk to you."

"Too bad," he said, grasping her arm tightly in his hand and dragging her to a secluded area behind the bathroom.

"You can't push me around, Jack." She pulled her arm from his grasp.

"Are you seeing that guy that hit me at your apartment?"

"What do you care? I need time to decide what I want and you pushing me doesn't help, but then again, you never did care what I wanted, did you?"

Trying to pull her into his arms, he said, "I can give you the things you like, Amy. I'll pay your rent, buy you things," he murmured, trying to nuzzle her neck.

She pulled back. "You want me to be your mistress?"

"If that's the name you want to use. I love you."

"Then why did you cheat on me and hit me?"

"It only happened once, babe. I swear it won't again."

"That's your story now Jack, but at the next stop, you'll find some skinny little bimbo to warm your bed while I'm at home working my ass off. No thanks." She stepped back, putting more distance between them as she continued. "You know, I considered getting back together with you, but now I know you don't care about me at all, my mind has been made up. You can't understand how someone could walk away from you, can you? I really hope someday you find the girl you are madly in love with and she cheats on you, just like you cheated on me." She pulled away from him. "And yes, I'm seeing that guy. Tanner cares about me for me, not what I can do for him and he's better in bed than you." She knew her raised voice could probably be heard all over the growing crowd, but she didn't care. "So take your proposition and shove it up your ass!"

"If you want to go to him, that's fine. You were nothing more than a hot piece anyway," Jack snorted.

"Fuck you." Amy turned on her heel and stomped out into the crowd just as Chris rounded the corner.

"Are you okay? I saw Jack push you in here."

"I'm fine, pissed off but fine." Her back ramrod straight, she quickly walked to her truck, disappearing around the front of her horse trailer. She sighed heavily and shook her head, her heart lighter as she realized her affection for Jack did not run as deep as she thought.

* * * *

For the rest of the two weeks, Amy's feelings for Tanner became more and more apparent. She sat by the phone, wishing he would call, but not giving in to calling him herself until after the full two weeks.

One day at the hospital, Chris asked her, "When are you going to give up and call him?"

"I can't, Chris. I caused him so much pain when he left and after our disagreement on the phone when he got home, I think I need to give things a little more time."

"Don't give him too much, Am. You might lose your opportunity. He might move on without you."

"I hope not."

Almost two weeks to the day he met her at the rodeo, she gave up. She picked up her cell phone. Her heart skipped a beat and her hands started to shake when she heard, "Hello?"

"Tanner?"

"Yeah?" The question in his voice gave her pause and made her nervous.

"It's Amy."

"Hey. How have you been?"

"Good. Working a lot."

"Yeah, I've been keepin' busy, too."

"Are you playing at the bar this weekend?"

"Tonight, yes."

She whispered into the receiver, crossing her fingers, hoping he hadn't given up on her. "Can I see you?"

"Are you drivin' down here?"

"I can, if you'll see me. I miss you," she murmured.

"God, baby, I miss you, too. I can probably get the guy to switch with me so we can have some time together," he answered. "I'll call him real quick and find out then I'll call you back. I don't want you drivin' down here for one day."

"I don't care how much time we have. I'll throw some things in a bag and leave in the next couple of minutes. Call me on my cell when you find out. That way I'll know where to find you."

"Okay. I'll call you back." She heard a click as he hung up and she headed into the bedroom.

She threw some clothes in a bag and grabbed a couple of things to eat on the way. Stuffing her phone in her purse, before she grabbed her keys and her bag, she locked the door and shut it behind her. Her stomach quivered like a thousand butterflies fluttering around as she almost ran to her car. She threw her bag in the back, and as she slid into the driver's seat, her cell phone rang again. She checked the phone number and smiled.

"Hello?"

"Hey. He said he'd take tonight." She thought she heard a smile in his voice and her heart soared.

"Where do you want me to meet you?"

"Can you find your way back to my parents' place?"

"I think so, but I don't have Chris' GPS. How about I call you when I get into town and you can direct me."

"Okay. I'll talk to you in four hours."

"I can't wait."

"Me either."

Apprehension clenched her gut and she sighed, trying to calm her nerves. She put on some music, but had to be aware of her foot on the gas pedal as the speedometer closed in on ninety.

About four hours later, she drove into the outskirts of Brenham and picked up her cell, hitting redial to call him back. Her heart thumped loudly in her ears as anticipation rolled through her.

When he answered, she said, "I'm here."

"Great. I got to thinkin'. Why don't I meet you at the burger place on the left as you come into town? That way I don't have to worry about you gettin' lost."

"Okay. I think I see it now so I'll pull over and wait for you."

"I'll be there in about ten minutes."

"See you then."

She sat in the car at the burger shop, nervously waiting for him to arrive, her stomach in knots. The drive from Dallas had been the longest she had ever made. Even the trip from Oregon didn't seem as long as this one. When he pulled into the parking lot, she got out of her car and walked around to the driver's side of his truck just as he got out. She stared for a few seconds, trying to take in everything about him that might have changed in the last two weeks. After a minute or so, she threw her arms around his shoulders, hugging him tightly as his arms slipped around her with a groan.

Stepping apart, he gave her one of his sexy grins. "Do you want to follow me back?"

"Sure. It probably wouldn't be a good idea to leave my car here." She stepped back a little. He raised her hand to his lips, brushing them softly across the knuckles, sending a shiver down her back.

"I'll see you when we get there."

"Okay," she said, heading to her car.

She followed him to his parents' place, pulling in behind him as his mother and father stepped out of the house onto the front porch.

Getting out of the car as Tanner came around to the driver's side, embarrassment colored her cheeks when she thought of how this must look to them. "This probably looks bad to your parents. I should get a room in town," she whispered for his ears only.

"Why?"

"I don't want them to think I'm loose or something if I stay here with you."

"Right now, all they know is you drove down so we could spend some time together. We'll worry about sleepin' arrangements later tonight." He slipped his arm around her waist as they walked toward the front door.

"Hello, Mr. and Mrs. Lewis."

"I thought we had that straightened out before. It's Scott and this is Mary," he said, introducing his wife.

"I'm sorry, Scott. It's nice to meet you, Mary," Amy replied with a smile.

"I'm glad you came by to visit. How have you been?"

"Good. I've been keeping busy."

"Dad, did I tell you Amy and her partner got first in the rodeo up in Fort Worth a couple of weeks ago?"

"No, you didn't tell me. That's great!" Scott exclaimed. "I'm proud of you."

Amy blushed under the compliment.

"Did you come down *just* to see Tanner?" Mary questioned skeptically.

"Yes, ma'am, but I thought I would visit Chris' parents, too. They were so nice to me when I visited."

"I'm sure Catherine would love to for you to visit. Lunch will be ready soon, Tanner. Don't disappear."

"Well, I've got work to do in the barn. I'll talk to you kids later," Scott told them as he stepped down from the porch.

"Your mother doesn't like me," Amy murmured to Tanner as she watched the woman retreat into the house.

"You're kiddin', right?"

"No, she's judging me for coming down here."

"No, she's not. She's protective of me. I'm sure she doesn't want me to get hurt again."

"I'm sorry. I probably should have thought about this more before I came down here, but I wanted to see you."

She met his eyes and the question burned bright in his gaze, the question she came to give him the answer to, if he wanted to hear what she had to say.

"What would you like to do?"

"Spend time with you. That's what I came here for," she murmured, sliding her arm around his waist and stepping in front of him.

"Mmm...I'm sure we can think of somethin'." Tanner groaned as her breasts pressed against his chest.

"I hope you are thinking the same thing I am," she whispered as she tilted her head back.

"Maybe. I want to get you alone so I can find out if we are thinkin' the same thing."

"Could be fun. But…"

"But what?"

"I think we need to talk," she said, pulling away from him. "Can we go up to your place?"

Raising his eyebrow questioningly. "Sure, but I have one question."

"What's that?"

"Am I going to like this or not?"

With a wry smile, she replied, "Maybe…"

"That isn't an answer."

"I know." She pulled away and headed toward the barn, Tanner close on her heels. They walked up the stairs to his apartment, and as he pushed open the door, memories of their time spent up there came flooding back. Making love with him had really been the start of her feelings. Even then she knew he had become important to her, too important to let Jack mess things up.

She walked toward the couch and took a seat as he asked from the kitchen, "Would you like somethin' to drink or eat? I think my mom expects us for lunch at the house, but I have a few things in here to drink."

"Whatever you have is fine." She nervously wiped her palms across the thighs of her jeans.

Tanner grabbed two beers from the refrigerator and handed her one as he approached the couch and sat down.

"So what's this all about?"

She took a long drink to steady her nerves. "I had a run-in with Jack at a rodeo ten days ago."

"What happened?"

"He pushed me into a secluded corner."

"He didn't hit you did he?"

"No. That's one thing I won't *ever* put up with again."

"And?"

"We had a conversation, and he told me I was nothing more to him than a 'hot piece'. I wanted to hit him so bad, I could taste it."

"But you didn't, did you?"

"No. I wish I had though. By the way, you left a pretty nice bruise on his chin."

He laughed and she smiled.

"I can picture you takin' a swing at him, but you need to be careful. He could have hurt you."

"I couldn't help it. When he said that, I realized he never cared for me, I mean, not the way he kept saying he did. He only said he loved me because he knew I was pulling away from him. I don't think anyone has ever told him no before. I'm sure his ego took a beating, but I don't care."

"Oh, darlin'. It doesn't matter now." He pulled her into his arms and she willingly slid into his embrace.

"I'm sorry about what happened at the apartment, Tanner." She rubbed her face against his shoulder, loving the feel of his arms around her.

A frown on his face, he asked, "Sorry we made love?"

"No! Never that," she exclaimed, pulling back in his arms. "I'm sorry that I made such a mess of things, the whole thing with Jack. I should never have told him I'd talk to him the next day or any day. He caught me off guard."

"It was obvious by how upset you were you still cared for him, even just a little. We can't always turn off our affection like a faucet." He looked down and she hoped her feelings reflected bright in her eyes.

"I know," she whispered leaning against him again as he stroked her back. "I know now, though, I don't want anything more to do with him. He's my past."

"So, what happens now?" Tanner murmured, kissing her hair as he pulled her closer.

"That depends." She slid her hand across his stomach, smiling when she heard him take a sharp breath.

"On what?" She heard the groan rumble in his chest.

When she lifted her face, the tight control he held onto his body reflected on his face, control she wanted desperately to take away from him. At this moment, she wanted nothing more than to feel his hands on her, his mouth on her breasts and let him make her feel loved.

As he finally opened his eyes, she stared deeply into them and said, "On you."

Chapter 14

"I'd do anythin' for you."

"There is something I need to say, but I want to make sure you understand what I'm telling you." Amy held his gaze with her own.

"What?" His voice came out in a tortured moan.

"I love you, Tanner," she whispered, not lowering her eyes.

"Amy, I..."

She wanted him to see the truth, to know what she said reflected the feelings in her heart, but when he wasn't able to finish, the pain nearly brought her to her knees. He couldn't say it. He couldn't tell her he loved her. She finally lowered her head, trying to hide the tears pooling at the corners of her eyes while she tried to stand. She needed to get away from here, from him. She thought the pain she experienced when she found out Jack had lied to her broke her heart, but nothing compared to this. The razor sharp teeth of the knife tearing her heart to ribbons was more than she could bear.

"It's okay," she choked out. "I understand this is a bit of a shock, after everything that's happened, but I'm going to go now." She headed for her escape route as Tanner came to his feet.

"Amy..."

"No, Tanner, it's fine. I'm just going to go home."

He followed her to the door. Right before she opened it, intent on getting away, he put his hand against the hard surface and slammed it shut again.

"You're not leavin' until we talk about this."

"Let it be, Tanner," she sobbed, not able to hold her tears any longer as she laid her forehead against the door.

"Look at me." He took her shoulders in his hands and tried to turn her around as he repeated, "Look at me."

Unable to stop him, she faced him and he put his finger under her chin to bring her face up to his.

"Give a fella a chance," he began as he swiped his thumb across her cheek to wipe away the tears. "You surprised me. I didn't expect this. I thought I was alone in my feelin's, but I guess not."

"What are you saying?"

"I love you, too, Amy Russell," he finished, pulling her against his chest and burying his face in her hair. "I never thought I'd say those words to anyone again, after Diane, but you've made me realize that I really didn't love her. My feelin's for her are nothin' like what I hold in my heart for you."

She pulled back in his arms. "Tell me again."

He smiled and looked deeply into her eyes. "I love you. I think I fell in love with you the first time I saw you as I walked across the round pen after my butt had been in the dirt." He ran his fingers down her cheek, and she snuggled her face against his hand.

"You were cute with your butt in the dirt," she murmured.

He bent his head and pressed his lips to hers, groaning as they met. She wrapped her arms around him, pressing close to him, a soft moan rumbling in her chest. His tongue brushed her lips, seeking entrance. She opened her mouth, and their tongues sought each other when he deepened the kiss.

The phone rang, and as the ring finally penetrated through the desire that raged between them, Tanner pulled away from her slightly. She followed, burying her head against his chest and kissing him where his shirt exposed the curling hair.

He whispered, "I need to get the phone."

She smiled when he groaned and pulled out of her arms to grab the receiver.

"Hello?"

She followed, continuing to kiss the exposed skin, smiling when his skin quivered under her touch.

"Yeah, Mom, we'll be there in a minute." He hung up the phone, before he wrapped his arms around her and said, "Lunch is ready."

"I kind of figured that out. Are you sure you don't want a quick cold shower before you go?" Her eyes wandered down the front of him, resting on his obvious erection outlined by his jeans.

He pressed his hand against the bulge between his legs as he smiled, "Maybe I should, but only if you join me."

She walked up to him, pushing against him as she whispered, "No way. We would never get to the house if we did. We can take care of your problem in a little while."

"You are a witch, you know that?"

She giggled and turned away to walk toward the door, pulling it open as he followed behind. When they reached the bottom of the stairs, she shot him a teasing glance and started to run toward the main house. He chased her to the front door, pushing her against the side of the house and giving her a quick but passionate kiss before releasing her.

Her rapid breaths mingled with his as he said, "I just wanted to make sure you are as wound up as I am."

"Mmm…you don't have to do anything to get me that way, cowboy," she murmured, before he opened the door and they walked inside.

* * * *

After lunch, Tanner helped Scott with a few chores in the barn as Amy helped Mary with the dishes. A huge smile graced his lips when he returned to the house. It thrilled him that his dad liked Amy so well. He chuckled softly when he thought about the conversation in the barn. His dad's protective side came out as they discussed the relationship between Amy and him. He knew his dad wanted to make sure his son had honorable intensions toward his good friend's daughter. *I'm glad we've already established our feelings for each other. Things might have gotten a little tense with Dad, if we hadn't.* As Tanner walked through the door after he finished the hay, Amy quickly moved to his side.

"All finished with the dishes?"

"Yeah," Amy replied, her voice sounding a little strained.

"Somethin' wrong?"

"No, not really. Can we go?"

"Uh…sure," he said, before he turned to his parents and said, "We'll see you later."

"Of course, son," Scott replied, flipping on the television.

Tanner and Amy walked out the front door and headed back toward the barn and his apartment with their arms wrapped around each other.

"Are you sure there isn't anythin' wrong? You seem distracted."

Amy smiled what appeared to be a little hesitantly, before she murmured, "Distracted by you."

He allowed a grin to cross his lips as he said, "Well, there is still the problem we discussed earlier."

"What problem?"

"This one," he whispered against her lips, moving her hand to his cock that pulsed behind the fly of his jeans.

"Oh yeah, I remember now. We'll have to see what we can do about that...problem," she replied, moving her hand against him. He groaned before he took her lips with his and pinned her against the wall behind her.

Pulling his mouth away, he rasped, "We should probably take this upstairs. I don't want my parents to catch us out here. I'd rather have you alone, in my bed, when we make love."

"That's probably a good idea." His hand slid up her side and moved across her breast

She moaned when he pulled his hand away to lead her up the stairs and through the door, shutting it firmly behind them.

He pushed her up against the wooden surface, taking her mouth in a kiss meant to weaken her knees. Their tongues danced while his hand found her breast again, raking his palm across her nipple. He pulled his mouth from hers to trail little kisses from her lips to her jaw and down her neck as she tipped her head to the side to give him better access. When his mouth found the spot at her collarbone, he felt her shiver and push her breast farther into his hand.

He was on fire. He wanted her so badly he could taste it; taste her, in the back of his throat, on his tongue. Knowing if he didn't get this under control, they would be fucking right there, he backed away, grasping her hand in his, before he led her into his bedroom. They stopped at the end of the bed and he took her in his arms again, taking possession of her lips with all the pent-up desire racing through his body. He ravished her mouth, his tongue sliding inside as his hands roamed her back, slipping beneath her shirt to work it up over her head. He unhooked her bra, moving around to take her naked breast in his palm. He lifted his head to see her face flushed with desire as she whimpered with need.

"God, I want you," he rasped, before he took her lips again in a heart-stopping kiss. "I need to fuck you so bad, I hurt."

Slipping the button free on her jeans, he worked them down her slim legs before his hands slid back up, grazing the inside of her thigh. Dropping to his knees, he kissed her belly while she stepped out of her pants. She inhaled sharply when he slipped two digits inside her pussy to find her slick and wet. Her hands grasped at his shoulders and her legs trembled as he pleasured her with his fingers, his thumb caressing her clit.

He sat her down on the edge of the bed, kneeling as he kissed her thighs, working his way to her swollen pussy. When his tongue found her, she bucked against his mouth and moaned before she rested back on the bedspread. His tongue slid along her folds, finding his way to her clit while he slipped his fingers deep inside, curling them up under her pubic bone to massage her G spot.

She gave into her desire as the moisture flowed across his fingers and his tongue. When she finally quieted and only small tremors rippled through her body, he toed off his boots and slid his jeans down, flipping them across the room. He moved over her, finding her breast with his mouth, sucking and pulling at her nipple, bringing it to a hard nub under his lips. Her body quivered as her desire rose again.

"Tanner, please," she whispered, trying to bring him up so that she could take his mouth with hers, but he would have none of it. He wanted her hot and panting beneath him. Continuing his assault on her senses, he let his hand slip down between them, finding her swollen pussy and sliding inside. "Oh God, Tanner, you're driving me crazy."

Lifting his head, he smiled as he whispered, "I know."

"You don't play fair," she grumbled, when he took the other breast in his mouth.

She began to whimper, telling him without words how close she was, without sending her over the top. He let go of her breast and took her mouth with his as he slipped his hard cock inside her, and groaned into her mouth.

"You feel so good. I've missed this," he murmured, not daring to move yet, lest things end too soon.

She whimpered again, putting her heels on the bed and lifting her buttocks so he could drive deeper, taking all of him inside her.

"Please."

His let his cock slowly slide in and out, bringing them both closer and closer to that blinding end they both sought. When she wrapped her legs around his hips and he began to pound his groin against hers, it was too much. His name slipped from between her lips on a strangled cry as she rippled around him, pulling his own climax from deep inside.

Resting his weight on his arms, he let his head rest on her shoulder for a moment while she ran her fingertips along his back.

He rose up enough so he could see her eyes. "I love you," he whispered, stroking her cheek with his fingers.

"I love you," she murmured, tears glistening on her lashes.

"Why are you cryin'?"

"Because I can't believe I found you." She choked back a sob.

"Don't cry, baby."

"I'm sorry."

"Nothin' to be sorry for. We just have to figure out what happens now."

They both groaned out loud when he slipped out of her warmth. They scooted up toward the middle of the bed and he pulled her into his arms while she rested her head on his chest, stroking the curling hairs.

"What do you mean we need to figure out what happens now?"

"It's kind of hard to be in a relationship if we live four hours apart." His let his fingers stroke her arm as she snuggled against him.

"I know."

Silence stretched between them for several minutes until he felt Amy drift off to sleep. He silently contemplated what their lives would bring in the months and years ahead. They could buy some land here in Brenham and raise horses and children together or maybe move up closer to Dallas. It didn't matter to him. As long as he had her by his side, he could do anything.

After an hour or so, she woke up when he let his soft lips played along her shoulder and his warm hand caressed her breasts.

"Mmm...that's fantastic," she whispered.

He lifted his head and gave her a smile before moving his attention to the soft mound near his mouth. Alternating between sucking and licking, it was only seconds before her nipple hardened under his ministrations. Arching her back, she pushed her breast into his mouth and wrapped her fingers in his hair.

I would love to wake her like this every day for the rest of ours lives. He took her hard nub between his teeth and nibbled.

He feasted on her skin while his hand slipped down her belly and through the curls, sliding over the hood protecting her clit from his touch, before he drove his fingers deep within her. Her pussy gripped him and trembled when he moved them in and out. His mouth left her breast to continue the journey down her stomach, kissing and nibbling, bringing a wild moan from deep within her. When he finally reached the spot he wanted, she almost screamed as his tongue rasped along her swollen clit. One, two flicks had her spiraling out of control and hot juices flowing over his fingers.

Her trembling slowed while she tried to catch her breath and he moved back up her body, taking her nipple in his mouth again.

She moaned as desire began to stir, but now it was her turn. He smiled as she pushed the hard surface of his chest, making sure he understood what she wanted as he lay on the bed, exposing everything to her wandering hands. She moved over him, taking his mouth with hers, their tongues dancing for a moment before she ripped her mouth away to kiss his jaw. Her tongue circled the shell of his ear, sending a shiver down his body. She moved to nibble his earlobe for a moment. A moan rose to his lips when she licked his neck, along his shoulder and shimmied herself down his body, taking his coppery disk in her mouth.

She sucked and nipped at the nub with her teeth, and he inhaled sharply, another groan rumbling in his throat. Her hand slipped between them, finding the crease between his thigh and his cock, skimming south until she could cup his balls in her hand. Her lips found a new path, down the center of his chest, following the line of dark hair. She kissed and licked as she moved, until her mouth hovered over his rock hard cock, standing tall and proud, begging for her warm lips.

The rough pad of her tongue rasped against the tip, licking the pre-cum as his body jerked at the caress. All he wanted was to have her mouth surrounding him, but he had a feeling payback was going to be a bitch.

She grasped his cock at the base before sliding up and down as his hips surged against her, trying to get her to move faster. She kept her rhythm slow while her tongue played on the tip and her hand moved along him. A tortured groan slipped from between his lips and he knew she loved every minute of his torment when she softly giggled.

Finally, she opened her mouth to take all of him inside as a sound left his throat that he didn't recognize and he groaned. "Oh God, baby."

Wrapping his fingers in her hair, he pushed her head down as she sucked. Her hand cupped his balls and they tighten in her grasp, bringing him to the brink of insanity before he grabbed her shoulders and forced her to stop. He pulled her on top of him, gave her a quick kiss on the mouth, and rolled her over so she lay beneath him. He slid inside her hot pussy as he moaned, "Fuck, you are so hot." He held on for a moment, his jaw clenched tight, trying to regain some control.

She wiggled her hips, causing him to moan out loud as he began to move, his own pelvis pounding hers. He pushed deep and hard, his movements almost frantic, bringing them both to the brink of climax before he surged against her. Their mingled cries of satisfaction filled the air around them.

Chapter 15

"What would you like for supper?" He watched from the bed as she slipped on her jeans, a sexy smile gracing his mouth.

"I don't know. It doesn't matter. I need food. You've made me hungry with all this activity."

Raising a questioning eyebrow, he grinned. "You'd better get used to it. I plan to keep you busy for the next century or so."

"Do you now?" She sashayed to where he sat on the edge of the bed and slid onto his lap, wrapping her arms around his shoulders and finding his ear with her tongue.

"All right, stop or we'll never get anythin' to eat." His ragged whisper did nothing to dissuade her from her task.

"But you said you were going to keep me busy," she whispered in his ear, before she moved to nibble at his earlobe.

"After we eat," he murmured, finally pulling away and forcing her to stand. "Let's go find some food."

"Fine, but remember—later."

"How could I forget?" He ran his hand down her backside as they headed for the door. "Italian sound good?"

"Perfect. I haven't had Italian food for a long time."

"Great. Marcellini's is awesome. Once we are done eatin', I need to stop of Pete's so I can tell Jerry thanks." He nuzzled her neck and whispered, "Besides, I want to dance with you. I love it when we move together, whether we are dancin' or making love."

"Mmm, me, too." She closed her eyes, loving the texture of his whiskered cheek rubbing over her skin.

When they arrived at the bar, he possessively held her waist as they moved inside, finding a small table off to the side of the stage. Tanner kissed her quickly and said, "I'll be right back."

"Okay. Do you want me to order anything in case the waiter comes by?"

"Sure. Get me a beer please."

"No problem."

Tanner made a bee line for the stage, stopping at the base as the singer jumped down. Amy watched as the two talked for several seconds, before the guy looked at her and gave Tanner a friendly shove. She smiled and shook her head as her eyes left the sexy ass of her lover to the others in the bar. Her gaze stopped on the four women two tables to her left, the same group who had draped themselves all over Tanner the first night they met. The glare thrown in her direction made her skin crawl. She was happy when Tanner returned to their table and slid into the seat next to her, pulling her close.

"What's wrong?"

"Nothing," she murmured as he slipped his arm across her shoulder.

"Then why the look?"

"Your fan club is here again." She glanced at the group behind him and he turned to see who she was talking about.

"So?"

"They obviously don't like us being together, by the looks I'm getting."

"I couldn't care less. I love you and I hope everyone in the bar knows by the time we leave."

The band started playing and Tanner took her hand, leading her onto the dance floor. He pulled her tight to his chest as they swayed to the music. His thigh slipped between hers. Her nipples tingled, aching for his touch and her pussy throbbed and filled as he forced her to slowly ride his thigh. Breathing sharply, she rested her forehead on his shoulder.

"You okay?" he murmured.

"Mmm. You should ask. You know what you're doing to me."

His soft chuckle met her ear. Her cheek rested against his and she closed her eyes while he whispered, "I love you" in her ear. *I don't think I'll ever get tired of hearing those words.*

When the song ended, they wandered back to their table and a couple of Tanner's friends came over. Tanner introduced her to his best friend, Brad and the two joked around for several minutes.

"We grew up together and hung out durin' high school."

"And competed for women," Brad teased. "So where has Tanner been hiding you?" Brad's appreciative gaze slid over her.

"Back off, buddy, she's mine," Tanner growled good-naturedly.

"Whoa, Tanner! Easy man! I'm not coming onto your girl." Brad raised his hands in defeat. "I wanted to find out where you've been hiding her, that's all."

She laughed when Tanner's eyes narrowed. "I don't live here in Brenham. I actually live in Dallas."

"So how did you and Tanner hook up?"

"I work with Chris, Tanner's neighbor. We came down here a few weeks ago to visit, and Tanner and I met then."

"That figures! Tanner grabbed you up before any other man even had a chance!"

Blushing under his compliment, she snuggled deeper into Tanner's embrace, still aware of the hostile glances coming from a few tables to the left.

"Get over it, Brad. I'm not letting go for a minute, so don't even think about goin' after my girl."

"Well, since this beautiful woman has taken you out of the pool of eligible men that just leaves more for me!" Brad teased. "I'll catch you later. I see several lonely females needing my attention."

As Brad left their table, she said, "I assume you two spent a lot of time pursuing the same girl."

"Not really. He makes it sound that way. We were both pretty good about it once one of us started dated someone exclusively, the other didn't try to cut in. I think a lot of the women around here like to compare the two of us, though."

"Why? I don't think there is much comparison myself." She let her eyes run over the handsome man next to her.

"Maybe because our features are so different. You know, him bein' blond, blue-eyed and me bein' dark hair with brown eyes."

"I prefer dark hair and brown eyes." She rubbed her nose against his playfully.

"You have to say that. You love me," he whispered as his lips wandered to her ear.

"Yes I do, and I can think of an exceptional way to show you." She let her hand wander to the crotch of his jeans, slowly massaging the semi-soft erection.

"You better stop doing that or we'll be leavin' here right now."

"I don't mind. I'm not into sharing you, anyway."

"Let's go then. I'd much rather be alone with you in my bed than let all these guys oglin' you, waitin' to find out if you are only with me temporarily." He took her hand before they headed for the door.

Their departure was stalled when the bartender waved for Tanner to come over from his spot at the bar. "Wait here. I'll be right back." He gave her a quick kiss on the lips and disappeared into the crowd.

A few moments later, Amy realized someone stood behind her as the hair prickled on her neck. She turned to find the black-haired woman who had been giving her dirty looks, standing intimidatingly close. She chose to ignore her, but the girl wasn't about to walk away.

"Something I can do for you?" Amy finally asked.

"Yeah, stay away from Tanner. He's mine."

Amy shrugged. "Not from where I'm standing."

"You won't be standing in a minute." The woman stepped closer.

"Go ahead and try it." She placed her hand on the girl's shoulder, pressing her thumb into the soft muscle, causing the other female to gasp in pain before she stepped back. "From what he's told me, I'm sure he's never whispered 'I love you' in your ear like he did mine after we had wild sex a little while ago."

"You'll be sorry you got between me and my man," the woman spat, before turning on her heel and stomping back to her table.

Tanner returned to her side a moment later. "What was that all about?"

"She wasn't happy we are together and she tried to tell me to stay away from you."

"Well, you don't have anything to worry about with her. I've never been interested in her. Now, there is a big soft bed at my house waitin' for two people to have really hot sex like you and me."

* * * *

Amy and Tanner sat on the couch in his apartment the next afternoon, snuggled together watching a movie. Before the movie was over, he flipped the television off and turned toward her as she gave him a confused look.

"Something wrong?"

"No." He shifted so he could look into her eyes. "I think we need to talk about how we are going to do things with us living so far apart. You're going back to Dallas tomorrow, right?"

"Yeah, I have to work the next day."

"Well, I've been thinkin' and I think you need to move down here." He told her in a stern voice, expecting a fight.

"What? You are kidding, right?"

"No, I want you with me."

"I want to be with you, too, but I can't quit my job, Tanner."

"I can support us. We can live here at my place."

She looked as though she questioned his sanity. "Wait a damned minute! One, I'm not living with you. Two, I'm not quitting my job at the hospital. What the hell would we live on? You don't make that much at the bar and I'm sure your parents don't pay you for helping around here."

"No, they don't pay me, but we wouldn't pay rent here."

"I'm not quitting my job, Tanner, and that's final. My life is nursing and I'm not going to sit on my butt while you work. Practicality is important here." She jumped to her feet and began to pace.

"But you shouldn't have to work."

"I want to. Why can't you understand?"

"So how are we going to see each other if you are four hours away?"

"We'll make the trips back and forth. I can come down when I'm off and you can come up there when you are able to."

"But I won't be able to see you as much as I would if you lived with me."

"You'll survive. We can be together as much as possible," she murmured, sliding back onto the couch next to him.

"How long are things going to go on like that? We can't do this indefinitely."

"I don't know. We'll figure things out, I'm sure. It's not like we're getting married or anything."

* * * *

The next words out of his mouth drove her head up sharply, and she contemplated whether he had lost his mind.

"Maybe we *should* get married."

He can't be serious. "We aren't getting married." She shook her head in denial.

"I know I love you. That's all I need."

"I love you, too, but we can't get married right now."

She stood up and began to pace again, nervous as to the direction of this conversation. His mother didn't like her, they lived four hours apart from each other, and now, he wanted to get married. *He's crazy. I've fallen in love with a crazy man.*

"Why?"

"This is nuts, Tanner. I can't even contemplate this at the moment. We need to get to know each other better." She continued to pace as nervous agitation rippled through her. "Let's just put this talk on hold for now."

"All right, we won't talk about this right now. You need to come here though," he ordered, as she continued to pace.

She whipped around to look into his face at his demanding words, but the smile on his lips told her he was teasing. Sliding next to him, she poked him in the chest as she said, "Don't get bossy with me, mister. I don't take orders well, never have. We'll continue this conversation another time. Now, are you going to make love to me again or not?"

"Oh yeah, I'm most definitely gonna make love to you several more times before you have to leave. I love to hear you scream my name as you come."

"Good. I can't seem to get enough of you," she murmured, her lips finding his neck, nibbling softly as she felt his hands roam down her arms.

* * * *

Amy slid out of the bed and headed into the kitchen to make coffee. His words of marriage the day before frightened her. She wasn't about to leave her job in Dallas. *We'll have to figure out something else.* She sipped the hot brew and waited for Tanner to wake up.

When he finally joined her in the kitchen, he asked, "Why did you get up so early?"

"Habit, I guess. I need to head for home soon. I have laundry and stuff to do before work tomorrow." She set her cup down and snuggled up to his chest.

"I know. I wish you didn't have to leave," he whispered, as he stroked her back.

"We'll manage. We just have to make a conscious effort to spend as much time together as possible." She buried her nose in his neck, inhaling his masculine musky scent.

"What days are off this next week?"

"Let's see, today is Sunday, I work Monday, Tuesday and Wednesday, off Thursday and Friday and work Saturday, Sunday and Monday."

"What if I drive up Thursday mornin' and stay until Friday afternoon? I'll need to be back here before nine to play so I would have to leave around four."

"That would be good. I don't have anything planned for those days." She stepped back out of his arms and grabbed her coffee cup.

"You do now," he whispered, giving her a quick kiss. "Do you want to shower before you leave?"

He gave her a suggestive, sexy grin and she said, "Oh no. If I do that, I'll never get out of here because you'll join me."

"You bet! Why do you think I suggested it?" he teased, wiggling his eyebrow suggestively.

Shaking her head, she smiled as she moved back toward the bedroom to pack her stuff and he followed.

"Can I ask you a question?" As she shoved her things into the bag she'd brought, doubts clouded her mind.

"Sure."

"How long has it been since you and Diane were supposed to get married?"

"Our weddin' date was set for the end of March. I found out she slept around the first part of January."

"March of this year?"

"No, last year." He took her hand in his, bringing her around and holding her close. She wrapped her arms behind him as she laid her head on his shoulder and he whispered in her ear. "Don't be jealous of her. What is in my heart for you is so much more than I ever felt for her. Why do you think I found it so easy to call off the weddin'?"

"I want to make sure you aren't on the rebound. Something your mom said made me wonder."

He looked into her eyes. "I love you. I haven't been with anyone seriously for over a year and even then, I don't think I ever loved Diane, not like I love you. My mom is only tryin' to protect me."

"I know."

"What about you? You thought you loved your bull rider? How can you say you love me if you were just in love with him a few weeks ago?"

Dipping her head, she answered, "I wasn't in love with Jack. I realize that now. I don't know, maybe I loved what our life might have been, him being in the PBR and all, but it wasn't real. When I found out he cheated, it hurt my pride more than anything, I guess."

"Believe I love you and don't question it. I know what I feel and I want you, no one else. We will just have to trust each other and believe what we feel is the real thing," he finished in a whisper, pulling her tight against his chest.

"I'm sorry, Tanner. I want to believe in this, I really do, but it's hard. It's going to take time."

"I know. We hold all the time in the world in the palm of our hands. We'll make the distance thing not a big deal," he said, pulling back so he could look into her eyes.

"I just hope it doesn't become too much."

"It won't. We'll make things work. I promise," he said, brushing his thumb across her face. She rubbed her cheek against his hand before she pulled back out of his arms.

"I need to get moving. Are you going to walk me to my car?"

"Of course."

They silently walked outside holding hands. He took her bag and put it in the back, shutting the trunk firmly before he returned to her side and pulled her into his arms. He bent his head, taking her lips with his, softly moving them over hers as he tasted her one last time before she left.

When they came up for air, he said, "You had better go or I won't let you in a minute."

"I know," she whispered, hugging him even though she knew she would be seeing him soon. "I'll call you when I get home."

"Please do. I want to make sure you get home all right."

"I will. I'll see you in a few days."

"I love you," he whispered, as he held her tight.

"I love you, too."

He let her go and she slipped into the driver's seat of the car, pulling the door firmly behind her before she started the engine. She waved tearfully before pulling out of his parents' drive to head back to Dallas and her lonely apartment.

* * * *

Getting out of bed the next morning seemed like a chore. Tired and miserable, Lord help anyone who got on her bad side today because she was in a very bitchy mood. She got to work, received reports on her patients and began her day. When time for lunch came, Chris couldn't join her, so went downstairs and walked to the sandwich shop next to the hospital. She brought her meal to an empty outside table and shocked rippled through her as Jack confronted her.

Rolling her eyes, she tried to ignore him.

"I want to talk to you," he demanded.

"Well, I don't want to talk to you," she replied, picking up her food and taking a bite with the intention of ignoring him completely.

He slipped into the chair across from her and grabbed her wrist as she started to rise.

"Get your hands off me." She pulled her arm from his grasp.

"Fine. What's going on between you and your lover boy?"

"None of your business. Our relationship is over, done, finished. What's between me and Tanner has nothing to do with you."

"Oh, yes, it does, if you want to keep your job," he snarled, his eyes snapping in anger.

"Are you threatening me?"

"I happen to know some higher ups in this place. Trust me darlin' when I say I can get you fired if I so choose."

"I don't believe you!" Her eyes widened in shock. *Will he really try to get me fired?* "Why do you care, Jack? Because I got out of our relationship and no one has ever turned you down before?"

"It doesn't matter what my reasons are, Amy. You're mine and I won't let you go until I'm ready."

"In other words, you don't care what I want and that you cheated on me." The reality of her situation weighed heavily on her mind as she contemplated his words.

"No, it doesn't. So from now on, you had better leave the loser alone and focus on me," he rasped.

"You know what? Do your damnedest. I love Tanner, not you, and if that means losing my job, fine. I don't think you possess as much power as you claim to, but if I have to go somewhere else to work, then I will," she shouted.

"You love him?" Jack laughed almost hysterically as the anger built in her.

"Yes, I do, and there isn't anything you can do to stop what's happening, Jack." She trembled as her rage grew, but she wasn't going to let him take control of her life.

"You'll be sorry you crossed me. Watch your back. Your life is going to be a living hell from now on," he threatened. He stood, knocking the chair off balance until it fell to the ground behind him as he turned and walked away.

Her anger deflated as her body shook as the adrenaline rushed through her. She stayed there for several minutes before she realized her cell phone vibrated in her pocket. She pulled it out and smiled slightly, when she recognized the number flashing on the screen.

"Hello?"

"Are you okay?"

"Yeah, why? I'm surprised you called. Something wrong?"

"I had a bad feelin' in the pit of my stomach that you were hurt, so I thought I'd call and check on you." Worry laced his voice. "Are you sure you are okay? You sound upset."

"Yeah, I'm all right. I had a bad run-in with Jack again."

"What did he say?"

"He wanted to know about us. I told him I love you and it didn't sit well with him."

"Are you sure that's all?"

"Everything will be fine, Tanner. No big deal." She paused a moment, trying to gain control of her emotions. Whispering in the phone, she murmured, "I miss you."

She did not want to tell him about Jack's threats. If she did, he would want to drive up here and punch Jack again and that would make matters worse. No, she would deal with this on her own.

"I miss you, too. I can't wait to see you again. Do you have any idea how miserable it is tryin' to sleep without you next to me?"

* * * *

He was worried. Her tone gave her away. Something happened between her and the other guy, but she wasn't going to tell him. When she changed the subject, he let her. For now. He'd find out soon enough and he would take care of the bull rider in his own way.

He could hear a smile in her voice as she said, "Yeah, actually I do. I didn't sleep well either."

"I can't wait to hold you again."

"I know what you mean, but I hate to cut you off. I need to get back to work. I still have medications I to give. Can I call you later after I get off?"

"Of course. I'll talk you then. I love you."

"I love you, too. Talk to you around seven-thirty."

Chapter 16

She hung up the phone and headed back upstairs. Total shock reverberated through her as Jack came out of the nurse manager's office with a smug smile on his face. *How in the hell does he know her?*

She could tell by the look on his face he had already started to cause trouble and she needed to be prepared. She didn't think that he could get her fired, at least not right away.

The next day, Carol called her into the office and her stomach tightened as apprehensive slithered along her arms.

"Can I talk to you?"

"Sure, Carol."

"Sit down, Amy. We need to talk." Carol sat down at her desk and she sat across from her with a sinking feeling in her chest.

"Jack Miller came into my office yesterday and gave me information that is pretty serious."

Amy hung her head for a moment, contemplating how she could handle this. *Honesty is the best policy.*

"Carol you know Jack Miller and I were in a relationship for a while."

"Yes, I am aware."

"I realize that, but what you might not know is our relationship is no longer. I split with him about a month ago, maybe a little more, and he's furious." She took a deep breath before continuing. "Now, he's trying to cause trouble. He threatened me yesterday because I told him I am in love with someone else. He doesn't take kindly to being told no."

"Well, I'm glad your relationship with him is over. It's the best thing for you, and I'm happy you've found someone else, but the truth is, Amy, he has friends, powerful friends in this organization. The accusation is you took narcotics from the floor."

"What?" Amy shouted, standing up. "I would never take narcotics out of the count for my own use."

"I understand but the dates he's mentioned are dates the count was off and also when you were here, it looks suspicious."

"Son of a bitch. I'm sorry, Carol," she said, shaking in anger, as she sat back down. "What happens now?"

"There will be an investigation, of course. Although due to your almost perfect work history here, you won't be suspended. Your record with this hospital is excellent so I don't anticipate a problem. You can continue to work until everything is concluded. I just needed to warn you ahead of time, before things came down from the board of directors."

"I appreciate your help. You have no idea how much this means to me. I'm sure the whole mess will work out fine. Trust me, if I run into him again, I may have to kill him myself, the bastard."

"I will, Amy. Just watch yourself around him if you run into him. And be careful with your threats. Should anything happen to him…"

"He really pisses me off to no end. Thanks again," she said, before she walked out the door and back to her patients.

* * * *

On Wednesday, anticipation zinged through her as she thought about seeing Tanner again. When Chris found her, she almost couldn't hold in her excitement.

"Tanner is driving up this afternoon so we can see each other on my days off." She shifted excitedly in her chair.

"You two are spending a lot of time together, aren't you? Didn't you just drive down there over the weekend?"

"Yes, I did."

Chris gave her a sly look before she said, "Jason was looking for you. He called up here on Saturday to make sure you didn't pull an overtime shift."

"Oh shit! I think we had a ride this past weekend and I totally forgot! I'd better call him." She picked up the phone at the desk and dialed Jason's pager number.

"You haven't told me what's up between you and Tanner."

"Nothing you need to worry about, Chris. Things are fantastic." The bright blush on her cheeks at the mention of the man she loved gave away her secret.

"Come on, Am, fess up. I already know you two have been together, so what are the red cheeks for?"

"You heard about our disagreement when Jack called."

"Yeah."

"Well, not seeing him for those two weeks made me realize my feelings for him ran deeper than I wanted to admit."

"And?"

"When I drove out to Brenham this weekend, I admitted to him and myself I love him."

"You're kidding? That's awesome, Amy!" Chris grabbed her in a huge hug as several of the other nurses looked at them questioningly.

"Ssshhh! The whole floor will find out what's going on."

"Sorry," Chris whispered. "I'm so happy for you."

"I'm happy, too, happier than I've been in a long time, I think."

"I knew you two would be perfect together, I just knew it!"

A frown settled on her face as they sat back down at the desk.

"What's wrong?"

"Jack. He's making trouble for me here at the hospital and I'm not sure how I can stop it."

"What's he doing now?"

"He's put a birdie in someone's ear and accused me of lifting narcotics from the count."

"You've got to be kidding me. There is no way you could steal narcotics. I don't think you take anything stronger than Tylenol."

She shook her head. "He must have some pretty influential friends her at the hospital to be able to accuse me and know dates the count had been incorrect."

"That bastard!"

"I know. I'm not sure what I'm going to do."

"Have you told Tanner?"

"Hell no! And I'm not going to. I can handle this myself."

"You should tell him, Amy."

"I'm not going to and you won't tell him either, Chris. This has nothing to do with him."

"Fine, I'll drop it for now."

The phone rang and Amy picked up the receiver.

Jason's angry voice zipped across the line. "Where the hell were you this weekend? We had a rodeo."

"I'm sorry, Jason. I completely forgot."

"Forgot? How could you forget, Amy? That's not like you at all. The rodeos are the most important thing to you."

"I know, but I had something to do."

"Like what?"

"I drove to Brenham, so the rodeo slipped my mind."

"You went to hang out with that guy, didn't you?" The disgust in his voice concerned her. Jason wasn't normally so hateful, especially with her.

"Yes, why?"

"I can't believe you! You jump out of the pan into the fire, don't you? You got yourself hurt hanging around Jack and now you are doing the same thing all over again."

"Jason, I'm sorry I messed up and forgot the rodeo. I realize I put you in a bind and if you want to find another riding partner, that's fine. As far as my love life goes, if I get hurt, it's not your concern."

"The hell it's not!"

"I'm not discussing this with you. What's between Tanner and me is just that. You are my friend, but I'll not let you ruin this for me. I'll talk to you later." She hung up the phone, refusing to let him say another word.

"Whoa, that was *not* pretty."

"No, it wasn't. I can't believe Jason would act like that. You'd think he's jealous or something."

* * * *

When the shift ended, the two women walked out to their cars as the warm summer air blew across the parking lot, drying the sweat on their skin.

"Have fun. Is Tanner meeting you at your place?"

"Yeah."

"Don't do anything I wouldn't do." Chris laughed as Amy blushed.

"Sure, Chris. I know what you would do."

"I hope you two have a good time."

"I'm sure we will. I'll see you on Saturday." Amy pulled open the door on her car and slid into the driver's seat.

When she pulled into the parking lot of her apartment complex, she turned the car off, grabbed her things and stepped out, locking the car.

Tanner slipped his arms around her waist and whispered in her ear, "Hey, baby, doing anythin' tonight?" His familiar scent wrapped itself through her senses and she sighed.

"Um…I don't know. What did you have in mind?" Shivers ran down her arms as he caressed the side of her neck with his lips.

"I'm sure I could show you a good time." His warm breath whispered against her ear.

"I don't think it would be wise. My boyfriend is supposed to be meeting me here and he doesn't like to share."

"You're damned right I don't," he growled, spinning her in his arms before his mouth came down on hers, slanting across her lips as she groaned. They were both breathing hard when he finally lifted his head and she smiled.

"You didn't happen to notice a very handsome stranger around here, did you? He just propositioned me." She laughed, rubbing against him as his cock pressed prominently against her stomach.

Tanner leaned in until her spine met the car behind her and his hands bracketed her shoulders as his forehead met hers.

"I chased him off for you. I knew you weren't enticed by his suggestion anyway."

"Darn it! I thought maybe you might be interested in a threesome. I've never tried that. Of course, you are more than enough to keep me busy." She ran her hands up his chest to wrap them in his hair and she felt him tremble slightly under her touch.

"No way, lady, you're mine."

"I like the sound of that."

She groaned as he pressed his lips to hers again, loving the feel of him next to her.

After a moment, he pulled away and wrapped his arm around her waist possessively as they walked toward the door.

* * * *

Tanner waved at George when they passed him on the way to the elevator. He remembered how the guard had kept Jack from going up stairs that night and when the police questioned him about the assault, George backed up his story of self-defense after Jack swung first. "He sure looks out for the residents of this building."

"That's his job I guess, but he sure seems to take things seriously."

"So what's the plan for our short time together?" He nuzzled her neck, wanting nothing more than to get her alone.

"I'm sure you can help me think of something."

The elevator finally opened and they moved inside. As the doors began to close, someone stuck their hand between the panels, stopping them from closing all the way. With a sly grin, Jack entered and the door shut behind him, enveloping the three in uncomfortable silence.

Amy stiffened next to Tanner as Jack said, "Well, hello again. Can you push five for me? Thanks."

Tanner pushed the button for the fifth floor as she snarled, "What are you doing here, Jack?"

"Relax, Amy. I'm here visiting someone. I know how much you miss me and all, but I have other interests besides you." His maniacal smile sent shivers down her spine.

Tanner pushed Amy behind him, stepping between her and Jack.

"Relax, wannabe. I'm not after your pretty little filly. She's worn out her usefulness to me, and once the hospital gets done with her, you'll probably need to move her down where you come from. She won't be able to work anywhere in Dallas." He laughed as the doors opened to the fifth floor and he stepped out. He tipped his hat to a young woman who waited for the elevator, right before she walked in and Amy wondered at the glance exchanged between the two.

When the door slid shut with Jack on the other side, she shuddered and Tanner wrapped his arms around her.

"Well, hello, Amy. I didn't realize you lived here."

Amy lifted her head to meet the intense stare of a co-worker from the hospital. "Hi, Anna."

"How is life treating you?"

"Good. I'm trying to stay out of trouble."

"I'm sure you are."

The elevator shuttered to a halt.

"This is our stop. Nice to see you, Anna."

"You too, Amy."

Amy and Tanner stepped out and as the door slid shut behind them, she wrapped her arms around his waist and buried her face in his shoulder for a moment before she whispered, "Jack's crazy."

"You need to stay away from him as much as you can. Who knows what the man will do to get back at you?"

"I feel sorry for who he's got his sights set on now. Lord knows if the girl has any clue what he's like. Maybe I need to find out so I can warn whomever he's hooked up with."

Tanner pushed her back so he could look into her face. "Don't get involved, Amy. I'm afraid you'll get hurt."

"I have to, Tanner. If I can prevent someone else from going through what he's put me through, don't you think I need to try?"

"You, my love, need to stay away from him." Tanner ran his fingers down her cheek. "Enough of this in the hall, I want you alone."

No more was said as they walked down the hall to her apartment. Once inside, she reached for Tanner, pulled him into her arms and slanted her mouth over his. Her tongue slid along the crease of his lips, caressing until he opened to her touch with a groan. She slipped her hands up his chest to the opening of his shirt, yanking until the buttons popped off and flew across the room.

He pulled his mouth from hers and grinned as he said, "In a hurry?"

"Yes, I want you," she growled, tugging his shirt out of his jeans, and slipping the material off his shoulders, before reaching for the belt buckle he wore.

Grasping her hands in his, he stopped her from unbuckling his belt and she looked up at him in confusion.

"Slow down. This ain't a race," he murmured against her mouth as he slowly caressed her shoulder, and then skimmed across her arm. Up her side his fingers played until he took her breast in his palm.

"I think you do this to torture me," she whispered as a shiver rolled down her spine.

He grinned as he looked into her eyes.

His lips licked at her flesh, until he took her nipple in his mouth and lapped at it with his tongue through the fabric of her shirt. A moan rose in her throat, escaping between her clenched teeth.

He reached for the tie at her waist, pulling the knot free and slipping her scrubs from her hips before he lifted her up and brought her long legs around his hips. The rasp of denim on her clit sent her need spiraling as she moaned.

Her bare ass hit the icy stone of the island countertop and she squealed, "Shit, that's cold!"

He chuckled softly as he slipped her shirt and bra off, before he pushed her back so she laid flat on the stone and kissed his way from her lips to her chest. He raked his mouth over her right nipple, nipping at the pink tip with his teeth. She threaded her fingers through his hair as she held his head harder against the aching tip and whimpered deep in her throat. His tongue licked at her skin as he worked his way down her abdomen and she spread her legs, begging for his mouth. When he reached her throbbing center and his tongue made a wide sweep from her vagina to her clit, her hips came off the cold surface beneath her, pleading for more pressure.

"God Tanner, please. Make me come. I need to, please." Her frantic appeal echoed in the stillness of the kitchen.

He lifted his head as she softly complained at the loss of tactile sensation. "I want inside you when you come, milkin' my cock, ripplin' around me."

Her eyes opened to mere slits at his words, and she watched him strip off his jeans. Grabbing her hips, he slid her across the hard surface until she her ass met the edge. She spread her legs wider as his cock nudged at her opening.

"Now. Fuck me now."

A tortured groan slipped from between his lips as he plunged into her pussy, his hips thrusting against hers. His finger found her clit, massaging the hard nub as he hammered into her and she almost came unglued.

"Faster, harder."

"Your wish is my command," he whispered as his tempo increased. The slap of skin and the grunts of pleasure rang in the air around them.

Blood rushed out of her head to her belly as liquid seep from where they were coupled together. Warmth spread quickly from her toes and up her legs, bursting over her in a rush tingles as sparks burst behind her eyelids and she scream his name. He joined her a moment later with soft cries of, "Oh God."

* * * *

Two shadows blended in the night as their tongues entwined, each seeking satisfaction from the other. The rip of material echoed in the apartment as the moonlight filtered through the window, casting the bodies in silver light.

"Now, I want you now," the woman whispered, fumbling with the buttons on the front of the man's shirt.

The man chuckled as he untied the pants at her waist, sliding the string out of the waistband and pushed them down until she kicked them off. "Impatient?"

"Yes. You've been teasing me for weeks. I need to feel your hard dick ramming inside me."

"Patience, my pet," he said, pulling her hands away and leading her to the couch. "You need to fill me in on the details first."

"Why? I've already told you."

"Everything is in place as we discussed?"

"Yes, damn it! I've done everything you asked. The narcotic count has been off for weeks, but only on the days she's there."

"Perfect."

"Now, will you fuck me?" she pleaded, her fingers finding her clit and massaging it with increasing force.

His lips trailed down her cheek to bite at the curve of her neck as the woman whimpered. He pulled her off the couch, pushed her down on the floor and lifted her hips as he spread her thighs. Reaching down, he rasped his zipper open and grabbed his enormous erection in his hand. Hips in position, he slammed into her, almost sliding her across the floor with the force of his thrust. His climax rushed through him on a strangled moan as the woman beneath him screamed his name.

Several moments later, he disengaged himself from her and buttoned his pants again. Walking toward the balcony door, he watched the skyline shimmer on the wave of the coming morning. The woman slipped up behind him and wrapped her arms around his waist. He turned in her arms and bent his head to kiss her neck. When he lifted his head, the string from her scrubs was wrapped tightly around her neck. He kissed her mouth as her hands grasped the binding, tugging and clawing while her breath became ragged and rasping.

"Sorry my pet, but I can't leave witnesses."

"But, I thought," her strangled words whispered from between her lips, "you loved me?"

"No, sweetheart, I don't. I only love one and it's not you." He pulled the string tighter until she gasped her last breath and slumped against him.

* * * *

The next morning found Amy and Tanner lying side-by-side in her bed sound asleep until the phone rang, bringing them both upright.

With a groan, Amy rolled over and grabbed the receiver as Tanner pulled the pillow over his head.

"Hello?"

"Amy?"

"Yeah, who is this?" she grumbled.

"Your mother."

"Mom? What's wrong?"

"Nothing, sweetheart. I wanted to check on you. I thought you might be upset." She vaguely heard the words as she settled back on the pillows trying not to go back to sleep.

"Why would I be upset, Mom? I don't know you are talking about."

"You haven't heard?"

"Mom, please," she said, coming alert, as Tanner rolled over beside her.

"They found a woman dead in your building this morning."

Amy dropped the phone into her lap as the words sunk into her brain and she gasped, making Tanner come fully awake.

"What's the matter?"

"Someone died in this building last night," she whispered.

Chapter 17

"What? No way!"

"Amy?" She heard from the bedding where she dropped the receiver.

She grabbed the phone again. "Sorry, Mom. I dropped the phone."

"Did I hear someone?"

"Uh…yeah, Mom. You heard Tanner."

"Tanner? Amy, who's Tanner?"

"I can't explain right now, Mom. Tanner is the guy I'm seeing now." The doorbell rang. "I need to go. I'll call you later."

She hung up the phone and, she turned to the man beside her. He rolled out of the other side of the bed, slipping on his pants. "I'll get it. You probably should get dressed. We need to find out what's going on."

She watched him button his jeans and head toward the living room before she slipped out of the other side of the bed and walked to the dresser to pull out some clean clothing.

"Who the hell are you? No, we don't have any comments concernin' the homicide in the buildin' last night. Now, please leave." The firmness in Tanner's voice drove her from the bed as she quickly put on her clothes. She crossed the threshold as Tanner forcibly shut the door.

"What was that all about?"

"Reporters. There are several outside who want a comment from you concernin' the murder here. Flip on the television." Tanner locked the door, before he moved to her side.

She sat on the couch, grabbed the remote and turned on the television. She gasped as the news channel showed the front of her apartment building and several reporters.

"This is Joyce Allen and we are live, here at the Mayfield/Rochester Apartment complex in the suburb of Hazelton, to report on the death of a young woman here by the name of Anna Cooper. She worked at Fort Worth

Metropolitan Hospital as a registered nurse on the tenth floor. Our question this morning is why was she found here in a hallway on the fifth floor of this apartment complex with obvious ligature marks on her neck?"

"Oh my God, I know her! I work with her. She's the woman in the elevator last night. How horrible," Amy whispered.

"Many questions go unanswered, but we are hoping someone here can unravel the puzzle. Another nurse who works with this young woman also lives in this building, but Ms. Russell is unavailable for comment this morning. We will continue to try to get a statement from Ms. Russell as the investigation continues. We will bring you breaking news as things develop. Back to you, Marty."

"What the hell is going on, Tanner?"

"I don't know, but we need to find out. Chris might be able to give us some insight. Let me call her," he said, picking up his cell phone and dialing.

When Chris answered, Amy heard their murmurs as she tried to wrap her mind around the facts. Anna died sometime last night, here in her apartment building. *Who could have killed her?* Her scattered thoughts ricocheted back to the present when Tanner said goodbye and hung up the phone.

"What did Chris say?"

"She doesn't know much, either. The buzz around the hospital is about her being found dead this mornin', but nothin' more." Tanner walked over and pulled her into his arms, wrapping her in a warm hug. "Everythin' will be okay. I'm sure the police will have questions, especially when they find out we may have been the last two to see her alive."

Within the hour, the police sent a detective to speak to her and they indeed had questions, several questions. Not supplying her much information, the only thing they did say was they were investigating her death as a homicide since she had ligature marks on her neck and defensive wounds on her hands. The reporters hovered outside in the parking lot of her apartment complex and as soon as the detective left, they swarmed around him. "Vultures, that's what they are. They just wait, wanting to feed off the flesh of the victims or perpetrators alike. They don't care if someone is innocent or guilty. I feel so sorry for her family. I wonder who could have done this to her?"

"I have no idea."

"I already have enough problems with Jack and his threats."

"I meant to ask you about that." Tanner shifted so he could look into her eyes.

She felt the blood drain from her face when she realized she'd slipped. She wasn't going to tell him about Jack's accusations, since she wanted to try and deal with everything herself, but now an explanation would be in order.

"What did he mean when he said you wouldn't be able to work in Dallas anymore?"

She dropped her gaze so she wouldn't have to look at him, but he put his finger under her chin, forcing her to raise her head.

"Amy?"

"I didn't tell you because I wanted to try to deal with him myself."

"How can we be in a relationship if you don't tell me about your troubles? Don't you trust me?"

"Of course I trust you, Tanner. I love you, and I wasn't trying to keep his threats from you unnecessarily. I didn't want you to worry."

With a questioning raise of his eyebrow, he waited. His look told her, he wasn't going to take no for an answer. She had to tell him. She had no choice now.

She sighed heavily. "He confronted me at work the other day, the same afternoon you called." He nodded in understanding. "He threatened me. He didn't like when I told him I loved you. Right after I talked to you, I saw him coming out of my boss' office with a smug smile. The next day she called me in her office to tell me he had given her information. For several days in the last month or so, narcotics have been missing from work. He told her because we had been seeing each other he knew for a fact I had been taking drugs."

"Can't you get into major trouble for that? I mean, get fired or lose your license?"

"Yes. My boss understood they were probably false allegations, but she had to report the accusations and an investigation will be conducted."

"So that's what he meant by you not bein' able to work in Dallas anymore."

"He wanted to ruin me."

"He obviously was workin' hard at it, yes. Did she say they had proof you took the medication?"

"No but things are suspicious. The drugs are missing on days I worked, but everyone who knows me should understand. I rarely take anything stronger than Tylenol or Ibuprofen."

"There shouldn't be a problem then. Can't they do a drug screen or somethin'?"

"Yes, but some drugs don't stay in your system long enough to be picked up unless it is done within a short time after taking them."

"We'll handle this together. I know you don't take drugs. I've been around you enough to know."

"I hope everything turns out to be so easy. If my license gets suspended or revoked, I don't know what I would do." Realizing she may never be able to work in nursing again shook her to the core. He gathered her to his chest, and she laid her head against his shoulder.

"You have to be stronger than you've ever been for a while. The accusations will be difficult. We'll deal with everythin' when the time comes. For now, just relax. There's nothin' we can do right now, anyway. I'll be here for you no matter what."

"You have no idea how much I love you."

"I love you, too." He pulled her to his chest again and bent his head to take her lips in a soft kiss that felt like butterfly wings against her mouth. Amy lost herself in the feelings of his lips, and she opened her mouth to receive his tongue. He deepened the kiss, pulling her even tighter against him, his hand finding her breast under her shirt.

"Come on." He took her by the hand and led her into the bedroom. She stood at the end of the bed while he pulled the covers back. She moved toward him while he slipped out of his jeans and then brought her down with him onto the soft mattress. He wrapped her in his arms and they lay in the silence until she finally drifted off to sleep.

Later in the afternoon, they sat on the balcony of her apartment. He had made a late lunch and brought the sandwich out to her while she sat staring out at the Dallas skyline.

"Here, baby. You need to eat," he said, placing the plate near her.

"I don't think I can. Thank you for making it, though."

"You are gonna eat somethin' if I have to feed you," he answered firmly. "Now, here, eat."

Amy dutifully picked up the sandwich and took a bite, chewing until the food tasted like mush in her mouth then swallowed heavily. She took a large drink of the milk he had set near her plate to wash the whole thing down, giving him a small smile.

"Not good enough. Come on."

Amy knew he wasn't going to let up until she ate everything, so she continued to take bites of the meal until everything disappeared.

"Good."

* * * *

The sadness in her eyes tore at him, as he watched the tears gather again on her lashes. He scooted his chair so he could pull her into his arms while the drops fell on her cheeks.

"Don't cry. I hate when you cry."

"I'm sorry. What am I going to do if they take my license? I can't bear the thought of not being a nurse, Tanner."

"We'll manage. Together we can face any obstacle, even this one."

"How am I going to face the people at work tomorrow? I'm sure by now everyone knows I'm being investigated. They'll think I'm some kind of drug addict."

"You're a strong woman. You'll do just fine," he encouraged, pushing her hair back behind her ear.

She shuddered as she sighed heavily, laying her head on his chest.

"Do you have to go home?" She stroked the fine hair near her cheek.

"I wish I could stay, but I can't."

She turned her head so her lips met his chest where his shirt lay open, kissing the skin beneath, and running her tongue along the ridges as he groaned deep in his throat.

"Amy," he moaned as a shiver ran down his arms, raising goose bumps along his skin.

"I need you, Tanner. Make love to me, please," she whispered against the firm surface under her mouth.

He stood, pulling her up with him. Swinging her up in his arms, he carried her back through the apartment and into the bedroom. Kicking the door closed behind them, effectively shutting out the crazy world that was about to come crashing down around them.

* * * *

Late that evening, after they had spent the afternoon making love, Tanner stood at the door as he kissed her goodbye.

"I wish you didn't have to go." She held tight as they stood near the door.

"I have to and you have to work tomorrow."

"Be careful going home, okay? Make sure you call me when you get to Brenham." He pulled away and grabbed his bag.

"I will, but it'll be late. It's already eight now."

"I don't care. I want to know you got home."

He grinned at her protective tone. "All right. I'll call you on your cell."

"I'll put it on your pillow."

"My pillow? I like the sound of that," he replied with a sexy smile.

"It will be yours as long as you want."

"How does forever sound?"

"Sounds good to me," she responded, right before she pulled his head down for another heart-stopping kiss.

"Mmm…" he moaned into her mouth before he finally broke the kiss. "I need to go."

"I know."

Amy stepped back allowing him to pull the door open.

"I love you," he said, stepping into the hall.

"I love you, too. Be careful."

She closed the door, putting her back against the wood with a heavy sigh. Morning would come early and things would probably be hell at work, but she knew she had to be prepared for the worst.

After her shower, she crawled into the bed, pulled his pillow to her face so she could inhale his musky scent, holding her cell phone close, waiting for his call.

When he called, she answered with a groggy hello.

"Hey, darlin'. I'm home."

"Good. I'm glad you're safe."

"I'll let you go back to sleep. I love you."

"I love you too, Tanner. I'll call you tomorrow after work."

"Okay. Sweet dreams," echoed in her ear, before she clicked the phone shut and drifted back off to sleep.

The next morning she was up and dressed early. George stood at her door, guarding it himself, and when he saw her, he told her he would show her a different way down so she could avoid the reporters out front.

"Thanks, George. You are such a sweetheart."

"I have to take care of my favorite resident, don't I?"

"I guess so since I'm not doing such a great job these days."

"Well, that nice guy you've got now will keep you out of trouble, I'm sure." His smile and approval made her day.

"I'm glad you like him, George. I do, too," she said as he escorted her to her car, and she slid onto the seat. "I'll see you tonight."

"Have a good day at work."

"I'll try," she replied, rolling up her window and pulling out of the parking lot.

* * * *

"Tanner?" his mother yelled out the front door. *"Tanner!"*

Working in the barn, he heard his mother call his name and the tone of her voice sent shivers down his spine. He raced for the house, terrified something had happened to one of his parents.

"What?" he asked, worry clear in his voice, as he reached the porch.

"You need to see the television," she answered, pushing the screen door open so he could enter.

"Now, coming to you live from Dallas Fort Worth Metropolitan Hospital Caroline Adams. Caroline, can you tell us what is happening there?"

"Hi, Marty. I'm here live at the hospital reporting on some breaking news. We have it on good authority that a large drug ring has been uncovered here at the hospital. Apparently a pharmacist and a registered nurse have been filtering drugs out to dealers on the streets to be sold for a very high profit. We have just learned that the Dallas Fort Worth drug task force has arrested Amy Russell, registered nurse, for filtering narcotics from the hospital with the help of Cory Harold, registered pharmacist. We will bring you more as things develop."

Chapter 18

Tanner watched as Amy, wearing her work uniform, was escorted out of the hospital in handcuffs and pushed into a squad car, before it drove away.

He talked over his shoulder as he walked quickly down the hall to his room to pack a bag. "Mom, I'm driving to Dallas. Call Pete's for me and tell them I can't play for right now. I'll be back as soon as I can, but I need to be there for Amy."

The ride to Dallas dragged by. He tried turning on the radio, writing songs in his head, anything to keep his mind off Amy and what she had to be going through. When he finally reached the outskirts of town, he headed straight for her apartment, only to find taped off with yellow police tape.

Next he called Chris, knowing his voice must sound frantic on the phone he said, "Chris, I need your help."

"Tanner? Did you hear about Amy?"

"Yeah, that's why I'm here. I need a place to bunk. They won't let me in her apartment. They are gatherin' evidence I guess. Can I stay with you for a few days until I help her get this straightened out?"

"Sure, no problem," Chris answered. "You know she didn't do this, right?"

"Chris, there is no way she could be sellin' drugs. She wouldn't have the heart for that type of activity."

"Then why do they think she did?"

"I have no idea." He ran his hands through his hair before he pounded his fist on the steering wheel as he drove toward Chris' apartment. "I'll be at your place in a few minutes."

"All right."

When he reached Chris' place, they sat down and discussed how the police could possible think Amy might be involved in selling drugs.

"You know Jack told them she had been usin' right?"

"Yeah, she told me, but there is no way, Tanner. Amy would never do anything like what they are suggesting," Chris paced, chewing her fingernail nervously.

"Someone must be settin' her up and I bet its Jack."

"What can we do about it?"

"I don't know, but I'm goin' down to the police department so I can see her." He pulled out the keys to his truck, heading for the door.

"Me, too."

"No, you stay here and keep an eye on the television. We'll probably be able to find out more from the nosey reporters than we will anywhere else. I'll make sure she knows we are here for her. I need to find out if she has a lawyer already. If not, we'll get one for her and go from there. Hopefully we can get her out quickly."

"I hope so, too."

"I'll be back as quick as I can."

Chris gave Tanner directions to the police station and once he arrived, he pulled out the card of the homicide detective they talked to at the apartment. Maybe the detective could help him see Amy.

"I need to talk to Detective Gilroy," he told the desk clerk.

"I'm sorry, but Detective Gilroy is unavailable right now. Would you like to wait?"

"Yes. Can you please tell him I need to speak to him as soon as possible?"

"Of course, sir."

Tanner took a seat in the lobby, his eyes looking around at the high ceilings, paneled walls, plastic plants gracing the corners and the bullet proof glass protecting clerk. Big double doors to his left led into the rear of the police station, and on several occasions, he could see people walking past looking at him curiously. *You would think they've never seen cowboy before.* He adjusted in his chair and pulled off his hat, hanging the Stetson on his knee as he waited.

After he had sat there for over an hour, the detective finally called him to come in the back. Once they sat down in a very stale, bland room with no color and only a small table and two chairs, Tanner addressed the man.

"Can you tell me why y'all arrested Ms. Russell?"

"I can't tell you, but I might be able to find the detective in charge of the drug bust. Let me see what I can do."

The detective left him sitting in the small room for several minutes before he returned with another man.

"This is Detective Harmon. He's in charge of the investigation into the drug ring. He might be able to help you."

"Thank you, Detective Gilroy. I appreciate your help." When the other man had taken a seat across of him, Tanner asked why they arrested Amy.

"I can't reveal the evidence we have, but let's just say we have reason to believe she is involved in pilfering drugs from the hospital and selling them to a dealer on the street." The detective's droll answer grated on Tanner's nerves.

"What makes you think she stole drugs? Have you tested her?" he growled.

"No, not yet but we will before the day is over."

"Then you will know she doesn't contain any in her system."

"Just because she hasn't taken any herself, doesn't mean she isn't capable of selling them on the street. We want the big man, not the small dealers. If she proves helpful, things will go easier on her."

"She's not involved!"

"We have reason to believe she is."

Tanner sighed in frustration. *I'm not getting anywhere with this.*

"I have two questions for you, Detective. Does she already have a lawyer, and can I see her?"

"Yes, an attorney has been appointed, and yes, you can see her, but only for a moment or two. I will even allow you to see her in here."

"That would be kind. Thank you," Tanner mumbled, completely aware they probably thought he and Amy would say something, suggesting a cover up.

After several tense moments, the door opened and a guard escorted her into the room. She looked like hell. Black smudges of mascara clung to her lashes like she'd been crying, an orange jail jumpsuit replaced her scrubs, and her hair stuck out of her ponytail in several directions, but she never looked more beautiful to him.

She launched herself into his arms as he wrapped her in his embrace and whispered in her ear, "Everythin' will be all right."

"How did you know I was here? I didn't even get a chance to call you," she mumbled against his shirt.

"The news at home, or should I say my mom caught it and called me into the house." She stepped back a little and he brushed the tears from her cheeks.

"Wonderful, now your mom thinks I'm a drug dealer. That will solidify her opinion of me."

"Don't worry about my mom," he replied. "Sit down and tell me what happened."

"I'm not sure," she began, as she sat in the one of the chairs and he took the other opposite of hers. "They came to the hospital and said I was under arrest for dealing drugs. You know that I couldn't do this, right?"

"I know, darlin'. It will be okay, I promise." He tucked a strain piece of hair behind her ear. "The detective said you already have an attorney."

"Yes, but he's just a public defender. He isn't going to give a shit about whether I go to jail for something I didn't do or not."

"I'm gonna call around when I leave here and find you a good one. Have they told you anythin'?"

"Nothing other than they hold evidence, but I can't imagine what."

"Well, I'm sure your attorney will get to the bottom of this. They have to disclose all the evidence to him from what I understand. I guess watchin' those episodes of *CSI* helped." He grinned, but she didn't respond.

"I'm sorry, Tanner. I wish I could joke about this, but I can't lose my license. My whole life will be over if I do," she cried.

"Oh, Amy," he said, stroking her hand with his thumb. "Your life won't be over. We will still be together when this is finished."

"Time's up," the detective said, returning to the room.

"I love you. Hang tough, okay?" he told her as the guard approached.

"I love you, too." She hung her head as she followed the detective out, with the guard right behind her.

He headed back to Chris' apartment and began furiously calling criminal attorneys until he finally found the one who said he could get her out. He and Chris met with the man in his plush office, giving him all the details of the case.

"I see," Daniel Arrington replied as Tanner told him the information he had. Tanner noticed how Daniel appeared overly alert and attentive to Chris from the moment they entered the office and he thought the whole thing slightly funny. The attorney's gaze rarely left the blonde beauty during their entire conversation. Daniel seemed right up Chris' alley even if she didn't know it yet. "So you have no idea what evidence they hold?"

"No, sir. They didn't tell me, but it must be somethin' pretty damagin' to arrest her, don't you think?"

"Not necessarily, Mr. Lewis. It could be circumstantial. The district attorney is up for re-election in a few months, and he's currently not favored to win. If he pins this case on your lady friend, it could shoe him in for another term."

"That's bogus!"

"I know, but to be able to wrap this case up nice and tidy would make thing much easier for him. Rest assured I'll get to the bottom of this evidence before it goes any further, and hopefully, I can get your lady out of jail before nightfall."

"That would be fantastic," Chris piped in, her eyes focused on the attorney across the desk.

"Of course, she'll have to stay in town until we either go to court or the charges are dropped. We'll be working on the latter as the best case scenario."

"No problem. She can stay with me."

"Good."

Tanner watched the exchange between the two. His focus needed to be on Amy, but the attraction between Chris and the attorney zinged through the air around them, even if they didn't notice.

"We'll head back to Chris' apartment, then. You'll let us know if they are going to release her so we can pick her up?"

"Um…yes. I'll call you as soon as I hear anything. I'm going to be headed to the jail when you two leave to talk to Amy and get her side of the story. That way I can present a strong case to the judge when we go in for the bail hearing in a few hours." Daniel stood to escort them out. "I'll be in touch."

"I look forward to it," Chris said, a small smile on her lips and Tanner just shook his head.

* * * *

The rest of the afternoon, Tanner and Chris spent pacing the floor in her apartment, waiting for the phone call. When it finally came, they both jumped, rushing for the phone.

"Hello?" Chris answered.

Tanner shuffled from foot to foot, anxious to hear what Daniel said while he listened to the one-sided conversation.

"Fantastic!" Chris exclaimed into the phone before she looked at Tanner. "They are releasing her. We need to pick her up in about an hour."

Tanner grabbed the phone from Chris and said, "Thanks, Mr. Arrington. You've been great."

"It's Daniel, and you're welcome. If I hate anything, its injustice and I'm afraid your lady friend has been the scapegoat for this one. We'll get everything straightened out."

"Okay, Daniel. Thanks again and we'll see you in a little bit." Tanner hung up the phone and grabbed Chris in a big hug.

"Let's go get her." Chris pulled out of his embrace and grabbed her purse before they headed for the door.

When Amy stepped out of the glass doors, wearing her work uniform again and without handcuffs, Tanner pulled her into his arms and she wrapped hers around him.

"God, you feel good," Tanner whispered, holding Amy so tight he felt like he would break her in two.

"Don't ever let go."

"Let's get out of here. This calls for a celebration," Chris said, wrapping her arms around them both. "Would you care to join us, Daniel?" she asked over her shoulder

"I'd love to."

Chris kept an arm around Amy's shoulder, Tanner on her other side as Daniel brought up the rear. "Daniel?" Amy questioned with a raise of her eyebrow.

"Don't start," Chris said. "It's nothing."

"Uh-huh."

"He's your attorney."

"So? Doesn't mean you can't be attracted to him. He is awful handsome."

They reached the waiting car as Tanner looked at Amy and teased,

"What are you doin' lookin'?"

"I'm just saying for Chris' sake." Amy planted a lingering kiss to his lips. "I have eyes only for a certain cowboy."

"Good answer." Tanner smiled before he kissed her again.

The foursome went back to Chris' apartment and ordered pizza so they could go over the case. Tanner and Amy watched as Chris and Daniel exchanged desire filled looks during the entire conversation.

"I've found out what the evidence is. Unfortunately, it does place you with access to the drugs."

"As they interrogated me, the detective kept asking me who I sold the drugs to. He wouldn't believe me when I said I didn't take them. I would never remove narcotics belonging to a patient or take extra's when I had access, for the purpose of selling them." Amy stood and started to pace. "I've worked in an emergency room and seen people die because of drugs, taking too many of something or swallowing a pill a friend gave them, not knowing what it contained. This is totally crazy!"

Tanner moved to her side and pulled her into his arms. "Everythin' will be okay. We'll get to the bottom of this."

"Do you know the pharmacist involved?" Daniel sorted through a couple of papers before he continued. "A Cory Harold?"

"Sure I do. He is one of the head pharmacists. If you mean on a personal level, no I don't."

"Do you think he would set you up to take the fall for this?"

Amy paused, chewing her lip nervously. "I don't believe so."

Daniel jotted notes as he asked, "Could he possibly be taking them himself?"

"He has access, of course. You hear everyday how another pharmacist had a drug problem. Cory never came across as someone who would be addicted, but if I understand the detective's correctly, they are looking for someone who is pushing these drugs out to the kids on the street. Do I think Cory could or would do that? Possibly."

"All we can do for now is try and figure out who else might be involved. Are there any other nurses with a drug problem that you are aware of?"

"No, I don't think so. How can they pin this on me, Daniel? Every nurse on the floor can get to those medications."

"From what I have been able to gather, this is all circumstantial evidence. Cory told the police he took the drugs from the pharmacy, gave them to you and you in turn, sold them to a dealer on the street."

"No way! He never gave me anything. Why is he doing this? Why me?"

"It sounds like he's trying to plea bargain with the DA. If he gives up his contact to the street, they'll go easier on him. For some reason, he decided it will be you."

"Can't you question him? Try to talk to him and find out why he's doing this?"

"I don't have access to him until he's on the witness stand if we go to trial. If he is indeed plea bargaining with the DA, we may never get an answer to those questions. Is there anyone you know connected to Cory who might hate you enough to try to pin this on you?"

Amy dropped her eyes, her gaze fixed on the coffee table in front of them, searching her mind as Tanner could almost see the wheels spinning in her brain. "No. I can't think of anyone."

"Do me favor tonight. Sit down and write a list of everyone who might hold a grudge against you. We may have to do a little investigating ourselves. I hope the police aren't ready to close this case without further investigation into the drug ring. We're missing something, someone else that is involved."

"Whatever you need to do, Daniel. We'll make sure it gets done." Tanner pulled her close as she snuggled against his side.

"Good. This may be a pretty long, drawn out process unless something busts wide open to turn the case away from Amy. I'll be in touch and thanks for the pizza as well as the company." Daniel stood, stuffing the papers he'd been working on into his briefcase before snapping it shut with a click.

Chris escorted Daniel to the door as Tanner watched from the couch. They said a few words to each other he couldn't hear, but a soft smile drifted across his mouth when Daniel lifted a hand and lightly brushed his fingers across Chris' cheek. He turned away from the other couple as he whispered what he hoped were soothing words in Amy's ear. He stroked her back while she buried her nose near his neck.

* * * *

Several days later, the group met to discuss the implications, attempting to brainstorm solutions for the situation. Daniel paced back and forth in front of the sliding glass door of Chris' apartment, agitation clear in his stride.

"I wish I knew how this connected together," Amy said as she leaned against Tanner's side.

"I'm not exactly sure. The convenience of Jack giving the hospital information and then for you to be arrested for selling them, is just too coincidental." He ran his fingers through his hair, making several pieces stick up in different directions. A small grin rippled across her lips. Seeing Daniel frustrated almost seemed funny. "Tell me again about your relationship with him."

"I don't understand how that helps. He's a rodeo rider. He would have no connection to this."

"Just tell me the details Amy. We're missing something here and I can't put my finger on it."

Amy sighed. "I met him at a rodeo several months ago. I don't usually date rodeo men. Relationships don't seem to work out. Anyway, we started dating and we even talked about moving in together and buying a piece of property outside of town. He started to get possessive and even though he loved riding bulls, he stopped going to rodeos as much and kept hanging out at my place. Come to think of it, he did seem to be able to acquire money all the time, not a lot, but enough to buy things even though he wasn't working and hadn't won any competitions for a while. He questioned everywhere I went, everyone I had dealings with, and accusing me of cheating. I couldn't even go to the store without him saying I had a thing for the checker."

Tanner snorted.

"He smacked me around a few times, leaving bruises, but never to the point of breaking a bone. I finally got tired of it and broke things off with him shortly before I met Tanner. He's confronted me on a couple of occasions since then."

Daniel asked, "About what? Where?"

"The last time I saw him, I was eating lunch at the deli around the corner from the hospital and he showed up. He demanded to know what my relationship with Tanner entailed and proceeded to tell me I belonged to him until he finished with me. I told him to go to hell basically and he left. I haven't seen him since."

"Are you sure he doesn't have connection to someone in the hospital?"

"He does, Daniel. He told me he had some powerful friends within the organization when he threatened to have me fired."

"We need to find out who his connections are."

"I'm not sure I'm following you." The frown lines settled between her eyes as she tried to understand.

"It sounds as if Daniel thinks Jack could be connected to this whole thing," Tanner added for the first time within the conversation.

"He's an asshole and vindictive to a fault, but what does that have to do with the drug ring?" Confusion clouded her mind for a moment before her eyes widened in realization. "You think he might be behind this? He doesn't do drugs. At least I don't believe so. I've never seen him use anything."

"He may not be using them for himself Amy. Drug dealing is a big business. Lots of money is involved. We need to find out if he knows or has a connection to the pharmacist," Daniel replied.

"But how?"

"That's where Arnie here comes in." Daniel nodded toward the balding man sitting next to him. "The DA's office could care less about you or how you fit into the whole picture. They want the dealer since the supplier has been apprehended. Unless Cory rolls and gives them a different name, they are content to let you take the fall."

"I can't go to prison, Daniel! This is crazy! I wasn't selling drugs!"

"I know you weren't, Amy, but we need to find evidence to point the finger in a different direction."

"Do you really think Jack could be behind this?"

"It's a distinct possibility."

"Okay. So what's the plan?"

"You may have to contact him again, Amy," Daniel suggested.

"No way! The man is crazy," Tanner objected. "He might hurt her."

"If I have to do this, then I need to. This must stop."

"You aren't gonna to put yourself in danger. I won't allow you to."

"Don't go getting all protective with me Tanner Lewis. I'm a grown woman and I can take care of myself."

"The hell you can! You said yourself, he can't be trusted. He's already smacked you around Amy. What if he really hurts you this time? I can't bear the thought."

"She won't be alone even if it seems she is. We can wire her and make sure we have back up," Daniel interjected.

"Y'all can't be serious."

"Do you have any other suggestions? If so, I'm willing to listen."

Tanner stood and began to pace, running his hand around the back of his neck as if he tried to loosen the tight muscles there. "There has to be a different way. What about talkin' to the police?"

"They don't care whether I go to jail or not Tanner. You heard Daniel."

"What if I hook up with him and convince him I'm lookin' to get into the business?" Tanner's suggestion held value, but when Amy's gaze found Daniel, he shook his head no.

"He'll never buy that Tanner. He knows you and wouldn't trust you. It has to be Amy if anybody. He might trust her. If someone else tries to infiltrate, it would take a long time to convince him," Daniel explained.

"I don't like this, not one bit," Tanner grumbled. "I have a bad feelin' about the whole thing."

She stepped in front of Tanner, sliding her hands up his chest as she looked into his eyes. "I'll be fine. This may be the only way to stop what's happening."

"What if you get hurt? I couldn't live with myself if that happened," Tanner murmured, stroking her cheek with his fingers. "I love you."

"I love you, too. I'll be extra careful. Besides, we don't even know if he'll buy me trying to get back together with him. I have to try."

"I think it's our only option at this point. If we don't get something to shine light on someone else being responsible, Amy will go to jail for a very long time."

"I don't have much choice from what it sounds like. You two have already convinced yourselves this is the only option."

Amy wrapped her arms around Tanner's waist and buried her face in his neck. "It'll be okay."

"You need to call him Amy and see what you can set up. Nothing says he'll even buy this," Daniel said from his spot on the couch.

She nodded reluctantly as she pulled out of Tanner's embrace. Grabbing her cell phone, she scrolled through the numbers, dialed and held her breath. She set the phone on the counter, putting it on speaker so everyone else could hear the conversation as well.

The gravelly voice growled, "What do you want?"

"I need to see you, Jack."

"Why? I thought you didn't want anything more to do with me and why is your phone on speaker?"

"I'm doing some cleaning around my apartment. I put the speaker on so I can still talk to you and do what I need to around here." She held her breath a second, hoping he would buy her explanation. "I've come to the conclusion that I miss you and what we had."

"What about the cowboy from down south?"

"You mean Tanner?

"Yeah. I thought you were in *love*?"

"I decided I didn't want a long distance relationship, Jack. I want you and," she fought the urge to throw up "I love you." Her eyes met Tanner's across the room, hoping he would understand those three words were for him and not the lunatic on the phone.

"So what are you saying, Amy?"

"I want us to get back together."

"This isn't just to get me to lay off on the allegations against you for stealing drugs?"

"No, Jack, but you know they are saying I'm involved in one of the pharmacists scheme to sell drugs on the street, right?"

He chuckled. "Yeah, I heard."

"I don't take drugs, Jack. I don't know why you told them I do."

"Because you pissed me off Amy, hanging around with the wannabe cowboy. He can't hold a candle to me."

She gagged silently. "I know, Jack. My relationship with Tanner didn't mean anything. So what do you say? Can I see you?"

"All right. Meet me at the motel six on East Market Street at three," Jack told her, "and don't be late."

"Of course not. I'll see you in a bit." Amy picked up the phone, hit end and shut it with a decisive click before she felt Tanner's arms slide around her from behind and she leaned into his embrace.

"Now what do we do?"

"How far is the motel from here?"

"About fifteen minutes," Chris answered.

"Perfect. We have three hours to get Amy wired so we can record her conversation with him. Hopefully, she'll be able to get him to say something that will incriminate him."

Arnie pulled a tiny wire connected to a small black box from his briefcase as he smiled. "I just so happened to have a wiring device."

A dry chuckle reverberated through the room from the rest of the group.

Her heart hammered in her chest as Daniel laid out the plan. Tanner, Daniel and Arnie would be close by, but confronting Jack terrified her. His temper had always been a problem between them and if he figured out the whole thing smelled like a set up, who knows what he would do, probably kill her. *I'm not sure he's even involved in this drug deal thing.* She shuttered. "What if we're wrong about him, about this and his involvement? This could all be for nothing."

"That's always a possibility Amy, but somehow I don't think so. For some reason, I think Jack is involved up to his eyeballs," Daniel reiterated.

"I guess I need to get wired up then," she said as she stood. "How does this work, Arnie?"

"I'll tape the wire to your body and the microphone will be nestled between your um..." his eyes shifted to her chest before ricocheting back to her eyes, "breasts. We'll be able to hear everything said."

"I'll be doin' the tapin', not you," Tanner growled.

"No problem." Arnie shifted in the chair and Amy smiled. Obviously Tanner wouldn't let the other man touch her, much less tape anything to her breast.

"You need to tape the end of this right between her breasts, trail the wire underneath and secure the small box to between her legs or somewhere it won't be felt."

"He better not be doin' any touchin', or I'll personally break his fingers." Tanner grabbed the device, a roll of tape Arnie had and following Amy into the bedroom, shutting the door securely behind them.

Chapter 19

She sat in her car in front of the motel. Her muscles bunched tight, her heart hammering in her chest as trepidation rippled through her. *I have a really bad feeling about this.*

"Can you hear me?"

The horn blew once somewhere off to her right, the signal from the group who watched her every move, listening to her every word. The sound calmed her nerves slightly as she waited. A few moments later, Jack's car pulled in next to her. She slipped out her keys and stuffed them into her purse as she grabbed it off the seat next to her.

When she stepped around the back of her car, Jack advanced on her, his eyes glittering in the sunlight. He grabbed her roughly around the waist and slammed her body against his, before he ground his lips over hers until she whimpered under the onslaught.

Finally lifting his head, he chuckled dryly as he said, "You always did like it rough."

"Do you have a room here?"

"Yeah. Let's go. I want you naked. You'll be sucking me dry in a matter of second's, babe." He grabbed her hand and tugged her toward the door a short distance away. Her gaze swung to the van parked against the back of the lot for a moment. Her breath hitched in her throat. *God, please don't let him hurt me.*

He pushed the door open on the motel room and yanked her by the arm until she stepped inside and he slammed the door behind them.

"Get rid of those clothes."

"Listen Jack, I think we need to talk a little. I mean, I haven't seen you in a while. What have you been doing?"

"What the hell do you care?"

"I want to know everything you've been up to since we've been together. I love you, and I want to be part of your life." Bile rose in the back of her throat. She fought to swallow it before she gagged.

He chuckled. "I've been keeping busy."

"Did you find a job or something?" She wandered away from his side, inspecting the dingy, smelly room, trying desperately to keep herself between him and door in case she needed to get out quickly.

"Yeah, you could say that."

"Doing what?"

"Let's just say I'm working inventory."

"Really? Where?"

"It's under the table. You know, that way I don't have to pay taxes."

"Ah, I see. Is it paying decent?"

He cocked an eyebrow. "Not bad. I'm making enough to survive."

"I noticed you got a nice new car, but I would think you could afford something a little better than this if this new job is paying well."

"I've got something real nice lined up. I'll be moving in a few days."

"Wonderful! What's it like?"

"A high rise apartment on the west side. Top floor."

"You mean like a penthouse or something?"

"Yeah. Great view of the city. I think you'll like it."

She cleared her throat as she tried to steer the conversation where her listeners needed. "Why did you tell the hospital I had stolen drugs?"

"I told you, you made me mad."

"You did a good job getting me in trouble. They are trying to say me and one of the pharmacists are selling them to someone on the street. A dealer or something."

"Sounds like a clever ploy."

"You know I wouldn't get involved. I don't want to lose my nursing license and doing something that stupid, would put it seriously in jeopardy."

He stood up from the spot he had taken on the bed and moved toward her, a feral look to his eyes. "I might be able to get you out of this *trouble* you're in."

"How?"

"I told you before, I have connections within the hospital," he whispered when he stopped in front of her.

"But how is that supposed to help me? The police said Cory told them he gave them to me to give to some dealer." *Hold your ground, Amy. Don't let him see how much he scares you.*

"I'm sure he could be persuaded to change his story for the right price." Jack picked up a curl that lay across her shoulder, caressing it with his fingers and she fought a shiver of revulsion.

"He might rescind his story, but I don't understand. Do you know Cory? How do you know he can be bought like that?"

The wild gleam still reflected in his gaze. "We are *acquainted* you might say."

"Oh?" She stepped back, trying to break the contact he had with her body, but she met the wall behind her as he moved closer.

"We have some mutual friends. Your pharmacist friend has a drug problem and financial troubles. I've put him in contact with someone who helps him with his predicament."

He bent his head, intent on kissing her until she turned slightly so he only grazed her cheek. It didn't stop him. He slid his lips along her cheek to her ear, biting the sensitive lobe and she had to fight herself to keep from shoving him off.

"You can't be serious, Jack. The police told me he stole drugs from the pharmacy at work. That's common knowledge, but for some reason, he's saying he gave them to me to give to the dealer."

He chuckled in her ear. "You wouldn't even know who to contact to sell drugs. You are too miss-goody-two-shoes."

"I'm glad someone believes me."

"Only because I know who his contact really is and who helped set you up for stealing the drugs," he said, his mouth moving to her neck as he sucked the soft flesh between his lips. His hand slipped up her side, making its way toward her breast.

"Who would that be Jack?" She shoved against his chest enough to break the contact of his lips.

"Where do you think all the money I have to get the new apartment and the new car outside?"

"You're his dealer?"

"Yeah. You could say that, honey. It's a very lucrative business." His eyes met hers. "You proved to be very easy to set up as the one taking the drugs from the hospital. A little help from a lonely woman and presto, instant access. Anna proved to be very gullible to my charms." He laughed cruelly. "She really thought I loved her, but I only love you."

"What do you mean Jack?"

"She took the extra drugs from the hospital and made it look like you did it, but when she started blackmailing me, saying she would tell everyone. I had to eliminate her."

Her startled gasp echoed through the room. "You killed Anna?"

"Yeah. Pesky bitch."

"I don't believe you!"

"Believe me, sweetheart. I met her in her apartment after she met you in the elevator. I fucked her brains out and then strangled her. She always did like the rough play."

His hand reached her breast and he cupped it in his palm, pinching her nipple through her shirt. She whimpered at the pain of his intrusion. He let go and slid his fingers under her breast, sliding down her rib cage. Suddenly, he stepped back, ripped her shirt open and exposed the wire taped to her stomach. "What the hell is this?" He grabbed the wire, tearing the tape from her skin. "You fucking bitch! You're wired!"

* * * *

Jack's words sent chills down Tanner's back. They heard a loud slap and a noise that sounded like shuffling before the wire went dead. All four people sat in stunned silence for a moment before Tanner reacted.

"I'm goin' in," Tanner growled, before he grabbed the door handle of the van where they sat listening.

"He might be armed. We have to be careful. The only gun we have is the one that Arnie has," Daniel insisted.

"I don't give a flyin' fuck. The sounds we just heard could mean anything. He could be tryin' to kill her right now."

He pushed the door open and the three remaining in the van jumped out behind him before they raced across the parking lot to the door Amy and Jack had disappeared through.

"Let me handle this. Hopefully we can get him to open the door." Arnie tapped the butt of his revolver on the door and called out, "Mr. Jack Miller. I have a warrant for your arrest. Open the door."

"Go to fucking hell!"

More crashes could be heard and a stifled moan reached their ears, sending shivers down Tanner's spine. "Blow the lock," Tanner insisted.

"Step back," Arnie instructed as he lifted the gun and pointed it at the door handle. "Mr. Miller, you have two seconds to open this door and give yourself up before I blow the lock."

Silence.

"One, two." The gun exploded in the heavy afternoon air, shattering the lock on the door, releasing it and allowing the others to push it open.

Tanner shoved his way inside only to meet Amy's terrified eyes where she stood held tightly to Jack's chest like a shield. A gun was pressed to her temple, and her face had already begun to swell. She whimpered as she attempted to wrestle his tight arm from around her throat.

"I should have known," Jack said as the other joined Tanner inside the door. "Come on in, lover boy, and join the party."

"Let her go, Miller," Tanner spat, trying desperately to control his temper.

"Not likely, dude. She's my ticket out of here."

"You can't get away, Miller. There are cops swarming around the parking lot as we speak. You'll never leave here with her as a hostage." Arnie calmly pointed out to Jack from somewhere behind Tanner.

"Then I guess I'll have to kill all of you," Jack said as the gun left Amy's temple and he pointed it at the four of them. "Who shall I blow away first?" His eyes narrowed as they fixed on Tanner. "I think lover boy gets it before anyone else. He's been such a pain in my ass since you met him, Amy."

"You'll only get one shot off, Mr. Miller, before I kill you where you stand," Arnie said as he stood pointing his own gun at the crazy man across the room.

"Well then, it will definitely have to be for Mr. Wonderful there. If I can't have Amy, neither will you." Jack leveled the gun at his chest.

"No!" Amy screamed as she knocked Jack's arm with her hand. Two explosions ripped through the air within a second of each other.

Tanner dove for cover as the guns went off, but as the smoke cleared and no more shots were fired, he searched for Amy. A few minutes later, police slipped inside the room, guns drawn.

"Amy?" He got to his feet, his eyes searching.

"Stay right where you are, mister," one of the blue uniforms demanded as Tanner tried to find the woman he loved.

"I'm not the one with a gun."

"We don't know that, so just stay put until we secure everything." One officer moved toward where Tanner could now see Jack lying in a rapidly spreading pool of blood. The rest of the officers ushered Daniel, Chris and Arnie outside, but he wasn't leaving until he knew where Amy could be.

When they finally let him move, he went around the other side of the bed as terror gripped his heart. She lay on her side between the bed and the wall.

"Amy?" He squatted be her side as he brushed the hair from her face. He looked at the officer next to him and said, "She needs an ambulance."

"One is already here," the officer told him. "You need to move back so they can work on her."

Two paramedics pushed their way inside the rapidly filling room and stopped next to Jack while two more ushered Tanner out of the way. They slipped a backboard next to her and rolled her onto her back, before securing her with several straps.

"Is she gonna be all right?" Tanner asked. She hadn't spoken or opened her eyes for several minutes.

"We aren't sure, sir. We need to get her to the emergency room. Are you family?"

"I'm her boyfriend," Tanner murmured, not taking his eyes off of her.

"Does she have family here?"

"Not really. They all live on the west coast."

"You'll need to meet us at the hospital then. Now if you'll excuse us, we need to get her loaded."

Tanner followed them out to the waiting ambulance. Just as they were about to load her inside, she opened her eyes and whispered, "Tanner?"

"Yeah, baby. I'm right here."

"I love you."

Tears pooled at the corners of his eyes. "I love you, too, darlin'. I'll be right behind you."

"What happened to Jack?"

"I don't know. Don't worry about it right now."

The paramedics slid the gurney into the waiting truck and slammed the doors.

* * * *

Tanner paced the waiting room as Chris, Daniel and Arnie warmed a set of chairs in the corner. Several minutes later, Chris moved toward Tanner with a cup of coffee in her hands.

"Here, drink this."

"Thanks," Tanner said, taking the cup from her hands and sipping the hot liquid for a moment. He ran his fingers through his hair as frustration curled in his chest. "Damn it!"

"What's wrong?"

"They haven't told us anythin'. This waitin' is drivin' me crazy."

She wrapped an arm around his shoulders as she replied, "I know. Hang in there and I'll see if I can find out anything."

He watched as Chris made her way to the nurses' station, before he turned and headed to where Daniel sat. Tanner took the chair Chris had vacated a few moments ago.

"She'll be okay," Daniel said.

"God, I hope so."

"At least with the information we gathered on tape, the police should be dropping the charges on her shortly. I have a call into the judge right now."

"It would be nice to tell her some good news once they let me back there."

Chris returned to their side a moment later. "They won't tell me much except that she's having some tests done, CAT scan and blood work mostly. It sounds as if she might have a concussion. The nurse called in the back and they said you could visit her in a minute or two."

"Thanks, Chris. How did you managed to get so much information? They wouldn't tell me anythin'."

"It helps working here. Even though we don't work in the emergency room, Amy and I are employees so they tend to tell us a bit more."

"Mr. Lewis?" a nurse called from the nearby doorway.

"Yes?" Tanner got to his feet quickly and approached her.

"You can come back now. Amy is asking for you."

Tanner followed the nurse to a curtained off area. She directed him between the panels and his heart dropped in his chest as he saw Amy lying on the backboard, still strapped down, her eyes closed and a large bruise forming on her cheek.

"Darlin'? Can you hear me?"

She moaned softly before she opened her eyes. "Tanner?" He leaned over her and softly kissed her lips.

"I'm right here."

"What happened?"

"You don't remember?"

"Not really. Where am I?"

"You're at the hospital in the emergency room. Jack must have pushed you or somethin' in the motel room. I'm not sure what's exactly goin' on."

"Is everyone else okay?"

He shook his head as he chuckled. "Listen to you, all worried about the rest of us."

She smiled.

"Everyone is fine except Jack. I'm not sure what's goin' on with him. I suppose the brought him here, too, but I haven't heard anythin'."

"Where is the nurse? I'll ask her what's going on. They need to get me off this damned board though. It's killing my back."

He laughed before he said, "I'll see if I can find someone."

* * * *

Chris shifted in her chair, trying to avoid looking at Daniel as she sighed. Her body had been on high-alert since she met the man. His gaze on her made her breasts tingle and her nipples harden. *He seems interested.* She stood up and began to pace. *Damn it! I wish I knew what ran through his mind when he looks at me. I can't read him like other men.* She stopped near the window and looked outside. Several moments later, he saw his reflection in the glass as he stepped up behind her.

Placing his hands on her shoulders, he said, "She'll be all right."

Giving into the attraction and his touch, she leaned back into his embrace as she let his strong chest shelter her. "I know. It's nothing major, but it could have been so much worse. What if Jack's bullet hit one of us? I can't bear the thought of losing you...I mean Tanner or Amy."

He chuckled at her slip of the tongue, his hands sliding down her arms. "You and I need to talk."

"We do?"

His eyes met hers in the glass. "I think so." The heat of his gaze even in the reflection as it moved down to her chest, sent her nipples into hard pebbles. He turned her around in his arms, before raking his fingers down her cheek. Her lips parted as a soft sigh escaped them when his thumb whispered across her lower lip.

"I'm dying to find out what your mouth tastes like," he murmured. "I want to know the feel of your lips, the texture of your hair as it wraps around my hand, and the softness of your skin under mine." His mouth moved toward hers.

"Chris?" Tanner's voice brought her out of the fog Daniel's touch wrapped her in as he called her name. Daniel stepped back.

Chris cleared her throat, resisting the urge to fan herself from the heat. "Yeah?"

"They should be releasing her in a few minutes."

"Did they say what's wrong?"

"Concussion I think and maybe a couple of bruised ribs. She'll be fine."

"That's great, Tanner." Her eyes met Daniel's again. "I guess we can take her back to my place tonight. You haven't heard from the judge yet have you, Daniel?"

"No, but it's getting kind of late so we probably won't hear anything tonight."

"I'll bring her out in a few minutes. They're doin' her paperwork now. We might need to get somethin' to eat before we head back to your place, Chris. I don't know about y'all, but I'm starvin'," Tanner drawled.

They laughed. "No problem," Chris said.

As Tanner returned to Amy's side, the silence between Chris and Daniel stretched on. Awareness zinged through the air between them as she sighed, stuffed her hands in her pockets and rocked back on her heels. "Would you like to join us, Daniel? You are just as much a part of this as any of us."

A small smile rippled across his lips. "I'd like that."

"Good. I'm sure Amy would like you to as well."

Tanner returned a few minutes later pushing Amy in a wheelchair. "I don't need you to wheel me out Tanner, I'm fine."

"Too bad. Let me take care of you for a change," he insisted as Amy rolled her eyes and Chris laughed.

"I'll pull the car around."

She grabbed her keys from her purse, and Daniel followed as he said, "I'll go with you." She shrugged as he fell into step beside her. Pushing the thought of his lips on hers out of her mind for now, she opened the door on the car and unlocked the passenger side. Once Amy settled into the rear seat, Tanner by her side, they said good bye to Arnie and left the hospital.

"What does everyone want as far as food?"

"I'm game for anything," Amy said from behind her.

"You sure you're up to this, Amy? You probably should rest," Tanner suggested.

"Don't get all protective with me again. I'm fine, just a little sore and I need food."

Chris shook her head and smiled as she saw Tanner pull Amy into his embrace from her rear view mirror. A moment later, she could feel Daniel's eyes focused on her and she turned her head for a second and caught his intense stare out of the corner of her eye.

Dinner gave them a chance to celebrate. The drug charges should be dropped by tomorrow evening and Jack wouldn't be a problem anymore or so they thought.

"Did the hospital give you any indication on his condition, Chris?" Amy asked.

"No. I only know he had been taken to the emergency room and they were working on him," she answered.

"Well, hopefully he'll be in there for awhile and when they do let him out, he'll go to jail for a long time."

"As long as he stays away from you, baby, that's all I care about."

Once they reached Chris' apartment, Tanner and Amy took a seat on the couch. Chris frowned for a moment as she watched them, her heart sad in her chest. *I want that so bad I can taste it!* Her eyes met Daniel's across the room before she got up from her chair and wandered out onto the back patio of her apartment. The night air hit her face and she sighed heavily, her thoughts focused on the disturbing presence of the man in her inside.

The door slid open. She didn't have to look. The hair standing up on her arms told her who stood behind her. His hands found her shoulders and she allowed herself to lean into his chest as his warm breath whispered across the flesh of her neck. *Good grief, just his touch sends me into a sexual frenzy.* He turned her around in his arms and the look in his eyes sent her heart slamming against her ribs in anticipation.

This wasn't the same staunch, trussed up in a fancy suit lawyer she'd come to think of him as. He was all male, obviously a very aroused male as his musky, sexy scent met her nostrils.

"Daniel, I—"

His mouth slanted across hers, grinding his lips against her softer ones. She moaned softly under his onslaught, and as she parted her lips under the pressure, his tongue darted inside to take possession. After several moments, he lifted his head, breathing rapidly as his big body pinned her where she stood.

"I couldn't stand being here with you and not feeling your lips under mine anymore," he whispered as his mouth trailed across her cheek and down her neck.

She moaned before she said, "But Amy and Tanner…"

"They've gone off to bed, and I expect they're doing exactly what I want to do to you right now."

"I…" She sighed as his teeth nipped at her throat.

He raised his head and looked into her eyes. "Make no mistake, lady. I want you. I want to bury myself inside you right now so badly I ache, but we need to get to know each other better before that happens. I don't want you to think this is just something sexual because it isn't." He trailed his fingers across her cheek a moment before he stepped back and disappeared into the apartment. Several seconds later, she heard the front door shut as he left.

Chapter 20

"Gilley's should be crowded tonight. I'm sure you'll get some great exposure," Amy said as they parked a couple of blocks from the club and Tanner grabbed his guitar from behind the seat.

"I'll take whatever I can get."

He wrapped his arm possessively around her waist as they stopped at the door and paid the cover charge. Tanner asked the doorman how to go about getting on the list to play and the man pointed toward the back where a small table sat in the corner.

"Thanks."

Approaching the table, a platinum blonde with a shirt low enough her enormous fake boobs almost spilled over the top, raked Tanner with her eyes as Amy bristled beside him. He leaned close to Amy's ear and whispered, "I love you," before moving away and stepping up to the table.

"I need to sign up for the open mic night."

"Sure, sugar. Sign on the line." The woman pointed her bright red fingernail to the spot on the paper.

She whipped the page around when he finished and smiled again. "Well, Tanner Lewis, I'm sure you'll do fabulous. I can't wait to hear your deep baritone voice."

Tanner flashed a dimpled smile at the blonde and Amy gritted her teeth so loud she thought for sure, everyone in the bar could hear it. Resisting the urge to elbow him in the side, she spun around with the intent of disappearing into the crowd without him. He grabbed her elbow and tugged her back. "Goin' somewhere?"

"I thought I might find a cowboy around here interested in a girl without size double D boobs spilling out of a shirt that is three sizes too small."

He nudged her ear with his nose and licked her earlobe, sending tingles clear to her toes. "I happened to like your tits just like they are. And I love you with all my heart."

She murmured as he nibbled her neck, "Women don't like them called tits."

He chuckled before he said, "She's nothin' more than another woman Amy, and you're *my* woman. The one I love and the one I'm goin' home with no matter who else tries to come on to me." He lifted his head finally and looked into her eyes as he stroked her cheek. "Do you love me enough not to be jealous?"

"I'll always be jealous, Tanner, when other women throw themselves at you, but I'll try to keep it under control."

"No one else holds a candle to you in my eyes." He leaned over and kissed her. "Let's find a table."

Sitting down just to the right of the platform positioned at the front of the bar, Tanner ordered them both a beer and took her hand in his.

"Are you sure you're up for this? You probably needed to rest a little more before trekking out with me."

"I'm fine. Quit being such a worrier."

"I'm gonna worry. Get used to it. I love you and worryin' about you comes with lovin' you." He kissed her fingers. Their eyes turned to the stage as a tall, lanky man stepped up to the microphone.

"Howdy y'all." A round of applause rippled through the room until he raised his hand to quiet the crowd. "For those of you who have been here before, you know tonight is open mic night. We have several people signing up to stand up here and sing their hearts out so let's give a big round of applause to our first performer. Come on up here Cole Wright."

For over two hours, different men and women stood up on the stage. Some strummed guitars as they sang and some had recorded background music as the lights focused on their faces. Tanner listened intently to each and every one, giving Amy his opinion of a few. She could tell which he thought were good. Those were the ones he didn't say a word about. When it came to his turn, he leaned over and kissed her quickly before he whispered, "For good luck."

"Okay, everybody. Let's give a hardy welcome a good looking cowboy from south of here near Houston. This is Tanner Lewis."

Tanner took the stage as Amy moved close to the bottom so she could be near his feet. "Howdy, folks. I would love to do a couple of songs for you. I wrote both of these myself so I hope you enjoy 'em." Her chest swelled with pride as the crowd grew silent when he started to pick his guitar. You could have heard a pin drop in the bar as his voice filled the space around them. No one talked and even the bartenders were quiet during his two songs. When he finished, he flashed his heart-stopping dimpled smile and the crowd erupted in applause so loud, the noise hurt her ears. The announcer moved up on the stage and said, "Wow!" He grabbed Tanner's hand and pumped it a number of times before he let go. "Let's give it up again for Tanner Lewis, y'all."

Tanner jumped down from the stage, wrapping his arm around her as he escorted her back to the table. He picked up the beer on the table, slamming the remainder down his throat. His eyes sparkled in the light as he leaned down and kissed her soundly on the mouth. Several people came over to congratulate him and bought both of them drinks while he talked and laughed. *He sure knows how to work a crowd.*

She tapped him on the arm and put her mouth next to his ear. "I'm going to the ladies room. I'll be right back." He smiled and nodded, his attention drawn back to the two men standing next to him.

The wait in the bathroom took a considerably long time, before she started to weave her way back through the ever increasing crowd in the bar. She had a hard time even seeing Tanner over the group of people, but she knew the general direction of their table as she squeezed between bodies. Finding a break in the horde of people, she could finally see Tanner and her eyes narrowed. Her man stood in the middle, surrounded by a group of women, two of which had their arms wrapped around his waist. *I'll kill 'em!*

Making her way to his side, she forcefully wormed her way between one of the girl's and Tanner, wrapping her own arm around him before she reached up and tugged on his hair until he brought his mouth to hers. She slipped her tongue between his lips as he moaned softly into her mouth. When she finally let him go, the group of women had disbursed into the crowd around him.

"Possessive, aren't we?" He chuckled softly as he slid his fingers down her cheek.

"You're damned right. You are here with me and as such, I expect you to pay attention to me, not them."

"They were only makin' conversation, Amy."

"Conversation doesn't require their lips on your face." She looked from one side of his face to the other. "You have red on one cheek and pink on the other."

"And yours on my lips." He pulled her tight against his chest. "Yours are the only pair that will touch mine."

He bent his head and kissed her, slipping his tongue inside her mouth as she melted into him until they heard someone clear their throat behind them.

"Excuse me. I don't mean to interrupt, but I would like to talk to you for a moment." Her gaze found an older gentleman wearing a simple dress shirt and slacks, with graying hair at his temple and a smile on his face, standing off to their left. "My name is Arthur Foster."

"Nice to meet you, Mr. Foster," Tanner replied, taking the hand offered.

"I have a proposition for you, son, but we need to go somewhere not so crowded and loud. Can I buy you a cup of coffee? There is a coffee shop around the corner."

"Uh...sure." Tanner grabbed his guitar case and her hand, before they followed the gentleman out the door into the cooler night air. She hadn't realized how hot the bar had gotten until they were outside and she could take a deep breath again.

They followed the man through the double glass doors and took a seat in one of the booths in the corner.

"What can I get for y'all?" the waitress asked as she approached the threesome.

"Coffee for me, Millie."

"Coffee is fine. Amy?"

"Sounds good."

The waitress disappeared and Amy turned her attention to the man across the table.

"I'm sure you're wondering what this is all about."

"Yeah, you could say that," Tanner replied.

Arthur pulled out his wallet and slid a small, flat business card across the table. It read, Arthur Foster, A&R Representative, Country Life Records.

Amy read the card from Tanner's side and when the implications of the man's title hit her, she gasped. "You're from a record label?"

"Yes, Miss and I'd like to have your boyfriend here, come by and do a few songs for some people."

"You're serious?"

"Yes, son, I am. You are very talented and we are always looking for new talent in country music. As I'm sure you know, it is also a very cutthroat business, but I think you have what it takes to make a great career. Are you interested?"

"Interested? Of course I'm interested." The smile that spread across Tanner's face melted Amy's heart. Singing meant everything to him and God meant to hand him his chance on a silver platter. "When and where?"

"Call me in a couple of days at the number on the card and I'll let you know. I need to set things up with the studio and make sure the execs I want are available."

Tanner sat in stunned silence for a moment as he studied the card in his hand, but Arthur just smiled.

"He'll call you. Thank you so much for giving him this chance. You have no idea how much this means to him," Amy said, watching as the man began to rise from his spot in the booth.

"I'll talk to you soon then, Mr. Lewis." Arthur dropped several dollar bills on the table to pay for the coffee.

"Uh, yeah. Thank you," Tanner replied as he stood and shook Arthur's hand, before Arthur turned and walk out of the diner.

Amy quickly slid out of the booth and hugged Tanner tight as she exclaimed, "Oh my God! This is fantastic! I never in my wildest dreams thought bringing you here tonight would result in this."

He finally seemed to come out of shock as a huge grin flashed across his face and he hugged her tight enough, she thought he might break her in two. "A record deal. Oh man! I might have a record deal! I can't believe this."

"Believe me, it's for real." Amy held on tight as trepidation rolled down her back. *If he makes it big, how am I going to handle all of these women throwing themselves at him? I can hardly stand even a few, much less thousands.* Flashes of rock concerts where women threw bras and underwear at the artists, rippled across her mind and she sighed. *Can I deal with the life of a star?*

* * * *

"You are awfully quiet. What are you thinkin'?" Tanner asked as they lay side-by-side in her bed later that night, his fingers stroking the arm lying across his chest.

"Nothing."

"I know you better than that. You're too quiet for nothin'."

She kissed his chest, sliding her lips over the expanse until she reached the flat copper disk and laving it with her tongue. He moaned for a moment before he pushed her back and forced her to look into his eyes. "Distractin' isn't fair. Tell me what's botherin' you babe."

She rolled away and sat on the side of the bed. "I'm just not sure I can handle the whole thing with you being a star."

"Amy, I'm a long way from bein' a star."

An unladylike snort left her mouth. "I've seen you perform, Tanner, and I know what I saw even tonight at Gilley's. You're a natural. Oh, it may take a few years, but you'll get there eventually and when you do, I'm afraid I'll be pushed to the back of your life."

He reached over and pulled her back into his arms. "I love you, Amy Russell, and you will never, ever be pushed to the back of my life, no matter what happens."

"I wish I could believe you."

"What do I have to do to convince you?"

"I don't know, Tanner."

"Tell you what. Let's not worry about this right now. I don't even have a record deal yet. We need to see what the next few days bring before we start assumin' anythin'."

"I love you," she whispered as she trailed her lips down his neck and nipped at the soft skin with her teeth. She gently sucked it into her mouth.

"No hickies. I can't go to the audition with hickies on my neck."

Anger zipped through her at an alarming speed. "Never mind," she spat as she rolled over and got out of the bed.

"Amy?"

"Is this the way it's going to be? I can't even make love with you the way I want to because I can't mark up their property?" Tears sparkled at the corners of her eyes and she angrily wiped them away. "This is fucking ridiculous, Tanner. The next thing you'll be telling me is you can't be near me because you can't go into the audition with a hard-on."

"This could be a huge break for me. Why can't you understand?"

"I do understand, Tanner and I'm happy for you, but I don't want this to change what is between us and it already is."

"No, it's not," he said rising from the bed and moving to her side. "If things are changin', it's because you are lettin' 'em"

"How can you say that? You just told me not to leave marks on you."

"Only where they can be seen." He pulled her to his chest and she buried her face in his shoulder. "I love you," he whispered in her ear.

"I love you, too. Please don't let this come between us."

"I promise it won't. I love you too much to lose you now." He pushed her back and looked into her eyes. "Let me love you. I need you. You are the other half to my heart and I can't live without you."

She couldn't tell him no. The love shining in his gaze melted her heart and she let him lead her back to the bed.

* * * *

Amy stood outside the recording booth and watched. The thick glass separated her from Tanner as he sang his heart out into the microphone in front of him. The audition had gone perfectly and now he sat on a stool inside the booth recording. After the label offered him a contract, he had moved in with her in Dallas to be closer to the studio. She loved having him around all the time, but she still felt like he held a secret in his heart, one he did not want to share with her. Their loving had become almost desperate, at least on her part.

"Perfect Tanner. Let's take a break," the engineer said into the microphone and Tanner nodded before he removed the headset he wore and walked through the door.

He planted a lingering kiss on her lips as he reached her side. "I'm starvin'. How about you?"

"I could use something to eat."

"Let's hit the café up the street."

After they ordered their food and took a seat, Amy said, "So when do they expect you to start touring?"

"Soon. I think they've set up a couple of dates already," Tanner replied taking a bite of the sandwich in front of him.

"Close by?"

"Not sure. They haven't given me the details yet."

She dropped her eyes as she picked at her food.

"What's wrong?"

She sighed heavily before she answered. "You're aware I won't be able to go with you if they are somewhere else than within a few hours drive. I have to work to pay the bills while you tour."

He took her hand in his. "I know. Everything will work out babe. They should be giving me an advance on royalties so I can pay for some of the tourin' stuff. That should help, too."

"It bothers me I can't go with you."

"I don't like you not with me either, but we'll get through this."

"I suppose."

They finished their lunch and made their way back to the studio. Tanner opened the front door for her and as they approached the front desk, the girl behind the counter told Tanner she had a message for him.

A confused look passed over his face before he asked, "For me?"

"Yep. Here you go." She handed him the folded piece of paper.

He unfolded the paper as a frown appeared.

"What is it?" He handed the paper to Amy. Terror ripped through her as she read the words:

> *Watch your back.*
> *You are a dead man.*

"My God Tanner. This is a threat letter."

"I'm sure it's nothin'." He took the scrap from her hand before he turned and asked the girl if she knew who left it for him.

"Some guy is all I can tell you. He didn't really notice. He just dropped it off and said to give it to you."

"It isn't nothing. Whoever wrote this is threatening your life. We need to call the police, Tanner," Amy said. "Maybe they can dust the paper for fingerprints or something."

"Fine, we'll call, but don't make a big deal out of this."

She forced an angry sigh out of her mouth. "This is a big deal."

"We'll talk to the police after I'm done this afternoon, okay? Will that make you feel better?"

"Better than nothing, but you need to take this seriously."

He ushered her back toward the recording booth. "Let's see what the police say about it before we go jumping to conclusions."

He took his place back in the booth, leaving her standing behind the glass again. *I don't believe him! He's going to blow this off.* She shook her head as he started singing.

The police met them at her apartment later in the afternoon.

"Are you sure you don't know who might have sent this?"

"Not a clue, officer," Tanner answered.

Amy watched the exchange as the officer took notes. "Can't you dust it or something? We need to find out who is threatening him."

"Ma'am, do you have any idea how many country music artists get this kind of stuff?"

"No and I don't care. You have to investigate."

"We'll do our best, but we are perpetually short-handed. Not that we are trying to say this isn't important, but really, it's not a priority."

"Everythin' will be fine, Amy. Stop worryin' so much."

"I'm going to worry. I love you."

"I love you, too, darlin'.

* * * *

Over the next several months, Tanner toured extensively, leaving Amy at home on many occasions. The tour seemed plague with accidents from pieces of the stage falling, to the bus blowing tires on the road. One stop had Tanner over twelve hours away by car. As they kissed and whispered I love you before he left, she felt tears burn behind her eyes. *I have a really bad feeling about this, but he's not going to listen to me.*

She went to work after he left and spent the entire day wondering, hoping and praying her feelings were wrong. He called her before he went on stage that night and she finally managed to drift off to sleep in their big bed once he said I love you and goodnight.

The next morning she woke to his lips drifting across her cheek.

"Mmm. You're home," she whispered before his mouth found hers.

His tongue slipped between her lips as his hand palmed her breast. She groaned and arched her back, pushing the hardening nipple further into his touch. She threaded her fingers through the curls at the back of his neck, fitting her mouth better against his. She pulled him down on top of her and moved to roll him onto his back. His painful hiss brought her eyes open with a start.

"What's wrong?"

"My hand hurts a bit."

She sat up in the bed, brushing her hair out of her face as she took his hand in hers and examined the palm. "My God, Tanner. Your hand has second degree burns across the palm. What the fuck happened and why didn't you call me?"

"It's nothin'."

"Damn it! Don't give me that shit. You're hurt."

"One of the speaker wires frayed and when I plugged it in, it caught fire."

"Did you go to the emergency room and have your hand checked?"

"No."

"Why the hell not?"

"I have a nurse for a girlfriend. Why should I go to the emergency room? Besides, what would they have done except put somethin' on the burn. I've been icing it all the way home. Now I need the love of my life to kiss me and make it better."

"You are impossible. Come on," she said, crawling from the bed, tugging him along with her toward the kitchen. She grabbed some ice from the freezer, putting some in a plastic bag and placing it on his palm. "Stay there. I've got some ointment to put on there." When she returned, she spread a thick layer of white cream on the burns and wrapped his hand with gauze. "Tell me exactly what happened."

"I already told you. One of the speaker wires caught fire," he shrugged.

"Are you sure it was an accident?"

"Don't read more into this than there is."

"It seems awful convenient. This is crazy, Tanner. All these accidents that keep happening aren't coincidental. You need to tell the police about this."

He stood up and began to pace. "I can't let this stop me from touring, baby. We need this."

"No, you need this, Tanner, not me. I'm happy with the way things were before. I hate you being gone all the time. I hate being here alone. I hate women throwing themselves at you, hoping you'll take them to bed before you come home to me." Tears slipped down her cheeks. "I'm sorry Tanner, but I can't do this anymore."

"What are you sayin'?"

She sobbed silently, squeezing her eyes shut, before she choked out, "You need to move out."

He stopped in front of her and took her shoulders in his hands. "You can't be serious. I love you."

She stepped back and he let his grip drop. Grabbing her purse and car keys, she slipped on her flip flops and walked toward the door. She could hardly see him through the tears as she said, "I'll be back later. Please have your stuff out before I get back."

She returned several hours later. The silence that met her ears as she opened the door almost brought her to her knees. He was gone, just like she had asked.

Chapter 21

"What do you mean, I'm pregnant?" Amy's startled voice echoed through the exam room where she sat on the table, naked from the waist down, only a thin sheet draped across her lap.

"Just what I said, Amy. You are going to have a baby in about seven months would be my guess," Dr. Conner answered.

"That isn't possible. I'm on birth control. Run the test again."

"Birth control isn't a hundred percent. Your cervix shows the signs, too, Amy. Not only the blood test."

She shook her head as she tipped it back on her shoulders. *Pregnant. Tanner's baby.*

"I'll let you get dressed and then we'll talk more." The doctor stepped out of the room, but she couldn't move.

She hadn't seen or talk to him since she asked him to move out three months ago. She missed him everyday and cried herself to sleep on many occasion. *Now what the hell am I going to do?* Sliding off the table, she grabbed her clothes from the chair and mechanically got dressed.

About an hour later, she walked out of the doctor's office, prescription for pre-natal vitamins in her hand. She slid inside her car and pulled the door shut behind her, before she pushed the key into the ignition. She picked up her cell phone and flipped it open. Scrolling through the numbers in her contact list, she found Tanner's number, but couldn't bring herself to call him. Shutting it with a click, she laid it back on the seat as she started her car and drove home.

The sun streamed through the sliding glass door of her balcony, lighting the room with a golden light as she opened her apartment door. Tossing her purse and keys on the island, she sighed heavily. *I have to tell him. It isn't fair to him not to know.* Her gaze caught the blinking light on her answering machine. Drawn to the red glow, she pushed the button.

"I'm trying to reach, Amy Russell. If this is your phone number, I need you to call me as soon as possible. My name is Doctor Jonathan Brooks. I'm an emergency room physician at a hospital near Chicago. I have someone in my ER who is insisting I call you."

Oh God Tanner!

"His name is Tanner Lewis, and he's been hurt. Call me immediately at seven-seven-three-four-zero-two-nine-eight-four-one."

Shaking hands scribbled the number down before she grabbed her cell phone and dialed.

"Mercy Hospital Emergency Room. Can I help you?"

"Yes. My name is Amy Russell. A physician, Dr. Brooks call me about a patient there. A Tanner Lewis."

"Yes, ma'am. Hang on and I'll put the physician on the line."

Elevator music met her ears for what seemed like forever before a rich, deep baritone voice answered. "Doctor Brooks."

"Doctor Brooks, this is Amy Russell. You called me about Tanner Lewis."

"Thank goodness you called me back. Your friend is driving me crazy!"

A choking sobbing laugh escaped her ears. Just like Tanner. "What's wrong? What happened to Tanner?"

"A bus accident. His tour bus flipped on its side and he's hurt."

"How hurt?"

"There is a small amount of internal damage, a concussion as well as a broken leg."

"You can tell me the real deal, doc. I'm a registered nurse."

"Okay. He's in surgery right now. His spleen sustained damage and they are removing it. Here in the ER, he kept asking for you. They might have to pin his leg. The tibia is fractured. How soon can you get here?"

"I…" Her hand rested on her still flat stomach.

"You are coming, right, Ms. Russell?"

"Yes. I'll catch the first flight I can."

* * * *

"Thanks," Amy said as she paid the cab driver and stepped out of the car. The imposing sight of the large red letters depicting the emergency room sent fear straight through her. *God, please let him be all right.* She moved toward the doors and the admission clerk sitting directly in front of her.

"Can I help you," the woman asked.

"Yes ma'am. My name is Amy Russell. I'm trying to find out where Tanner Lewis is."

"Are you family?"

Family.

"No, ma'am."

"Then due to privacy laws, I can't tell you anything."

"I'm aware of the privacy laws, ma'am. I'm a registered nurse. Doctor Brooks called me."

"Excuse me," she heard a deep male voice from behind her. "Miss Russell?"

"Yes?"

"I'm Doctor Brooks."

"It's nice to meet you. Where is Tanner?"

"He's in recovery right now from what I understand. Follow me and I'll show you."

Amy followed the handsome blonde to another desk where he explained to the clerk the situation and the woman quickly buzzed them into a restricted area.

"I believe he's behind the last curtain."

Amy held out her hand and said, "Thank you so much for calling me."

His appreciative gaze moved over her face and she blushed. "You are very welcome. I wish we had met under different circumstances."

"Thanks again," she murmured, pulling her hand from his grasp.

She hesitated at the curtain for a moment, before pushing the linen panel aside to get her first real look at Tanner since that fated day in her apartment when she told him to leave. His eyes were closed and a huge bruise covered the left side of his forehead. She choked back a sob as she moved to his side. Her eyes found the monitor over his head. It reassured her to see his vital signs were stable as she listened to the steady beep of his heart. Slipping into the chair left at his bedside, she grasped his hand and softly called his name.

He moaned once and his eyes flittered open. His voice came out in a strangled whisper as he turned his head toward her. "Amy?"

Tears rolled down her cheeks as she murmured, "I can't leave you alone for a minute, can I?"

"Where am I?"

"A hospital near Chicago."

Frown lines appeared between his eyes. "I don't understand."

"You were here for a show. The bus rolled."

"Wait a minute. How did you get here if I'm in Chicago?"

"The physician in the ER called me."

He closed his eyes for a moment before opening them again. "You came because of me?"

"He said you were asking for me. If you don't want me here, I'll leave."

His hand gripped hers so tight, she thought he might break her fingers. "No, don't leave. I need you." His eyes drifted shut and his grip slackened on her fingers, but didn't let go completely. "I love you," he whispered.

His words echoed through her mind as she watched him drift off to sleep, tears rolling down her cheeks. I need you. I love you. Could he really mean what he said? Did he still love her?

* * * *

Dread rippled down her back as she stood outside his hospital room door. He had still been asleep when she left to find something to eat, but the grunts and yells coming from inside the room, told her that wasn't the case anymore.

She took a deep, fortifying breath before she pushed the door open and said, "I'll warn you right now, yelling like that will only piss the nurses off more and you won't get anything."

"What the hell are you doin' here?"

Cocking an eyebrow, she said, "You don't remember?"

"No," he grumbled.

"The physician in the ER called me and said you were asking for me."

"Must have been the concussion."

"Probably, but I'm here now so suck it up because I'm not going anywhere."

"I don't need you here."

"That's not what you said last night in the recovery room."

"Probably the drugs."

She closed her eyes for a moment, fighting the anger rising inside. *He just angry. I can't let his anger get to me.*

"I brought a couple of hamburgers. Would you like one or do I have to give it to one of the nurses for lunch." His stomach growled and she smiled. "I guess that is a yes."

She handed him the bag as he shot her a scowl, before digging inside and pulling out the food.

"A thank you would be nice."

"Thanks."

"You're welcome," she said handing him a cup. "Has the doctor been by?"

"Yes."

"And?"

He scowled again. "Why do you care?"

"Because I do, Tanner. I wouldn't have come if I didn't."

"You were the one who told me to leave. You said you couldn't handle things the way they were anymore."

"That doesn't mean I stopped caring." She forced herself to swallow the greasy hamburger in her hand. *I can't throw up in front of him, I won't.*

"What's wrong?"

She swallowed, hard. "Nothing."

"You look green. I've never seen you look that color before and I know very little makes you sick."

"I..." she squeaked and then dove from the chair, rushing for the bathroom, barely reaching the toilet it before she threw up everything in her stomach.

His concerned eyes met hers as she walked back into his room.

"I've got a flu bug or something."

"You don't look like you are running a fever."

"Never mind." She took her chair again, but stuffed the remainder of the hamburger back in the bag. "Did the doctor say when they would release you?"

"In a couple of days. I haven't seen anyone from the band. Did anyone else get hurt? How bad is the bus?"

"I didn't lay eyes on the bus, but from what I've heard, it's totaled. No one else got hurt as bad as you. Bumps and bruises mostly."

"Thank God."

"I'm glad your injuries weren't worse."

"Are you?"

"Of course. I would never want you to be hurt."

Silence stretched between them as he continued to eat and she fought the rising nausea in her stomach. She got up and moved toward the window. Looking out over the parking lot below, she wondered what would happen now. *I have to tell him about the baby, but I don't want him to feel obligated to be with me because of it.*

"I need to tell you something Tanner, something that has come up in the last couple of days."

"Okay."

She closed her eyes as she tried to form the words on her tongue. "I'm going…"

"Hello again," a chipper voice said as the tall, lanky man barged into the room, interrupting her thoughts. "I'm Doctor Allen. I'm the one who did the pinning on your leg."

"Nice to meet you. When can I get the hell out of here?"

"Patience, son. You'll be out in a day or two, but you'll not be doing much running around the countryside for awhile. The cast needs to stay on your leg for at least six weeks."

Tanner groaned and Amy smiled. *That will go over like a lead balloon.*

"And, you will need to do some therapy afterwards to strengthen the muscle again. I realize you aren't from around here so we will discharge you with instructions to follow up with a physician in Dallas."

He's still living in Dallas?

"Fine. Just get me out of here," Tanner grumbled.

"I will check on you tomorrow, and we'll see what we can do to get you home."

"I would appreciate it tremendously, doctor." Tanner's gaze slid to her. "I have some important things to take care of at home."

"I certainly understand, young man. See you in the morning."

Once the physician had left, his gaze whipped back to her where she continued to stand against the wall. "As you were saying."

She took a deep breath and said, "I'm pregnant."

"You're what?"

"I'm going to have a baby, Tanner, your baby."

"You can't be serious."

"I'm dead serious. I had a doctor's appointment a few days ago."

"But you were on birth control."

"Yes, but it's not one hundred percent effective either. Obviously, I am within the two percent margin."

He sighed heavily and laid his head back on the bed, closing his eyes. Not moving for several minutes, she almost wondered if he'd gone to sleep but the tense tick in his jaw told her he definitely wasn't sleeping.

"Say something, please."

"What the hell do you want me to say, Amy? I'm happy? Because I'm not. We aren't even together anymore and you spring this on me."

"I didn't plan to get pregnant either, Tanner. The last thing I need right now is a baby."

He looked her square in the eyes as he said, "How do I know it's mine?"

Anger zinged through her as his words met her ear. "You son-of-a-bitch! How can you even ask me that? I never once cheated on you."

"I haven't seen or talked to you in three months and now all of the sudden you show up on my doorstep per se, telling me you are pregnant with my child."

"You know what, never mind. Obviously you've turned into an asshole over the last three months." She shook with rage and indignation as she grabbed her purse and keys. "I almost thought we could work things out, but forget it. I don't need you and you obviously don't give a shit about me."

* * * *

"You are an ass, Tanner Lewis," Chris yelled as she paced his living room. "I can't believe you turned your back on her."

"I didn't turn my back, Chris," he grumbled.

"Yes, you did. She told you about the baby and you asked her if it belonged to you. You might as well have accused her of cheating on you, and I know damned well Amy would never do that and so do you."

He raked his fingers through his hair. Six weeks, six long, agonizing weeks since he had seen her and she had told him about the baby she carried, his baby. The cast on his leg would come off tomorrow and as soon as it had been taken care of, he planned to visit her and talk. "I know she wouldn't, but she sprang everythin' on me out of the blue."

"That still doesn't mean you accuse her of cheating."

"I'm going to talk to her tomorrow."

"You better." Chris stopped pacing. "Did they find out what caused the accident on the bus?"

"Yeah, severed brake line."

"Then someone is trying to hurt you."

"Looks that way, yes. That's part of the reason I haven't tried to get back together with Amy in the last few months. I couldn't stand if she got hurt in the process."

"She still loves you, you know."

He shook his head. "I'm not so sure anymore. I thought she might when I woke up at the hospital to find her by my bed, but after our argument about the baby, I don't think so."

"You don't know her at all, do you? She jumped on the first plane when she heard you were hurt. She wanted to be by your side and I'm sure it about killed her to see you in that bed. She wouldn't have done those things if she didn't still love you. Question is, do you still love her?"

He paused and looked at Chris. "I never stopped lovin' her. She's my whole world."

"Then what's stopping you?"

"I won't get her hurt in the process of lovin' me. I have to figure out who is doin' this and why."

"But you are going to see her tomorrow right? Straighten things out about the baby?"

"Yes, Chris, I am."

* * * *

The next day, the doctor's removed Tanner's cast and he could drive again. Chris told him Amy bought a house outside of town so that's where he headed. He knocked on the door. She opened wood panel and her eyes went wide, right before she tried to shut it in his face. He swiftly stuck his foot between the wood panel and the doorframe, preventing the green painted entry from closing all the way.

Pushing it open, he walked inside and closed it behind him.

"Get out, Tanner. I don't want to see you."

"Well, too bad. We need to talk or at least I do and you'll listen if I have to tie you to a chair." Her eyes widened again at his threat. "Sit down."

Her eyes narrowed into tiny slits, but she did as he told her.

"First of all, I'm sorry I said what I did about the baby. If you say the child is mine, I believe you."

She opened her mouth to speak, but he held up his hand and she closed it again.

"Second, I still love you. I never stopped lovin' you even when you told me to leave. I know bein' with me is difficult at best, with the tourin' and bein' gone all the time, but you have to trust me. I would never do anythin' to hurt you and I could never cheat on you. You have to be willin' to work with me on this Amy, if we are gonna work this out."

"Third—." He watched her stand up and walked toward him, tears shimmering on her eyelashes.

"Third, I love you. I wouldn't have come to Chicago if I didn't. This child," she took his hand and laid it on her still flat stomach, "was conceived in love. It's ours, yours and mine and I want nothing more than to raise this baby with you. I know trust is earned and you've earned mine even if I hate every time another woman looks at you. It's something I'll have to live with because you are doing what you love to do and I can't take that away from you."

"They can look and want all they care to. You are the only woman I want in my life on a permanent basis. The money is better now so you won't have to work as much." She started to protest, but he silenced her with a quick kiss before he continued. "I know you want to and you can if you'd like, but you don't have to. You can come on the road with me, be by my side." His fingers trailed down her cheek before he swiped his thumb across her bottom lip. "I love you." His lips found her mouth again, slipping between the crease to invade her mouth with his tongue.

* * * *

She slid her hands up his chest and wrapped them in his hair as she moaned under his mouth, pushing herself against him. He wanted her as much as she wanted him. His rock hard erection strained against the zipper of his jeans and she felt every inch of it trapped between them.

"Amy," he whispered, pulling his mouth from hers and nibbling the corners.

"I want..." His lips moved to her jaw and along her neck, his hand sliding down her arm to take her breast in his palm. When she felt his palm slide across her aching nipple, she moaned, "Oh God!"

He lifted his head for a moment as he murmured, "Tell me. Tell me what you want."

She opened her eyes to meet his as she whimpered, "I want you."

He smiled the smile that made her heart leap in her chest. "Good," he replied. "Because I want you." He swept her up in his arms and headed down the hall to her bedroom, kicking the door closed behind him.

He walked to her bed and lay her down softly on the coverlet, kissing her hard on the mouth before releasing her to toe off his boots. She sat up when he reached for his shirt and pushed his hands away. Her own fingers sliding the buttons from the holes as she kissed the skin revealed with each one that was undone. His body shook as she moved down his chest, tracing the small line of hair that ran to the waistband of his jeans with her tongue.

She reached for the belt buckle at his waist, but he stopped her with his own as he murmured, "Not yet."

She sat back on her heels while he moved toward her, reaching for the small straps at her shoulders, sliding his fingers under one as he pulled it off. His lips following the path down her arm. She moaned when his hot mouth fastened on her already hard nipple through her shirt. She threw her head back, clutching the back of his neck to hold him in place, almost bucking under the pressure of his tongue and his teeth.

While he feasted on her breast, his hand moved to the button on her jeans, slipping it free, before his fingertips slid down her stomach. She felt his fingers slide inside her hot folds, his thumb finding her swollen clit, and she groaned above him, feeling warm liquid spill from between her legs.

He lifted his head as his fingers slid out, and gave her the warmest smile. She scooted to the middle of the bed as he followed on his hands and knees. She reached to remove her shoes and socks, but he stopped her with his hand on her leg. She looked at him questioningly, but all he did was smile again, turning her inside out.

She finally lay back against the pillows as she watched him reach for her shoes, pulling each one off slowly, followed by each sock. He ran his hands over her feet, rubbing each one, kneading them with his hands. She thought she would go crazy with the sensation of having him rub her feet, but when she felt his tongue slide from her ankle to her toes, taking each one in his mouth to suck, she closed her eyes and melted against the pillows behind her.

When he finally finished torturing the toes near him, he slipped up her body and grabbed her jeans, pulling them off her hips and down her legs, taking her lace panties with them. Her eyes opened to slits when he tossed her pants across the room and divested himself of his own. She watched in appreciation as his finely sculpted chest moved back over her, and he settled himself between her thighs. His tongue found her knee, moving along the ridges and up her thigh as she moaned deep in her throat. His mouth finally settled on her swollen pussy and she almost screamed as he ran his tongue from her labia to her clit. Swirling the rough pad of his tongue across her aching bud, she made soft mewing sounds in the back of her throat while he stroked her until she couldn't stand it anymore. She almost screamed in frustration as his mouth left her. *So close!*

Without giving her the satisfaction she sought, his mouth moved up her belly to her breasts, sucking and nibbling while she held the back of his head tight against her.

His hips now between her thighs, she tried to move so he would take her, sliding inside until he reached her core, but he held back.

She opened her eyes to see him above her, a wicked smile gracing his gorgeous face as he waited. She didn't know what he wanted. Did he want her to beg? It didn't matter. She would do whatever he wanted, as long as he finished what he started.

"God, Tanner, please!"

His smile got bigger and more wicked if that was at all possible.

"Tell me what you want. I'll do anything. Please fuck me," she whimpered, hoping he could see the desperation in her eyes.

He pushed slightly inside her pussy with just the head of his penis until she groaned again. She closed her eyes as tears formed at the corners and slipped silently down into her hair.

"Why are you cryin'?" he whispered, sliding a little more into her warmth as a tortured groan slipped from her mouth.

"Stupid hormones," she grumbled on a laughing half sob. Her body shook as he slid inside, his hard cock reaching her deepest core and he groaned as if in pain. She wrapped her legs around him to pull him even deeper as he started to move, the friction driving them both ever closer to the magic spot where they would float together, enveloped in love.

Drifting back to reality, Tanner withdrew from inside her with a heavy groan, before he rolled on his side, pulling her with him. Their breathing slowed as she rested her cheek on his chest and she traced the curling hair with her fingers. She whispered against his skin, "I missed you."

He smiled as he murmured in return, "I missed you, too."

Several hours later, they were startled from sleep by a loud noise outside the bedroom door.

She sat bolt upright in the bed as she whispered, "What the hell was that?"

"I don't know," he answered softly. "Were you expecting someone?" His tone became indignant, as if he thought she had invited someone to her apartment.

"No," she whispered angrily, turning on a small light on the bedside table.

He bent over the side of the bed to grab his jeans and slip them on.

"I'm going to check it out," he said, right after he kissed her hard on the mouth. "Stay here."

"Tanner?"

"Yeah?"

"Be careful. There is a baseball bat in the corner. Take it with you."

He grinned. He grabbed the bat and slowly opened the door. "I don't see anythin'," he whispered before he slipped out the door, pulling it shut with a soft click behind him.

She got up and pulled her jeans and shirt on as she waited. He said to stay put, but it drove her crazy not knowing what was going on outside her bedroom door. She was terrified. If she lost him now, she didn't know what she would do.

She moved toward the door, listening for any sound, anything that would tell her where Tanner had gone. Since he took the bat, she didn't have a weapon. She slowly opened the door, peeking out into the hall. She didn't see anything, so she crept out and slowly walked toward the living room.

When she reached the main hall, she could tell someone sat on the couch. She moved slowly forward when she realized it was Tanner, but he shook his head no right before she felt the cold muzzle of a gun in her side.

"Let's join your boyfriend, Amy, shall we?" The man beside her pushed her forward toward where Tanner sat, his eyes narrowed to slits as he watched.

She walked into the living room keeping her eyes on Tanner until the gunman moved into the light that had been turned on and she could finally see who held them at gunpoint.

"Jason?"

"Surprise, sweetheart. I knew I would find you rutting around like a couple of dogs in heat. You never could keep your hands off him, could you? Move over by Tanner. I want you both where I can see you."

She moved to the couch and sat down as she asked, "What's the meaning of this, Jason?"

"I said you would be sorry, didn't I?" he growled, waving the gun in front of the pair.

"I don't understand."

"You just don't get it, do you? You always seemed so smart. Everyone loves you. Jack, Chris, Tanner, even me, but I wasn't good enough for you, was I? I gave you everything I had. I tried to be your friend, and then he came along," Jason spat angrily, waving the gun at Tanner.

She looked at Tanner as their gazes locked and she tried to communicate to him how crazy she thought this all sounded.

"Stop that! I'm not crazy."

Her gaze swung back around to Jason. "But, Jason, I do love you, as a friend."

"I didn't want to be your friend! Don't you see?" His angry voice reverberated around the room. "While he buried himself inside you, I stood on the outside wanting in."

"I'm sorry, Jason. I don't care for you like that."

He laughed manically for a moment before he stared at them again.

"It doesn't matter anymore. You'll be mine, one way or the other, when I kill him."

"You can't do that."

He appeared not to hear her as he continued, "Oh, yes. You'll be mine all right." Jason paced back and forth for a moment. "I swear to *God* you must have nine lives, mister big shot country star. It didn't matter how many times I tried to get rid of you."

Amy whispered out loud, "You are the one who has been trying to hurt Tanner?"

"Yeah, pretty smart I'd say. You never even suspected me, did you? I figured if I got rid of him, you would come back to me Amy, just like before." Jason's voice dropped almost to a caress as he looked at her.

"We were never a couple Jason. You are my friend, but nothing more."

"You loved me once, I know you did."

Amy started to rise from her place near Tanner, but he tried to stop her. She shook her head as she stood and approached Jason, the gun wavering between them. She had to get the gun away from him before someone was hurt.

"Jason," she whispered, tears sliding down her cheeks.

"I love you, Amy," he told her as her hand touched him.

"I know, Jason, but you can't hurt Tanner. I love him," she murmured, as she reached for the gun. "I'm carrying his baby."

"No!" Jason screamed, the gun coming up between the two of them. Tanner dove for the gun and managed to knock it from Jason's hand before it went off. Two men rolled across the floor as Amy watched, her heart in her chest. The weapon skidded across the floor out of reach as Tanner balled up his fist and hit Jason as hard as he could.

"Call the police Amy, now."

She grabbed the phone and with shaky hands, managed to dial. Several minutes later, sirens blared as they pulled up in front of her house and more than half of a dozen police officers bound up the steps. They burst in through the front door, guns drawn. Training their weapons on Tanner, Amy yelled, "Not him." She pointed to Jason who moaned softly on the floor several feet away. "Him!"

The police handcuffed the semi-conscious man as Tanner wrapped her in his arms whispering, "Ssshhh. It's over now."

4

Epilogue

Seven months later ...

"Come on baby, you need to push."

She grumbled, before she groaned again and he smiled.

"You get up here and push this bowling ball out."

His hand moved over her swollen belly, feeling the contraction ripple across the surface. He was behind her, bracing her shoulders as she leaned against his chest and tried to push their child out of her body. He put his lips near her ear and whispered, "I love you."

Tears sparkled on her lashes as she surged against the pain, pushing with everything she had as the baby slipped from her body.

He could see the squirming bundle between her legs and a ragged sob shook his frame. "It's a girl, love."

"A girl?"

"Yes, and I'm sure she'll be just as beautiful as her mother."

"No bias there, huh?"

He chuckled as he slipped out from behind her so she could lie back against the pillows and rest. He tenderly brushed the wet tendrils of hair from her face as her eyes met his and she brought her own hand up to wipe the tears from his cheek.

"I love you."

"I love you, too."

"Why don't you go see our daughter for a minute while they clean me up?"

He smiled. "I'll be right back. Don't go anywhere."

"I'm too tired to do much of anything right now."

A wistful smile crossed his lips. He knew her better than that. They had been playfully arguing over her riding during her pregnancy for several months.

A moment later, he returned to her side with the pink wrapped bundle in his arms, laying the baby across her chest as she wrapped her arms around their child.

"We never did agree on a girl's name," she whispered as her eyes met his.

He chuckled. "No, we didn't."

She touched his cheek as a tear slipped down her face.

"Thank you, sweetheart," he whispered, his lips brushing her cheek, taking the salty tear in his mouth.

"For what?"

"For our daughter."

THE END

www.romancestorytime.com

ABOUT THE AUTHOR

Sandy Sullivan is a romance author who, when not writing, spends her time with her husband Shaun, riding her horses, playing with their dogs, relaxing in the hot tub and enjoying the rolling hills of her home.

She lives on a farm south of Nashville, Tennessee, where they moved in 2005 from the state of Washington where she grew up.

She is an avid reader of romance novels and she enjoys reading Nora Roberts, Jude Deveraux, and Susan Wiggs.

She would love to hear from you, so please visit her website at www.romancestorytime.com, and feel free to leave feedback about any of her novels that have been released to date.

Siren Publishing, Inc.
www.SirenPublishing.com

LaVergne, TN USA
12 April 2010
178971LV00002B/53/P